You are not going to believe t

Julian 'Cla.

The 1st Battalion the Gloucestershire Regiment and the 1st Battalion the Royal Gloucestershire, Berkshire, and Wiltshire Regiment

Prologue

The Rifles

julianheal@yahoo.co.uk

Comments welcome!

First Edition 2022

julianheal@yahoo.co.uk

Table of Contents

Introduction

1RGBW Support Company, Ballykinlar County Down, Northern Ireland, September 2000 – April 2002:

Chapter 21
Lamp Posted:

Chapter 22
NAFFI Brawl:

Chapter 23
Belize Bedlam:

Chapter 24
Snakes and Ladders:

Chapter 25
Mexican Madness:

Chapter 26
Meanwhile, back in Belize!

Chapter 27
1RGBW C 'Criminal' Company Cavalry Barracks, Hounslow, West London. Public Duties. April 2002 – September 2005:

Chapter 28
NCO Cadre:

Chapter 29
Four Ton Truck Drama and Scandal

Chapter 30
Brummy Playing the Numbers Game:

Chapter 31
Cardiff Cluster Fuck:

Chapter 32
Kenya Exercise Grand Prix - Kenyan Kerfuffle:

Op Olympic 2012.

Chapter 46
Kenya and Flood Relief Operations 2012-2014:

ENDEX

About the Author

'Clarence'
Is a retired veteran who has spent the majority of his life in uniform. He found a home a life & a wife in the Army. He now lives 'quietly' in Chester UK with his wife and extended family. His main passion in life being family, old comrades, his godchildren, and travel. Especially Whanau in New Zealand.

BOOK INTRODUCTION

> *"This is a brief life, but in its brevity, it offers us some splendid*
> *moments, some meaningful adventures."*
> *Rudyard Kipling*

"You are not going to believe this lads, but what happened was!"

THE LIFE AND TIMES OF CPL 'CLARENCE' HEAL:

This book is dedicated to all the various characters and amusing situations I encountered during my time as a soldier of the Queen.

This book covers my service in the 1st Battalion, The Gloucestershire Regiment and the 1st Battalion the Royal Gloucestershire, Berkshire, and Wiltshire Regiment. 1990 – 2007 The Rifles, including Rifles Support team and the 1st Battalion the Rifles 2008 – 2014.

This book is not a war story or an autobiography. It is an insight into good times and laughs that I experienced during my military service including op tours and foreign travel. It does not detract or disrespect in any way the memory of my fallen comrades and the casualties of war.

All the characters in this book are real people, but in the interest of my continuing health and various possible legal actions and some of the lad's irate ex-wives and birds, nicknames have been used to protect identities. It also will hopefully save some various bits of embarrassment and give you, the reader an insight into my personal odyssey and adventures, during my time as a soldier of the Queen.

"Writing a book is an adventure". Winston Churchill

PROLOGUE

My own nickname was given to me in my second week of basic training at the Depot of the Prince of Wales Division, Litchfield - Which has now stuck with me for the last thirty years.

This book is dedicated to all the lads that I have served with, The British and Commonwealth forces, and the United States Marine Corps. The proceeds of this book will be going to the **Blesma** - The Limbless Veterans, which is an Armed Forces charity dedicated to assisting serving, and ex-Service men and women who have suffered life-changing limb loss, or the use of a limb, an eye, or their eyesight.

I am not a hero, but I had the honour and the privilege to serve with a Company of heroes and loveable rogues. Standing together with my sword brothers in the shield wall, then drinking and laughing with them in the hall of heroes. Some of my brothers are now drinking mead with the Gods in Valhalla.

'There was only one colour in the Regiments I served in, and that was green! It's all about growing up son! And growing up is tough for any kid.'

'Clarence' Heal

> *"No, a merry life a short one, shall be my motto."*
> *Bartholomew Roberts*

CHAPTER 1

> *"Yes, making mock o' uniforms that guard you while you sleep... For its Tommy this, a' Tommy that' Chuck him out, the brute! But it's Saviour of his country when the guns begin to shoot!"*
> *Rudyard Kipling*

Depot - Prince of Wales Division, Litchfield, Staffordshire, England. AKA The Hitler Youth. September 1990 - March 1991.

Bumpers, Block Jobs, and the C.H.U.D:
Basic Training was every soldier's nightmare. The trick was to keep your head down, play the game, and get to the Battalion ASAP. Do the whole thing once, and once only. Get it done in a oner.

But me being me, I had to drop myself in the shit, doing 'Block Jobs' which were the holy grail of cleanliness in training. Any infringement or skiving off - there was a one-way ticket to the Pokey! The offender went straight to jail - no get out of jail free card!

My own nickname was given to me in my second week of Basic Training at the Depot of the Prince of Wales Division, Litchfield. To all recruits 'Crows', the Gym at the depot is the lair of the Beastmaster's.

I will quote Big Phil the QMSI - Gym bloke, King of PT "I will have you lot sweating through the floorboards of my gymnasium" in his Northern tones.

To this end, the Gym PT lessons were a subject of fear and apprehension for all of us recruits. So, as an 18-year-old Bristolian half-caste, mocha, immature, Jack the lad with a squint in my left eye; I was on the PTI's radar like a lamb to the slaughter lit up light a Christmas tree. Trust me, there were some scary PTI's at the training depot. 'Midnight' was Mike Tyson reincarnate and our Platoon PTI 'Woody' was the Welsh cyborg.

Woody was a lovable rogue from 1RWF. Hard but fair, plus he had a few scams and money-making schemes going from his mobile burger bar on camp; and in later years his clothing empire. I would have a brew and shoot the shit in the NAFFI in Ballykinlar, when he would come round to the various camps in Ulster in his white van selling 'designer' clothes.

So, I am stood in the gym in three ranks, with the Platoon awaiting our fate. Woody, who is the God King for the next hour, is walking up and down the squad taking the piss out of us all. I am stood next to Arthur Daley from the Cheshire's, who is also on the radar and getting ripped for his Manchester, Kevin Webster accent. Then it is my turn for personal motivation and banter. 'Who are you looking at son? Hey lads its Clarence the cross-eyed lion!' This was taken from the old Daktari 1960s TV show in reference to the cross-eyed lion. Cheers Woody! 30 years down the line, 'Clarence' is still jogging on - the name stuck.

One dark winters night, me and Arthur Daley were doing block jobs i.e., scrubbing the floor of the landing outside the Platoon lines.

'Arthur' was a fellow recruit from the Cheshire Regiment, whose last name was Daley, hence the nickname Arthur. Just like the TV character, he was a loveable rouge always ducking and diving. If anything, dodgy was occurring, Arthur was not far away. He went on to have a full 22-year career reaching the rank of Colour Sergeant. His sidekick in the Platoon was another Cheshire Regiment recruit 'Molly', who was the 'Daddy' of the Platoon. Strong as an ox and was always getting ripped for his North Wales/Manchester hybrid accent. We have all stayed friends for the last 30 years and by a strange twist of fate live in the same Chester/North Wales area.

We had just finished the task when some young lad walked straight across the landing, which pissed me off. Arthur was motioning to me to *shut the fuck up and let it go,* but me being a bit gobby thought, *fuck it* the lad had just destroyed all our hard graft. "Oi dickhead we have just spent an hour scrubbing the fucking floor - you on drugs?!"

Wrong answer! The 'Lad' was a Corporal 'full screw' from another training Platoon, and I had just shot myself in the foot massively. To cut a long story short, I went straight to jail. Did not pass go. Or collect £200. Arthur had a look of total disbelief on his face, followed by sniggering tinged with sympathy because he knew the score on going down the Pokey! I had just booked a one-way ticket on the pain train! What a prick I was. The Corporal in question was a known dickhead and bully from the Royal Hampshire's who had an evil reputation.

The Pokey, or jail to us CROWS 'Combat Replacements of War', was a place to be avoided and feared. You were made to suffer and atone for your sins. I was shitting myself as I was waiting on the line outside the guardroom for the axe to fall.

In the late 80s there was a B grade horror film doing the rounds called C.H.U.D - Cannibal Human Under Dweller. So, I'm stood to attention on the line outside the Guardroom awaiting my fate, when the Guard Commander, who had already heard my tail of woe via the jungle drums, was laughing his head off and told me with great amusement that CHUD was Duty Provost Corporal. Look in for a look out son!

Nobby is the nickname most used in English for those with the surname of Clark or Clarke.

Nobby arrived in my life as the Anti-Christ. I heard him before I saw him. A mixture of Welsh, English, and swearing hit my ear drums like a tomahawk submarine launched super-sonic cruise missile. CHUD, aka Nobby, had like a combat pinkie, squashed boxers' nose, slight cleft lip, and a light welter weight boxer build. *Fuck!* I thought, *I am dead. My life is over!*

Enter mistake number two of the evening; I was thinking to myself, *fuck he looks like CHUD from the film,* so I am trying not to laugh and failing badly. This makes Nobby even angrier! I am now taken to the cells for a re-education on my failings as a solider. Plus, to my horror, I realize Nobby is an NCO from the Gloucestershire Regiment - the same Regiment that I'm hoping to join. *Shit! Shit! Shit! Why me Lord?* After some language difficulty and readjustment to my attitude, I was introduced to the dreaded 'Bumper'.

The 'Bumper' is a very heavy weight attached to a broom handle. It is designed for the sole purpose of buffing up a laminated or painted stone floor. Once you have as the operator attached a cloth or rag to the base of it, as with all things Army, it has been converted and redesigned as an instrument of torture for us recruits. So, Nobby then has me on his own personal attitude adjuster bumper blitzkrieg! Hours later, my arms are like jelly, and I am sweating like a pig. Plus, all the floors are shinny and gleaming. I became an expert on making brews for the provost staff. Top tip: of the day -Engage brain before gobbing off. 30 years later, Nobby is one of my closest friends and I am a proud 'God-Father and Uncle' to his stepdaughter.

Flipper the Dolphin - This an interesting tale of a lad who joined our Platoon due to him being a back squad from another Platoon, due to injury or something. The story, according to 'Smasher' from the Cheshire Regiment goes like this. Smasher was the Platoon 'Daddy'. A big, strong Manchester lad, with a colourful history before joining the Army, who got his nickname on his ability to break various bits of equipment and vehicles. I digress - back to Flipper. The story goes that when he was a teenager back in Liverpool; Flipper and his mates were involved is a bit of petty thieving.

Flipper and his mates had just robbed some sweats from a corner shop, and while being chased by the police, Flipper thought it was a good idea to jump in the canal and swim away from danger, and getting his collar felt by the law. The only problem with this cunning plan was that Flipper forgot he could not swim! So, the police had to fish him out before they arrested him. Hence the nickname, 'Flipper the Dolphin'.

Infrared Ted was one of our training corporals. A very professional but also chilled out solider, who was firm but fair, and would go out of his way to share guidance and advice when needed to us CROW's. He was also a Grade A gun nut! If he were a Yank, he would have been a fully paid-up member of the National Rifle Association. One night on guard duty, with I think it was either Arthur or Molly, we were doing the rounds down by the rifle range when heard all these pinging sounds off the metal work of the butts; followed by the whistle of incoming pellets in and around us. We took cover. Next thing we know, Ted appears in his Barbour jacket with the Gucci space age, smart as fuck air rifle, complete with sniper scopes and flashing lights. 'Evening lads. Like my new .22? I saw you clowns miles away through my super-duper new infrared sight'. So that cold night, the legend of Infrared Ted was born.

Chapter 2

"By our deeds we are known"
Motto of the Gloucestershire Regiment.

1st Battalion, Gloucestershire Regiment, Alma Barracks, Catterick, North Yorkshire, England, April 1991 - April 1994:

I was a day one, week one CROW, sent to B Company. Fresh out of training, learning the ropes the hard way and the easy way. B Company was your typical county Regiment set up, with various characters, saints, and sinners within the Company. The Company Sergeant Major's nickname was 'Poll Tax' because nobody liked him, and he was extremely popular - Not!

As a Fucking New Guy (FNG), I was lower than whale shit, and had to prove myself, keep my head down and learn the ropes. Sink or swim, nobody gave a shit, because as the new bloke you had to gain the respect of your peer group within the Company and the Regiment. The Army in the early nineties was a hard and unforgiving mistress.

Christmas Tree Light Up!
Christmas 1991, the Battalion was deployed to Ulster on an emergency tour. B Company was deployed to Portadown and Armagh City. I had a lot to learn, was still finding my feet, and I was a little scared on my first tour. Lucky for me, my team commander was 'Skin'.

Skin - an old-time Sergeant Major who looked like Skeletor off He-Man, the Masters of the Universe cartoon. He was a legend who had been there, done that, and looked after us young'uns. We had just come off patrol when we heard an explosion a few miles away. Paddy PIRA had blown up the health centre in Craigavon, the fucking muppets. No early night and eating shit food in the RUC canteen for this callsign! Gutted. So, here we go then. Operation: Let's Get Fucked Around by PC Plod and the Head Sheds.

After a few hours on the cordon things had quietened down and Skin decided it was time to explore and have a sniff around the partly destroyed health centre. First bit of good news for the boys is that the phone lines were still up and running. You must remember this was the early nineties and the days before mobile phones and the internet. Doing an 'ET' phoning home was a green BT plastic pre-paid phone card of a good old Twenty pence 'piece of eight'. So, word soon spread - free phone calls home! Happy days! A right result for B Company 1GLOSTERS.

This when things went a bit crazy with the lads doing a bit of liberation of various bits and pieces of kit laying around, including a pallet load of baby milk, a framed picture of a blue whale, and stationary. As a new bloke I used the free service and did what I was told and kept my trap firmly shut.

The next morning after returning to camp, the shit hit the fan! Poll Tax was not a happy teddy bear. To cut a long story short, he was happy for a bit of taking the piss and doing an ET, but having a rather large Christmas tree, including lights sticking up through the top cover hatch of one of the companies Land Rovers lighting up the two top covers, was taking the piss! Moral of the story: Do not steal Christmas trees and parade them round Lurgan, popping up through the top cover hatches on the Company snatch Land Rovers.

The Man-Hole Cover Kid!
Patrolling in the urban environment was always busy and eventful. During one patrol we were hard targeting, zig zagging, sprinting up the hill back into the security forces base in Armagh City. I was front man, so as I got into camp first, I waited as the rest of the 'Brick' four-man patrol to marry up and do our unload drills and post patrol checks. To all our horror we were missing a man. Where the fuck is 'Neil'? Quick, back out!

As we ran back out of the base, about twenty meters from the front, there was a helmet upright in the road. Skin was laughing his head off, and like Paul Daniels pulling a rabbit out of the hat, he was pulling Neil out of the road. Some scrote had removed the man-hole cover and Neil had fallen in! He was alright just a few bumps and bruises, but the pressure was off the rest of us for the piss taking and getting ripped, because Neil was now known as the Man-Hole Cover Kid.

Super Solider SAS:
Within the old system of the County Infantry Regiments, there are always larger than life Battalion personalities, and 1Glosters were no different. 'SASs was one of these people. He had come to the Regiment via a roundabout route. From the TA on an S Type Engagement, with an option to transfer into the Regular Army which he took. SAS being an elder gentleman and not rifle Company material was posted to the MT Platoon. This little anecdote has become part of Battalion myth and legend.

During a Battalion exercise in Northern Germany, SAS was alone and driving his four-tonner truck when he became separated from the rest of his convoy. When the convoy reached its final destination in the middle of a forestry block in the middle of nowhere in Northern Germany, the troops started to cam up the wagons and go tactical, no lights etc. Between the lads, the big subject of conversation was, where the fuck was SAS? The lads were taking bets whether he would end up in Denmark or back in the UK. To everybody's utter amazement, 10 minutes later, SAS and his truck appeared out of the darkness in the correct location - all in good order. Well-done SAS! Happy days!

'Bodge' the MT Sergeant was one happy teddy bear. After congratulating SAS on his performance, he asked him to produce his map. According to the witnesses that were present at the time, the look of disbelief and total bewilderment on Bodges' face was a thing of beauty! SAS had only managed to navigate his way round Northern Germany with a map of the Salisbury Plain Training Area in the UK. Thus, the legend of SAS was born.

SAS was sent on an especially important mission to go to the shop and buy fags for the MT lads. The brief he was given was 20 B and H, if not, anything will do! Being that a lot of the MT lads were avid smokers, SAS on return produced a chicken and mushroom pie! 'They didn't have any B and H, and you told me to come back with anything…', was SAS' answer when 'Moggy' was trying to get his head around the no fags' drama and trying not to fold SAS up like a deckchair on Blackpool Beach.

Sweating Through the Floorboards:
The Battalion had deployed on exercise to the USA. Fort Lewis was bloody huge, and for a 19-year-old crow like me, it was an experience of a lifetime on my first trip across the pond. The biggest downside was, being only 19, and in the USA, 21 was the legal age for pissing it up. I just cracked on with the training, enjoyed the experience, and tried not to fuck up and incur the wrath of 'Cyborg' my Platoon Sergeant.

The American barrack blocks were massive, straight out of Full Metal Jacket. Five Platoon B Company were sharing with the B Company Mortar Detachment. This was an experience and learning curve for me, due to the Mortars being the senior Platoon in the Battalion, which was full of interesting characters, and old and bold soldiers. I was lucky in the fact I had bumped into a few lads that were a few years older, but recognized me from the neighbourhood back in Bristol, so I was taken under their wing and introduced to Mad Metal Mortars.

Two of the lads were '63' from Gloucester, and 'Fred Star' from Bristol, who would be major influences on my Army life for the next few years. The story goes as follows:

These two lunatics went out on the piss and got hammered. In the morning they were still drunk and in shit state. This didn't go down well with the Head Shed, as it wasn't the first time, and support were taking the piss, if you'll excuse the pun. Examples had to be made that this behaviour wasn't going to be tolerated. The gym bloke, QMSI was summoned to exact punishment to the miscreants, witnessed by the whole Battalion.

63 and Fred Star were given the PT session from hell. They started off in sports kit and ended up in their full kit, including bergens, and were run ragged in front of the Battalion and some passing US Army Rangers for the morning. It was like something out of the old Sean Connery film, 'The Hill'.

Fair play, by lunchtime they were sober and experiencing rapid weight loss. Hence, the new Battalion saying, 'Sweating through the floorboards of the gymnasium'. I learnt a valuable lesson that day from 63 who gave me the benefit of his wisdom that night. "Do the crime, do the time son, and getting caught is the crime. Don't whinge and wine when you get rumbled, take your punishment on the chin." More from these two lads in later chapters.

On the flipside, Cyborg was my Platoon Sergeant. He was the God King in my little world. The man was also a fan of going on the piss, but unlike 63 and Fred Star, he would turn up the morning after, kick me out of bed because I was the team medic, to go and get him some paracetamol from the Platoon Team Med Pack, and then he would run the Platoon ragged on morning PT showing no after affects and beating us all in the sprints. Hence his nickname Cyborg.

He was proper old school but looked after us young'uns and went on to become RSM and commission. He was a hard taskmaster, but he was fair and always looked out for me as I progressed through the odyssey of my Army career.

On one occasion, I made sure I was remarkably busy sorting out my medical while he 'educated' the Platoon Commander.

Embo and the Fish Tank Fuck Up:
Weekends on the piss in camp in Catterick were always crazy, especially in Support Company. 'Uncle Wayne' was the Company Sergeant Major, and in my humble opinion, was the best CSM and future RSM I ever had the privilege to serve under.

Uncle Wayne was a character and one of a kind. He would lead from the front and would always look after his lads with tough love and a wicked sense of Welsh humour. Here is an example of his Welsh wit! On his daily Company Detail, on the Company Noticeboard he posted, 'Congratulations on Private Beasant, ATGW Platoon, on getting married. Take 10 extra duties for skiving son. Also, could 'Clarence' be round Wayne's for babysitting duties at 1900 hours, bringing his Dolby (washing) with him'.

With Wayne, if you were in the shit you would go into his office to tab the mat and roll Uncle Wayne's Magic Dice. The Magic Dice was a large wooden six-sided dice, and instead of a six there was a Back Badge. A Regimental Honour of the 28th North Gloucestershire Regiment, who had fought back-to-back against the French during the battle of Alexandria 1801. The only Regiment in the world to wear two cap badges, front and rear. If you had the misfortune to roll the Back Badge, you had 28 extras.

Rolling the Magic Dice was better than going through the official military discipline system, if you took your punishment like a man at the end of it, the slate was wiped clean. Old school, big boy's rules - Happy days. Rolling the dice was a Support Company rite of passage. It was always entertainment within the Company when the dice roll was on.

One weekend I was out on the piss with 'Embo Greengrass' and 'Welsh Roger'. Embo was a Regimental legend due to his thick West Country, Devon 'Jethro' accent, battered teeth, and a weather-beaten face only a mother could love. His likeness to the character Claude Greengrass from the TV series Heartbeat was uncanny. Like his namesake, Greengrass Embo was a lovable rouge. He was always in the shit, on the piss, banging birds, and living life to the full. He is still a good friend after all these years, and a source of amusement to all who know him.

Welsh Roger was an old and very experienced solider who was the voice of reason within the Company. He was also a bit of a miserable git when he had a monk on, so was always good to wind up. After a skin full of ale down the Fleece Pub in Richmond, followed by an RV with 'Punchy Blacky' and some of the reconnaissance lads and the rest of the Mortar Platoon in the 'Scorpion' nightclub, it was home to bed in Support Company lines. Mainly due to the fact that none of us had scored with the delightful maidens of North Yorkshire. Not wishing to point the finger of blame or suspicion, but Embo came up with the bright idea of us being good blokes, and always thinking of others to go and feed the Company Sergeant Major's fish.

The fish tank in the CSM's office is a thing of wonder and awe! It had all the mod cons: bubbles, shipwrecks, and top of the range fish. In a word, it was the crowning glory of the office, and Uncle Wayne's pride and joy.

Welsh Roger being a Lance-Jack, and more adult than myself and Embo, made like a Genie and disappeared in a flash. Everything was a bit of a blur after that, but I think during our early morning visit to the CSM's office there was a bit of drunken confusion over fish food, alcohol, cleaning products, and a broken door lock.

Monday morning, everything was fine and dandy. All was quiet in Support Company world, when a request from the CSM came – 'Could Embo and Clarence please report to the Company Office? The CSM has a special job for them.' Happy days.

So, over the road we go, saying hi to 'Steve' the Company Clerk as we entered the hallowed ground of the Company Offices. 'In you go lads, the CSM is in a good mood and has a special job for you both' says Steve. Happy days! I am thinking, *what a fantastic weekend on the piss! Now we're in Uncle Wayne's good books what a result! Life is surprisingly good.*

On marching into the CSM's office and standing to attention, the CSM has a massive grin on his face. "Relax lads, I've got a special job for you two. How does Bristol Recruiting Office for a week selling the Regiment sound to you?" "Bloody great Sir!", was our answer. Cheers! What a result.

Then I sensed movement behind me and heard the door lock click. Spider senses were now starting to alarm. Embo was totally unaware of this and was still talking to the CSM.

"Right, you pair of smeggs, who killed my fucking fish?" was the CSM's first belt fed question. To my total horror, I looked at the fish tank which looked like it had been nuked. All the fish were floating on the top. Shit! You could have heard a pin drop. Embo, to his credit, was trying to get his words out with some bullshit excuse, green-grass style. I could not help myself. I started to laugh at Embo's pantomime performance.

The CSM's second belt fed question came. "You find this amusing Clarence?" Before I could reply, with the speed of a striking Cobra the CSM was over his desk, and with the dexterity of his former boxing days I was given a combination of pain and suffering, followed by a complete head dunk in the fish tank! Bobbing apples was given a whole new meaning that day, and I still hate the smell and taste of dead tropical fish.

Embo was by this stage was trying to get out of Dodge City, but the door was locked, so he was then introduced to the CSM's brand of Welsh justice, with him also experiencing a fish tank dunking.

After the CSM had calmed down he was now, in his words, a 'sensitive' mood. So, to add to Embo and I's pain and suffering it was time to roll the Magic Dice of desire! Clarence = 3. Embo = 4 + 2 because he was a Lance-Jack. Me being a lowly Private, I was happy with three extra duties.

The office door was then unlocked from the outside. 'Mick' the Company Quartermaster was there waiting with his billing book, ready to take some of our hard-earned cash off our hands for the broken door lock. Fair play, he did taken pity on us due to our red faces and sodden uniforms, because I was half expecting a slap for breaking his shit.

Not wishing to call 'Steve' the Company Clerk a grass, but he had made himself remarkably busy in the Company Office while the fish tank fun and games had played out. The final insult happened as Mick was throwing our sorry arses out of the Company Office, when the 'Boss' Company Commander who had been enjoying the show from his office, asked us if we had had a good weekend with a big grin on his face. The word quickly spread about dramas at the Company Office, and the Mortar Platoon being in the shit.

A few days later when sanity had returned to the Company, the fish tank drama returned with a vengeance, and this time, I was an innocent bystander watching with great amusement as a fellow member of the Mortar Platoon incurred the wrath of Uncle Wayne.

'Billy Butler' also had a minor fish tank in his room, so as Uncle Wayne was in the process of restocking his fish tank, Billy thought it would be a good idea to gift Wayne one of his fish. Happy days - good results all round with that damage limitation exercise. Unbeknownst to us all, Billy's golden gift fish was a miniature apex predator shark.

The morning calm was shattered by an explosion of rage and swearing from the CSM's office due to the fact his latest addition to the fish tank had eaten every other fish in the tank. The CSM was well and truly on the war path with the Mortar Platoon thanks to Billy. To cut a long story short, a scene from the Titanic was replayed as the Mortar Platoon abandoned ship and its accommodation to escape the ongoing iceberg that was Uncle Wayne, with Billy B begging for forgiveness which fell on the CSM's deaf ears.

The following week the fish tank was moved to the CSM's Married Quarter, so the fish could live in peace just like Free Willy. To this day, Billy still has nightmares reference sharks and tropical fish tanks.

The Three Feather's Tattoo:
Uncle Wayne, being a proud Welshman, had the Prince of Wales three heraldic feathers tattooed on his forearm. This tattoo was the CSM's badge of honour, and symbol of a proud Welshman. Embo being Embo couldn't help himself.

One day, when he was Company Orderly Sergeant, we had some new lads straight from Depot join the Support Company. These were noticeably young lads who were going to the Drums - Machine Gun Platoon. As the young lads were wating outside the Company Office, Embo told them that when they went in to see the CSM, if they were asked if they had any questions that they should reply with, "What are those three weeds on your arm sir?" It was the Company standing joke, and the CSM would see the funny side.

The three young lads went into the Company Office to see Uncle Wayne, and they repeated exactly what Embo had told them, including the fact the Embo the Company Orderly Sergeant had given them a really nice introduction to Support Company.

That night at scoff, Embo looked like a giant panda and was also in a foul mood because he had rolled the dice and got some more extra duties. Top tip: Don't mention the three feathers!

CHAPTER 3
"When I read about the evils of drinking, I gave up reading."
Henry Youngman.

Incoming Sniper Fire and the King of Comedy While Reading Company Detail:
Company detail was the daily bible. It was the most important bit of paper on the notice board. Failure to read it was not an option. It what was happening the next day, and week: exactly who was doing what, when, and where. Most of the single lads would read it after evening scoff at about 1800hrs.

'Tom' was a gun nut who was bought up on the farm down in Devon, who loved engines and guns. His car was a supped-up boy racer Renault 5 that went like shit off an aluminium shovel! Tom's greatest love was his air rifle - the thing was like something off Star Trek - laser spec ops, the dog's bollocks of air rifles.

So, reading detail soon became an exercise in hard targeting and trying not to get a pellet up the arse! Due to Tom's room being on the top floor of ATGW, lines were in an ideal position to watch over the Support Company notice board. Reading Company detail thus became a bloody nightmare if Tom were up in his nest taking pot shots. You would have to zig-zag be as quick as you could to avoid the first warning shot - the ping of the lamp post - followed by the second pellet on your leg or arse. To this day, I never hang about reading outdoors.

'Andy the King of Comedy' was the Battalion comedian who had recently returned from special duties. Andy was always telling jokes and leading the banter within the Company. He was also one of the best soldier's I ever served with. His talent meant he could create complete and utter chaos in a 30-mile radius, and still come out the other end smelling of roses.

Andy also had a room on the top floor; so instead of shooting you, he would destroy you with banter and abuse! On this particular day, I was in the shit with the CSM due to being not particularly good at Drill, thus labelled a Drill Mong. So, I was on op low profile avoiding any of the Company head shed. Reading detail, minding my own business, and the next thing I hear is the CSM's voice shouting at me to "Drop and do 20 press ups!", because I am a Drill Mong, followed by a load of other abuse.

By this stage, a few blokes were watching from the Company lines, enjoying my pain, and suffering as I was being destroyed and humiliated, followed by a large cheer and clapping. Bloody Andy had done a word-perfect impression of the CSM, shouting from his window - he had got me! Left, right, and Chelsea. Wanker. More on the King of Comedy to follow.

Cookhouse Commandos:

Payday weekend within Support Company was a cross between Neighbours and Black Hawk Down. What I mean by this is, that the lads with wives', birds, or girlfriends either on the Pads, army married estates, or downtown/ back home in the county would disappear for the beast with two backs for the weekend.

The single lads left in the block would be on the piss all weekend - no excuses - it was the Support Company way. This would start straight after the Battalion Friday morning run with beers in the TV room. This weekend was no different. Myself being not particularly good at drinking, was classed as a lightweight, and trust me, within Support Company there were some heavy weight drinking champions of the world.

The following tale of woe was told to me by the lads involved in this disaster. 'Fred Star' was a nightmare on the piss with a surname like his. Everybody knew and liked him because the lad could drink and have a good time. His main partners in crime were 'Wanger Webb' who was a Rugby Head! Before he joined up, he was a semi-pro rugby player down in Gloucester. But beer and going out on the piss with the lads was his favourite pastime if he was not egg chasing. He was also a wind-up merchant who was always playing jokes on people.

One weekend he broke into one of the lad's rooms, left male porn in there, then reported the lad to our boss for coming on to him in a gay manner: the boss needed to check this lad's room. Everybody was in on the joke apart from the lad who was in a complete state of shock. Hilarious! '63' was the final member of the posse. 63 had a common Welsh name, so in Army ancient tradition he was called after the last two of his army number. 63 was a Battalion character, another rugby head, but would do anything to avoid PT. His favourite trick was his neck brace. Due to a minor rugby injury, 63 was signed off and given a neck brace by the doctor. So, every time the Company would parade for PT, 63 would amazingly appear with his neck brace on. It used to be white but was now black due to constant use.

So, after two days of the piss the dream team return to camp at stupid o'clock in the morning feeling hungry. Wanger decided to become Spiderman and climb up onto the roof of the cookhouse to do the initial breaking and entering phase. They entered the cookhouse via the sky light. After letting the rest of his motley crew in, Spider decided to cook a midnight feast of Chili Con Carne. By this stage, the master criminals had changed into the chef's whites, including stove pipe hats, and were having a write old knee up in the cookhouse. This came to a very abrupt end with the arrival of the Battalion Orderly Officer and members of the guard. It was great entertainment for the lads on guard, plus it was priceless gossip for the Battalion rumour mill. Unfortunately, it has a long night of paperwork for the Battalion Orderly Officer. The Battalion Orderly Officer had the last laugh though because Spider and co have the pleasure reporting to 'Honest Harry' who oversaw discipline for the Battalion. Drama and scandal! The hammer was going to get dropped Monday morning on the cookhouse cowboys.

Honest Harry was the Sheriff and the main man in the Battalion for sorting out the saints and the sinners. The phrase, 'It takes a poacher to be a game-keeper,' was made for Honest Harry. He was a cross between the Terminator and Sgt Bilko because Harry could be a right bastard when he wanted to be. On the same hand, he was old school in the sense of *you do the crime you do the time.* At the end of your punishment - no hard feelings, normal jogging. Plus, he had his fingers in loads of pies and was always doing a bit of business. It was a healthy pastime to keep off Honest Harry's radar. If you did happen to find yourself on the radar and in the shit with Harry, there was a dark art, black magic trick within the guardroom if a £20 pound note were found in a certain flowerpot by Harry - amazingly your extra ten o'clock rock parade would disappear Harry Potter style! Hogwarts had nothing on Alma Barracks.

I personally have great respect for Harry, who all joking aside stopped me one night doing something really silly and stupid which could had landed be in prison doing serious time in a civilian jail. After locking me up, calming everything down for the night, and having a brew and a chat with me the morning after when I had sobered up was a life changing moment in my life. Plus, I was never bullied again.

If you're reading this, cheers Harry, you are a good man. Where is that £20 quid, I lent you back in 1993? Harry was also responsible for Wanger Webb's nickname. During one of Wangers previous infringements, Harry was going mental and could not get out Pte Webb, so it was 'Wanger' instead. Due to the damage, they had done to the cookhouse skylight, Harry decided that the building was insecure, so the Lads had to Stag on and guard the cookhouse. Monday morning arrived and the following tale of woe was told to me by Spider Webb.

Honest Harry was not a happy man! Fred and 63 had reported to his office to receive their punishment but there is no sign of Spider, which has put Harry in a rage. There was going to be tears before bedtime tonight in the Mortar Platoon lines tonight. Spider had decided to go dark and hide it out in the Mortar Platoon TV Room and hopefully, it would all blow over because he had rugby that afternoon. Wrong answer. Very wrong answer. Spider had poked the bear and was going to get clawed. Harry's system of informers had located Spider's hiding place and was on the hunt. On trying to gain entrance to the Mortars TV Room, Spider had locked him out and refused to open to the law. Harry being Harry, always had a Plan B - he simply sprinkled and deployed some CS tablets smoking away in an ashtray under the door and waited for Spider to come to him after being gassed! It did not take long for Spider stop resisting; the law had already won.

Crime and punishment were quickly dispensed due to Wanger's Battalion rugby career. The cookhouse commando's punishment was passed, and the gabble was banged.

All the civilian catering staff we given a 3-day rest while in work. The commandos were now doing all the Dixie bashing, 'washing up', peeling spuds, wiping tables down etc in the Battalion cookhouse. For the commandos it was hell on Earth reporting to the Duty Chef at 0500hrs in the morning. Dixieland till after breakfast at 0800Hrs, followed by lunch scoff 1230Hrs-1345Hrs. Worst of all, the evening meal sloop out 1730Hrs till whenever all the pans were cleaned, the cookhouse was washed down and tided up - usually about 2200Hrs because Honest Harry took great delight in making sure the Queen herself would be happy with cleanliness of 1GLOSTERS cookhouse.

Wanger and his partners in crime told the lads it was the hardest, less Colchester nick, this was the worst punishment they had ever received. To add insult to injury, they were made to wear the civilian contractor's uniform while they were plate scraping and peeling spuds. The final nail in the cookhouse commandos' coffins was the trip the following week down to the Quartermaster's Department, reference the bill for the replacement sky light from the cookhouse roof. It was not a cheap visit; followed by another ear bending. Top tip: of the day - do not break and enter the cookhouse. The next generation of cookhouse commandos were also from the Mortar Platoon plus Support Company attachments during the Royal Gloucestershire Berkshire and

Wiltshire Regiment two-year residential Battalion posting to Ballykinlar Northern Ireland 2000-2002. This is a yarn for another chapter.

CHAPTER 4

"Pandora opened the box with the new high-heels, put them on, and went out to town".
Ljupka Cvetanova.

Grand Theft Shopping Trolley Auto:

The final yarn and tall tale of this chapter revolves around another pair of characters from the Mortar Platoon who incurred the wrath of the local Catterick Garrison Royal Military Police, regarding motoring offenses.

'Fozzie the Fritter' was a right good laugh and as camp as 'Lukewarm' off the TV show, Porridge! One of life's jokers. Always in a good mood, nothing could phase him. Fozzie was always good entertainment, especially when on the piss downtown. Plus, he was senior solider within the Platoon and was always happy to show us young lads the ropes and help us out. Plus, he was also a fellow Bristolian and a Bristol rovers' fan, so we got on like a house on fire.

'Norm' was also a lanky Bristolian with thick, wire rimmed glasses. He was also from one of the toughest neighbourhoods in Bristol west of the river, so he had his shit together. Norm was also a true gentleman, he would always put others first, and was the ultimate team player. Norm's only downfall was when he got pissed up - he was a complete fucking lunatic. Norm would not get punchy or aggressive, he would just do crazy shit. Like taking a dump in the fireplace of the Fleece Pub in Richmond for a bet.

This tale of woe starts, as always, in the Fleece Pub in Richmond. This watering hole was always the Support Company 1Glosters, unofficial meeting place for going out on the piss with the lads. This was in the days before mobile phones and the internet, so come the weekends there was always a member of Support Company supping ale in the Fleece Public House, surrounded by the bright lights of Richmond, North Yorkshire.

After firing the beers and bottles of twenty 20 Mad Dog down our necks, the night was progressing well. The lads would split up - either to the 'Pit' plastic night club in town which had a wobbly wooden floor upstairs that one day would give up the ghost and fall like the walls of Jericho; or the other choice was to jump in a taxi to the one and only real nightclub on the Garrison - The 'Scorpion,' AKA 'Scabs'.

To all the troops on the Garrison, Scabs was a rite of passage. It was a spit and sawdust shithole, with warm beer and loads of whores and slappers - the troops loved it. There were always inter-unit punch ups and fighting with the civilian population or F.B.A.R - army slang for 'Fighting in Bars and Restaurants'. The bonus was pulling one of the local slappers with excellent nicknames like Wendy Shell Shock, and the Old Woman Who Lived in a Shoe! Wendy Shell Shock was a legend in Scabs - trust me - some of the lads that had woken up next to her the morning after would be traumatised and in shell shock after doing the dirty deed. Also, there was the Old Woman That Lived in a Shoe, who had a football team worth of kids from various squaddies from the different Regiments and units that had passed through Catterick Garrison.

Getting home from Scabs was a bloody nightmare if you had survived the takeout scoff and had avoided getting throw down the stairs by the bouncers. You had to put your life in your hands at the taxi rank. Waiting for a taxi was a nightmare with the various dramas associated with drunken squaddies and slappers that would inevitably play out. Camp was a three mile walk away, so either way you were in the hurt locker.

According to Norm, he and Fozzie decided to tab back to camp. Due to them both being well pissed up, they acquired a shopping trolly for transport, taking it in turns to push or ride in the trolly. It was all going well until they hit the camp centre roundabout. Because of the copious amounts of alcohol, they had consumed, they hit the roundabout downhill with the wind behind them, in full sail, both riding the trolly on the wrong side of the road! Unfortunately for them, this was witnessed by a mobile patrol of the Garrison Royal Military Patrol. The RMP's, 'Monkeys' were not exactly known for their sense of humour. To cut a long story short, Norm and Fozzie went straight to jail - they did not pass go, and they did not collect £200 pounds. Happy Saturday night lads.

The trouble with being lifted, 'nicked' by the Monkeys, was that everything then goes nuclear. It is going to end in tears before bedtime, and the unfortunate offenders going on orders. Going on orders was a pain in the arse because the Company boss-man had to get involved and it meant either a fine or jail time; leading from that worst case scenario was going down the road to appear in front of the Commanding Officer, 'Marvellous Martin'. Guilty, you could end up in Colchester Military Nick - The Glasshouse - followed by discharge.

By this stage, the Mortar Platoon Head Shed, had had enough of the constant dramas and fuck ups. The Yemminator now deployed the Sword of Damocles down on our collective heads.

'Yemminator' was a bear of a man from the Forest of Dean. A cross between The Terminator, and a Native American shaman wise man. He was, in my little world, the ultimate warrior king! He was an old school Senior NCO and the non-commissioned boss of the Mortar Platoon. In the big man him selves' words, when being given the benefit of his wisdom; 'Clarence, your cavalier attitude is starting to piss me off. Grow up son or you will feel my wrath'. This was a measure of the man; we were his boys, and nobody fucked with his Platoon. We were *his* children. But he was also Victorian father to us all. When he said, "Jump", you asked, "How high.?" I still had a lot to learn, and one of his favourite one liner to me was, 'Life is hard son, and growing up is tough for any kid'. To this day I will always be grateful for his no-nonsense approach to bringing up his Platoon solider children.

Monday morning was the last straw for the Yemminator. Thanks to Fozzie and Norm - those pair of jokers being the last straw that had broken the camel's back. The Sword of Damocles now fell on the Platoon. Reference Fozzie and Norm being on orders and possibly in even bigger shit. His attitude was now hardening into, 'Dry your eyes mate. You are in the shit. Suck it up buttercup. Take your punishments like men'.

The Sword of Damocles now fell on to the Platoon, our Mortar Platoon Senior NCO's hit us with a surprise room and full kit inspection. The whole living in the block lads got picked up for various infringements. Staff and extra cleaning parades were handed out like confetti at a wedding. Honest Harry had a busy couple of days with the Mortar Platoon. At one stage, the ten o'clock rock staff parade stretched from Battalion Headquarters all the way down to the Guardroom. Worse was to follow!

Thursday morning at 0600 hrs the Platoon paraded at the Mortar Store in CEMO - Complete Equipment Marching Ordered - i.e., Belt kit and bergens for a Tab. Tactical advance to contact, a fast forced march over rough terrain. We were then issued our own mortar equipment including base plates, bipods, and barrels. I, being a signaller, ended up with radio kit which was fucking heavy, but not as much as a pain in the arse to carry as a bipod or barrel. We then boarded 4Tonners provided by the MT Platoon, dropped 20 miles from camp on the North Yorkshire moors, given maps and told to Tab back to camp dickheads!

It was an awfully long and very painful day. I will always remember my back killing me. Coming down and over the last ridgeline and looking down at the bright lights of Alma Barracks as dusk was falling, I was thinking *thank fuck this little walk was over and done with*. Everybody was fucked and, on their chinstraps, Endex. Life lesson learnt - big time.

Company Commanders orders were the next long-awaited event within the Company. Norm and Fozzie were duly marched into Big Steve's, the Company Commander's Office to face the music. Fair play to the OC, he did find the shopping trolly grand theft auto rather amusing and could have thrown the book at them both, but he was feeling generous. They went in one at a time, and both were awarded seven days ROPs, Restriction of Privileges and getting grief from Honest Harry.
Fozzie was marched out and away back to the accommodation. Norm wasn't marched out due to the OC having to take an important phone call, so Norm being Norm, took the OCs hand wave as his cue to jog on out of the office. As per ROPs standing orders, before commencing their punishment they had to go and report to Honest Harry for a brief and Do's and Don'ts for their action-packed adventure down the guardroom on ROPs a week of fun in the sun.

This is where Honest Harry played an absolute blinder regarding due processes. Because Norm had not been marched out and due process has not been followed, his seven days of ROPs were invalid. Whereas Fozzie was marched out, so his punishment stood. Unlucky son. Life is full of disappointments. Norm had got away Scott-free for a few weeks and was renamed McVicar. Top tip: Don't go joy riding round camp centre roundabouts in a shopping trolley.

CHAPTER 5

> *"Twilight drops her curtain down and pins it with a star."*
> *Lucy Montgomery.*

Twilight of empire

Twilight of empire, 'Marvellous Martin' or MM was the last of his kind. MM was the last Commanding Officer of the 1st Battalion, Gloucestershire Regiment 28th/61ST. MM was a soldier's soldier; both feared and respected in equal measure. The last of the old breed of commanding officers who lead from the front and spent most of his career within the same Battalion. He knew everybody's nickname, always up for a laugh, and would like nothing better than having a beer downtown with his lads. His main effort was always field soldiering - no bullshit. His motto was, 'A happy ship, was an efficient ship'.

One incident I will always remember, was that I was in the shit over something and the RSM wanted a word in my ear. So, there I was standing to attention outside the RSM's office shitting myself, when I heard the RSM tell the CO he has got Private Heal outside for being a Dickhead. MM then says, "Who is Private bloody Heal? Do I know him?" The CO then sticks his head round the door and says to me; "Oi, Clarence! Who The bloody hell is Private Heal? You know him?" I stammered out that it was me! He started laughing told me to, "Get lost! Fuck off! Don't be a dickhead or I'll give you a slap myself!" I broke the record for running up the hill back to support Company lines that day. MM what a legend.

Years later in 2005, I had the honour and the privilege to take MM, now a Brigadier, on a ground orientation of the A Coy 1RGBWs area of operations in Kabul because I was an independent call sign under USMC command. Fair play, the great man was good Company for the day and was even telling jokes and having a laugh with the US Marines. He also took time to send me a thankyou letter. MM - strength and honour to a great man.

The last thing the Regiment did before laying up the colours were the Freedom Marches, and final parade of the Glorious Glosters. All this was done down the shire, with the Battalion working out of RAF South Cerny for a few weeks. Enter Evo and the Support Company Good Idea Club.

Evo is, to this day, one of life's enigmas. He comes across as a jovial, slightly overweight fellow - not the image of a battle hardened solider who puts holes in skulls. The DS solution to the saying, 'Don't ever judge a book by its cover', is Evo. He has natural fitness, passed the all-arms commando course, and is still serving as a CSM for the Rifles Reserves at the time of me writing this book. He and his fellow partner in crime 'Cain the Train', will be mentioned in more detail later, are good soldiers. Always up for a laugh and a piss up. Plus, when it comes to being relaxed professional Riflemen, they are up there in Jedi orbit.

Evo always drove a shit car but had a top of the range motor bike. He was a petrol head who raced bikes for the Army.

Evo being a native of Gloucester decided to take the boys sightseeing with a difference. So, a jolly boys outing was arranged to the Fred West House of Horrors, 25 Cromwell Street; followed by a trip down some dodgy pub that Evo had family ties to.

So off we go down the lanes to Gloucester in Evo's latest shit car - a beige Renault 18 which he had bought of Tony 'H' Holford from Mortars. Seven of us squeezed into the wagon. Me in the passenger footwell, Evo driving, Shads commanding whilst trying not to squash me; Ryan K, Bots and Dock-ray in the back, and Harry Crumb in the boot. After the usual Evo rally driving experience, bickering and banter, we arrived at the infamous 25 Cromwell Street House of Horrors.

What a let-down it was! Some grubby end Victorian Terrace 2 up with a copper stood outside, and half of the gaff was covered with tarps. I was thinking it would be something out of a Stephen King novel. Well done Evo - this is not Scooby Doo you clown! Let us go to the pub, which was also a drama. The County Arms, Millbrook Street, was a right shit hole, a typical spit and sawdust joint. Wipe your feet on the way-out son! The highlight of the trip was Ryan K saying, "I'm not going in there as the windows are cardboard". Top tip: Don't let Evo organize any jolly boys outing because his admin is shit.

In all Regiments there is always a bloke that tells tall stories and is a bit of a bullshit merchant. On route back to camp after some airmobile infantry exercise, wait, fly, dig, and die! Our wagon was passed by some big Eddie Stobart HGV. 'Mark Tell me a Story' piped up. "Good old Eddie, I helped him start that business back in the day, lent him my last £200 quid". Evo looked at me in disbelief! Roger and Embo started sniggering, so the saying 'Doing an Eddie Stobart' was then used as Support Company slang for somebody talking bullshit. Also, if you were telling outright lies you were known as a Pinocchio!

Another one of Mark's tell me a story claim to fame, was that one day he was out parachuting with the Commanding Officer, when the aircraft flew over

Mark's hometown. According to Mark, the Commanding Officer said to him, "See you Monday Mark!", so off Mark jumped. Home for tea and crumpets.

CHAPTER 6

"He who neither drinks, nor smokes, nor dances, he who preaches and even occasionally practice piety, temperance and celibacy, is generally a saint, or a mahatma, or more likely a humbug, but he certainly won't make a leader - or for that matter a good soldier".
Sam Manekshaw.

1st Battalion the Royal Gloucestershire Berkshire and Wiltshire Regiment, Alma Barracks, Catterick, North Yorkshire England.

Amalgamation: April 1994 – September 1994. UNPROFOR, Bosnia, September – April 1995:
On return from Easter leave the amalgamation of the two Regiments was done and dusted. A major problem was that the two Regiments were vastly different in character, especially regarding the head shed. The Gloucestershire Regiment had a relaxed way of doing things and were not into bullshit - polishing boots etc. The Duke of Edinburgh's Regiment loved their green belts and muster parades. There would be interesting times ahead.

Fair play, the newly formed Support Company was overall not too bad. Some good lads across the board from the former Regiments getting on with it, plus some new characters were added into the Support Company mix. The main thing for us was that we kept our OC - Big Steve who was a good bloke and treated everybody fairly and cared about his lads.

Unfortunately, the new Commanding Officer, in my humble opinion, which is shared by the rest of the lads, was a wanker! Typical Cold War warrior stuck up snob who had his own little hand bell which he would ring when he had finished looking down his nose at you when you were in his office for whatever reason. He played favourites and wasn't a great fan of the Glosters relaxed way of doing things.

Several things stick in my mind. Firstly, was the first Support Company piss up of the new Regiment. We were on a beat-up exercise and the Company head shed decided to have a 'smoker' piss up. So happy days. Everybody was making the effort to get on and have a laugh getting to know each other when in walks the new CO. Instead of having a beer with the boys, he drinks a can of pop and only talks to the officers. Then, when he says a few words of wisdom to the newly formed Support Company 1RGBW, he comes across as Lord Fucking Snotty looking down his nose at the peasants! So, it starts to kick off. Led by some of the ex-dukes that knew what this clown is all about.

I have to say in hindsight, I think it was a member of the Anti-Tank Platoon that threw the first empty beer can in the direction of the CO – Andy, the king of comedy looking rather guilty and Dai from the Dukes trying to look like butter wouldn't melt in his mouth. Fair play to our outgoing Company Commander, just as it was about to go nuclear, he stood up all relaxed, raised his hand, and told us all to calm down and enjoy the evening. Instant obedience. It was all good in the hood and the look on the CO's face was a picture. Top tip: one does not go on a Support Company piss up with a can of pop.

CHAPTER 7

"If there is ever another war in Europe, it will come out of some damned silly thing in the Balkans".
Otto Von Bismarck.

'Mick' was our new Platoon Sergeant in Mortars. He was a monster of a man - bloody huge like a grizzly bear. Most of all was an absolute beer monster. I have seen some big drinkers in my time, but Mick takes the biscuit! He smoked like a chimney, couldn't run for a bus, but could carry mortar kit like a carthorse. Life was never dull when Mick was around, plus, he had a few world-famous party tricks.

His favourite one, which I discovered to my detriment, was when he was pissed up. He would stand next to you, engage you in conversation, flip his knob out and piss in your pocket. Welcome to Mick's Magical Waterfall! His other party trick was to punch you in the solar plexus when we used to take the piss out of him and give him grief. Trust me on this one, getting a punch in the solar plexus off Mick was not a good idea or life experience. It was like getting kicked by a rather large mule on steroids. Going out on the piss when Mick was out and about was a nightmare. Top tip: Stay well clear of bears with sore heads called Mick from Mortars!

UNPROFOR Bosnia September 1994 – April 1995:

Bosnia was a shithole and a nightmare. To put it in simple terms, The Serbs, Croats, and Muslims were all at it. They all had blood on their hands, hate in their hearts, and had been at each other's throats for years. The winter was bloody and bitterly cold. Plus, the standing joke amongst the Brits was that the UN stood for useless.

Embo - Dropping me in the shit with the Bosnian Serb Army:

As per usual, the banter and messing around continued during the tour. This tale of woe personally involved me getting grief from the Bosnian Serbs and the New RSM. Checkpoints in Bosnia were a bloody nightmare, and anything could and would happen. On this day it went nuclear because of Embo, who could not help himself and keep his big trap shut. My Land Rover FFR - Land Rover Fitted for Radio Communications, was always at the front of the convoy due to me being the convoy leader's driver and radio operator. Now, my boss Captain S was a good bloke for a Rupert, he could speak the lingo like a native, plus was a subject matter expert on upsetting the various Bosnian warring factions, because they were all as bad as each other and on the make.

So, on this day were having a drama at the Bosnian Serb checkpoint. 'Rog a tits up', due to there being on large can of OMD 80 engine oil unaccounted for on the convoy manifest. The Serbs being the Serbs were their usual argumentative selves and basically accused us, the Brits, of supplying their Muslim enemies. They wanted the engine oil for themselves - wankers.

Captain S was in the middle of having a row and decides to play the Serbs at their own game. He pulls out his knife, then starts punching holes in the oil can so all the oil starts seeping down the road. The Serbs then go ballistic, and the situation starts to escalate and go nuclear, so Embo decides to get involved in the fun and games. Embo goes up to the biggest Serb that looks like the 'Grizzly Adams' of the group and points to me. He then informs 'Grizzly Adams' that I am a Muslim even though I am a bloody Methodist!

Boom! Embo has now caused an international incident! Here we go, Captain S has already pissed the Bosnian Serbs off big time. Now they have another target for their wrath and general hatred of the UN. Talk about how to gain friends and influence people! Weapons are now being cocked and loaded for bear; the engine oil is forgotten about, it's all about me now.

Next thing a know is Grizzly Adams comes storming over to my Land Rover FFR and starts gobbing off, finger pointing, and giving it the big un in Serbo-Croatian - fucking great! Well done, Embo. Me being me, I just laughed at the prick because I was thinking, correct answer - this fool looks like Grizzly Adams.

Then, Grizzly has picked me up in a bear hug and slammed me against the side of my Land Rover in a bearhug, showing off in front of his mates, the cheeky bastard. So, I knee the prick in the balls. He lets me go with a roar as I have just poked the bear. He then gives me a slap, which is like getting hit by lightning which then starts a bit of a melee with me being used as a human rag doll.

Embo is just stood there laughing at me for having a slap and enjoying the entertainment, before he jumps in and a gives Grizzly a WWF smackdown. Captain S manages to calm things down and peace is restored – off we go following the yellow brick road to Gorazde.

To add insult to injury my face looks like I'm a giant panda, my uniform is in rag order, and I have Big Ben ringing in my ears for a day. All the while Captain S is laughing his head off, taking the piss and asking me if a would like a bamboo shoot to eat.

I was one relieved teddy bear when the convoy finally made it into the UNPROFOR base at Gorazde. Captain S disappears into the ops room leaving me to sort out the convoy delivery and RV with 'The Penguin'. Reference what stores, what equipment was on what wagon, the order of march on the unload, and check the manifest. I had 'contraband' hidden in my Land Rover battery box from prying Serb eyes. The contraband was shiny items of kit, sneaky beaky that was for UK eyes only.

CHAPTER 8

'If you had been in charge of The Last Supper, it would have been a takeaway.'
Del-Boy Trotter.

The Penguin and The Riddler:
The following were larger than life characters, that were both former Support Company Senior NCO's from the Glosters who had acquired their nicknames way before I joined up. They had got their nicknames during the Battalion's previous two-year Northern Ireland tour.

Andy the King of Comedy was responsible for the nick names, he had gotten his ideas from the old 1960's Batman TV show. According to Andy, every day before they went out on patrol all you would hear was 'The Penguin' shouting 'Mac, mac, mac, mac, mac...', flapping about something or other.

In return 'The Riddler' would always answer a question with a question or riddle – 'Can I get some batteries for my torch? Please colour.' The Riddler's reply would be a riddle, 'In what country does the sun set and rise in the east?' So, The Penguin and The Riddler were christened. Two good blokes who took it all in good grace. Plus, The Penguin was into jap slapping marital arts, not a bloke to upset.

So, I'm in the process of having a chat with The Penguin and sorting things out with the convoy. With him being a support Company SNCO, he would make sure I'm doing ok and would square me away. The Penguin was one of the most kind-hearted blokes in the Regiment, always looking out for the lads.

The next thing I know, the new RSM appears out of thin air. Don't forgot he's a green belt wearing, ironed kit clown that doesn't like the Mortar Platoon and Glosters in general. The only thing he's worried about his career. I still have no respect for the clown after all these years the muppet. "Heal you're a fucking disgrace! Look at the state of you!" He is ranting and roaring my face with his green belt on, ironed jacket, waving his pace stick about - typical barrack room bully boy style going mental.

I then think *fuck this* for a game of soldiers. I was at the end of my tether - the bell end. So, I told him straight I had been beaten up by the Serbs, had numerous vehicle and radio dramas, and was fucking knackered after four days on the road; bloody freezing cold and generally pissed off with life and Bosnia to boot. To that end, I did not give a fuck what he thought of me or the world in general. I also mentioned that at least the old RSM of the Glosters said that belts were for ammo pouches, not prancing around this shithole giving brigade of guards' bullshit. As you can imagine this went down well with him – me, a mere private solider gobbing off to the RSM. I had just signed and sealed my own death warrant.

As my life was going down the Bosnian drain at a rapid rate of knots, the Yemminator grabbed me by the ear and extracted me from the situation before it could escalate even worse. He then took me round the back calmed me down; told me he was happy with my work, but to avoid the new RSM like the plague and not be a dickhead! Wise words from a top bloke, followed by an almighty bollocking for gobbing off to the RSM. I was lucky not to be in serious bother because of my actions. Mind you Ivor, the last RSM of the Glosters laughed his head off when he got wind of the story off the jungle drums. He thought it was hilarious, but said if I had gobbed off to him, he would have shoved his pace stick up my nose. His Top tip: for me was to avoid the new RSM like the plague and keep my head down. Wise words indeed.

EOD and the Hitman:
Here is a very funny story from Wanger. When the lads first arrived at the OP locations, the weather was still good, so the Hitman decided to make some improvements, including the installation of a picnic table. There was plenty of timber lying about to make this happen. However, one small problem arose due to the wood splitting when the lads were knocking the stakes in with a sledgehammer. The Hitman came up with a cunning plan!

To prevent the wooden stakes from splitting, The Hitman decided to use a discarded 105mm empty shell case as a thumper, or top cover for driving the wooden stakes into the ground for this ongoing construction project. It was a hot day, so The Hitman had stripped down, was flexing his muscles, and was ready to begin some sledgehammer logging. As his first swing contacted top of the 105mm shell casing, which was covering the wooden stake, there was a loud bang followed by a flash and smoke.

When the smoke had cleared, Wanger and the boys ran down to the area of the picnic table. They were greeted by the sight of The Hitman looking like a black and white minstrel, with flash burns to his face and hands, and no facial hair! Wangers exact words when retelling the story was that The Hitman looked like looked like a Victorian chimney sweep that had been electrocuted. There had been a live percussion cap in the base of the 105mm shell casing. The blokes were rolling around in fits of laughter at The Hitman, who was now known as EOD - Explosive Ordnance Disposal. Luckily, nobody was seriously hurt. The Hitman got grief for weeks afterward, as the news quickly spread about picnic tables and Mortars EOD dramas.

CHAPTER 9

'Multi-tasking is the ability to screw everything up simultaneously.'
Jeremy Clarkson.

Wangers Top Gear Driving School Special - Central Bosnia:
On one convoy out of Gorazde, 'Ronny Parker' was driving his Saxon APC, and Wanger was commanding up in the turret with no troops in the back, the wagon was going back to Kiseljak for repairs and maintenance. As Wanger jumped down to have a slash during a piss stop from the turret and stretch his legs; Ron had his headphones in and stayed in the wagon listening to his country and western tunes on his Walkman. The convoy moved off again to continue its journey towards Sarajevo. About an hour into the journey, I was driving my Land Rover as the lead vehicle, when I had a VW Golf car up my arse beeping his horn and flashing his lights for about two miles going mental.

'Here we go then', Captain S says. 'More bloody drama and scandal with the toothless pissed up locals.' As the vehicle cut me up and bought the convoy to a halt, I am expecting World War Three to break out! To my total shock and amazement, Wanger gets out the passenger seat of the VW Golf. He was looking very relived and happy to see us.

What happened was, that Ron had not bothered to check if Wanger was up in the turret before he had drove off, listening to Johnny Cash, totally oblivious to what was going on up top in the turret. Wanger having been abandoned in the middle of Bosnia with no weapon or kit had been incredibly lucky to have flagged down a friendly local who chased the convoy down. It could have gone very badly and ended in tears. Wanger was one lucky teddy bear! For obvious reasons everybody involved kept their traps firmly shut about this little episode of 'Top Gear'. Top tip: always makes sure you do a head count.

John, Dogs Arse; and the Kiwi Bar in Split Croatia end of tour April 1995:
John and Dogs Arse were the lads responsible for the Battalion rear link in Croatia. John was an old-time Sergeant Major who had returned from a posting under a cloud being told his career was over; having been naughty in the eyes of head shed. The lads thought he was a legend; he was a soldier's soldier that ran an incredibly happy and efficient ship. The army of the early 90's was still in the 1970's Cold War mindset, where one mistake or upsetting someone, could ruin a man's career overnight - as John had found out.

He is now a gentleman farmer in New Zealand. We remain good friends, and I always look forward to my yearly trips down under to visit him and Wanger with our respective families. Dogs Arse was the Battalion scrum half and senior private solider who had been there, done that, and got the t-shirt. He was also a fully paid-up member of, Do What the Fuck You Like Club. A good lad and a good man to have on your side. Dog's Arse acquired his nickname from various rugby club songs.

With Spilt in Croatia, being the main logistics hub for UNPROFOR every man and his dog, REMFs, head shed, UN Civics, and bottle washers were located and living in large former Yugoslavian army base down on the waterfront. The Brits being the Brits soon combined with the Canadians and the New Zealanders. John being John, and Dogs' Arse being a rugby head where soon joined at the hip with the Kiwi's. The Kiwi bar/Koru Club soon became the official headquarters and administration hub of the Battalion. I would do a bit of business with John and the Kiwi's due to there being a lot of souvenirs available on my travels in the former Yugoslavia that would just be laying around and looking for a new home.

The Koru Club/Kiwi Bar was a rather large portacabin and BBQ patio area out the back of camp by the helipad away from it all - the idea location. It was run by friendly Kiwi lads and all-round top fellows; Pete, Smalley, and Māori Phil - ably assisted by John and Dogs Arse, when they were required. The two can beer rule was not well enforced, if you played the game, it was a great night and good banter. If you were a pissed-up prick you were out on your arse via a 'Jake, the Muss' Kiwi bouncer Māori Phil who was built like WWF's The Rock. It was semi-official, but you needed an invite from the Kiwi boys to enter. John and I are still in contact with the Kiwi lads 20 years on and John settled and now lives with his family in New Zealand. I always enjoy my trips down the Southern Cross to reminisce and shoot the shit with the Kiwi's.

John being John, and in the twilight of his career was in his element and would square the boys away when they came down to slipper city from up country. With his connections, he made sure that his support Company crew were always invited into the Koru Club.

At the end of tour a few members of the Battalion got well pissed up in the Kiwi bar, Dogs Arse decided to play 'Madness' through the sound system which ended up with a massive failure in the Croatian school of dancing, and one of the walls of the portacabin becoming a new door/patio entrance with half the RGBW lads falling through the wall. The Kiwis were not impressed with the destruction of the wall of their bar, so John had to call several large favours in from the Royal Engineers and other interested parties to repair Anglo Kiwi relations as well as the wall. Not wishing to point the finger of blame and suspicion but, Fat Lewe from ATGW Platoon was the first through the breech in the wall.

CHAPTER 10

'A lady came up to me one day and said, "Sir! You are drunk," to which I replied, "I am drunk today, madam, and tomorrow I shall be sober, but you will still be ugly.'
Winston Churchill, former British Prime Minister.

1st Battalion the Royal Gloucestershire Berkshire and Wiltshire Regiment

Salamanca Barracks, Episkopi, Cyprus, April 1995 – April 1997:

Cyprus sunshine posting - not! We as a Battalion were constantly on duty. It was guarding either the Episkopi Garrison, or the RAF Base at Akrotiri. There was the added bonus if you were unlucky of staging on up the mountain, Troodos Defence Platoon. Mind you, if you were not on duty, Cyprus - especially in the holiday season was a 18-30 piss heads paradise.

Ron the Dog:

'Ron the Dog' another member of the Mortar Platoon that had acquired his nickname because of his surname MacDonald, hence Ronald/Ron, and the Dog being his ability to sleep anywhere when drunk like a Dog. Ron the Dog's party trick was to get drunk, and the morning after forgetting where he had parked his car. It was a regular Sunday morning tradition for one of us to drive Ron around town looking for his car on the garrison or town.

Ron took to the Cyprus lifestyle like a bear shitting in the woods. Support Company Block was on the hill at the top of camp, and out of the way for obvious reasons. With a New OC and CSM, life was surprisingly good for the single living lads; apart from the CSM's pet hate of the Support Company car park.

The Support Company car park was a cross between a scrap yard and a car show room. At the bottom of the scale was Airy Neave's 1975 Datsun Cherry, held together with black nasty; my own burnt by the sun, 1982-mark one VW golf; and finally, Caesar's trail motorbike that was only held together by the rust.

The middle of the scale was Kev's Surf bum Suzuki Jeep, Embo's Mazda 929 which only had a couple of dents due to Embo's amazing parking skills; and Hitman's S Ford Sierra XR4i. The top of the scale was Tex and Gary's ivory white, brand-new Mazda 323, and Big Tels Brand spanking new RAV4.

Now we come on to 'Ron the Dogs' pride and joy. The light blue Mazda 626 Estate - complete with orange flashing magnetic portable roof light. The car was known throughout the Company as the 'Helen Daniels car' after the Neighbour's Australian soap opera character.

Ron the Dog's School of Driving.

Ron's automotive party trick was to cram as many blokes as he could in the Helen Daniels car, attach the orange flashing light to his roof, then drive us all down to the Limassol strip Duke of Hazard style. After getting well pissed up we would get a taxi back to camp. Then usually on a Monday morning Ron would try and remember where he had parked his car, with no recollection, the whole Company would play, let us go and find Ron's car downtown.

During one heavy drinking session watching the 6 Nations Rugby, Ron had a full-blown heart attack. Ambulance flashing lights - the full Monty. After retiring somewhat in shock, the lads were taking bets on how long Ron would be laid up in the hospital. To everyone's utter amazement, just before last orders, Ron rocked up in the bar - hospital gown and wrist tagged up. He had been treated and could not be bothered to stay in a Cypriot hospital, so he thought, *fuck it lets have a beer*. Lunatic.

CHAPTER 11

'Alcohol may be man's worst enemy, but the Bible says love your enemy.'
Frank Sinatra.

The Penguin's Desert Odyssey:

The Penguin was responsible for resupplying the Company whilst the Battalion was deployed on exercise in Kuwait desert. I was then in COY HQ, and one freezing cold desert night The Penguin decided to stop the wagon for an impromptu, 'Let us give Clarence an astrological navigation lesson'. Boring!

Plus, it was fucking freezing! Let us just get back to camp and into our gonk bags.

After getting cold and bored to death for half an hour, I start driving back across the desert. The Penguin is giving it the big un, reference his new super-duper Gucci hand flask, so I thought I would give him a nudge. I hit the brakes due to trying to avoid a jerboa! The Penguin's hot drink from his flask ends up all over him - bloody hilarious I thought as I started sniggering. For about 30 seconds nothing happened, then he lost his shit. I mean, he goes fucking mental. I am laughing at him which was not a good idea. He is a Jap-slapper karate expert, so I ended up getting another lesson that night in karate and shown the error of my ways.

Revenge is sweet so I had a cunning plan to get him back for giving me a slap. During a bad sleet and rainstorm, I let his side of the tent down so all his R and R kit got wet. I'm trying not to laugh as he is going off - one because his kit got wet, unlucky Penguin. A few days later at stupid o'clock, The Penguin asks me to get the water on for the boys. This involves lighting the Puffing Billy.

The Puffing Billy is basically a metal B and Q bin with a petrol heater in it for boiling water. These days, under health and safety rules they are illegal due to fire hazards and the like. Unbeknown to me, The Penguin let the petrol drip all night. The fumes were condensed, so I am monging trying to light the bloody thing with numb hands. The only thing I can remember was seconds before the explosion, hearing the woosh before the flash and the bang. According to The Penguin, there was a large explosion - a sheet of flame about three meters high, followed by the bang of the bin returning to Earth.

As this was happening, I was crawling around on the deck due to being temporary blinded and losing my eye lashes and moustache. By this stage all I could hear was the blokes laughing their heads off and calling me Michael Jackson. Even Des, the Medic Sgt was laughing his head off when he was sorting out the flash burns on my boat race. Top tip: - do not mess with The Penguin and petrol.

Andy's Car Crime:
As the Battalion was preparing to move back to the UK, I was put in a position of trust which certain parties then used and abused. I was called into the OC's office to be told I would be, driving Miss Daisy for the next two weeks i.e., driving the CO because I was a signaller and the Commanding Officer's car had

a phone and radio fitted. So, I am cutting around in a brand-new Toyota Corolla. Enter Andy with a master plan: to cut a long story short, Andy promoted himself to Commanding Officer for the day.

Andy has got me driving him around in the CO's motor, flag on the front, and Andy is sat in the back with the CO's beret, wearing the commanding officers spare rank slides getting salutes etc. He then had the brass neck to walk into the Garrison Officers' Mess. Cruising past 'MH' who nearly fell off his mountain bike. The jungle drums were soon beating - to cut a long story short - I was sacked and went straight to jail because I had cut up a car being driven by the Commanding Officers wife. I kept Andy's name out of the frame and fair play all the provost staff thought it was hilarious, so they went easy on me. Top tip. one does not get easily led by Andy the king of comedy.

Murph's 4 Tonner Kebab Collection:
Murph was a right laugh - a multi-talented solider who was in the Mortar Platoon but was also an Assault Pioneer who liked building things and blowing shit up. Murph also liked a whisky. The Platoon was preparing to go on duty up in Troodos the following morning, so all the kit was packed and the wagons ready to go. Murph got pissed and decided he was hungry and wanted some scoff, so his kebab compass kicked in. Murph could not be bothered to walk down the hill to the Mughals beer and take out joint. He took the 4Tonner. 4-ton Bedford army trucks were driven on an HGV licence, plus as a driver you had to be familiarized on them - Murph had neither. In all due respect to Murph, his driving skills did get him to the kebab house to pick up his takeout. It was a pity he hit a trailer, several kerbs, and a fence. Let us just say Murph had an interesting time explaining his kebab collection to the CSM.

CHAPTER 12

'I couldn't be more chuffed if I was a badger at the start of mating season.'
Ian Holloway – Bristol Rovers FC Manager.

Football Focus:
Andy, the King of Comedy, was also responsible for a major incident on Cyprus, involving an RAF Wing Commander, the RSM, and the Royal Military Police. Andy was the Battalion football captain because he had been a high-level, keen amateur player in his youth down in sunny Devon. He still does a bit of youth coaching and a bit of management to this day down in Devonshire. The military

football league in Cyprus was very keenly contested in Cyprus, but also political due to the RAF thinking they were Manchester United of the military football league in Cyprus. The rest of us mere mortals, were Bristol Rovers. One Saturday evening I had arranged to meet Andy and Ness, another keen footballer, at the Sovereign Club after the match for the prize giving and a few beers.

The Battalion team had won the match 2-1, and everybody was thinking, 'Great! The Battalion had won the cup - happy days, let us get on the piss!' So, in the club everyman and his dog from the 3-services football cohort were present having a jolly old time until it kicks off - thanks to Andy big time. Andy was being told by some Biggles RAF Wing Commander lookalike, that we may have won the cup that day, but were getting stripped of the league that we had won because the Battalion had played Chris Dunn. Chris was the RAPTC king of the gym attached to the Regiment. They said he was an illegal player, so the Battalion was disqualified and not getting the double. It went nuclear!

The look of complete shock and awe on Biggles's face was a thing of beauty when Andy called him a fucking cheat to his face. Then it all kicked off in the bar with a bit of pushing and shoving. The RAF do not do bar room brawls. So, the police were quickly called followed by the RSM. To prevent the RGBW lads leaving the bar to smash up the RAF, we, the RGBW, were locked into the back bar of the Sovereign Club. As we were waiting for the RSM and some more RMP reinforcements to arrive, the powers that be forgot to tell the bar staff what was going on. So, Andy said, "Are you still serving?" "Yes, of course", was the reply. So, we were drinking Cyprus brandy, cheap as chips for a double.

We were all pissed up and singing when the RSM rocked up. To calm it all down the RAF cheating bastards gave us the cup we won that day, but we were stripped of the league. We were all escorted of the premises and the whole incident was put down to high spirts. Fair play, I do not think the RSM and RMP's wanted the hassle of dealing with the football focus drama and scandal.

Bouncing Bomb:
This disaster was down to me. The Company Commanders Land Rover FFR was always reversed in outside the Company office. This day, I had finished work late, and with vehicle kit being prime shinny items liable for getting nicked, the radio antenna and spare wheel were locked in the back of the wagon.

The Series 3 Land Rovers had the spare wheel bolted on the bonnet. I climbed up on the front of the wagon to take off the wheel and fucked it right up! I slipped and the wheel fell off. Instead of landing flat, the bloody thing bounced then rolled down the hill gathering speed! Just like the dam busters bouncing bomb, it sailed over the road narrowly missing traffic and disappeared into the scrub, past Battalion headquarters.

Monday morning the Company was in extended line, walking down the hill through the scrub looking for the spare wheel. 'Slack Mac' the Company signals guru made sure everybody knew it was my fault. I was about as popular as a rattle snake in a lucky dip that day for messing the Company around.

Callout Tab Down to RAF Akrotiri:

The Battalion had a practice callout which involved the Battalion tabbing down to RAF Akrotiri, a nice 12-mile morning walk in the Cyprus sunshine. But first we had to do the assault course as a Company.

TM a member of the Anti-tank Platoon fell off the 10-foot wall and complained of having hurt his leg. This got zero sympathy from his Platoon who thought he was being spineless. He was dragged round the tab by the boys.

On arrival at the end of the exercise, the doctor noticed TM was in ruin. After a brief medical inspection followed by X-Rays, it was confirmed that the poor bloke had a fractured leg. TM was a legend within the Company for doing a 12 miler with a broken leg. Also, Big Tel was giving us grief all the way round, then ended up getting on the jack wagon due to blisters much to everyone's amusement, he should have saved his breath.

Sympathy for the Devil:

Andy, The King of Comedy, was always upsetting the Commanding Officer, which wasn't exceedingly difficult because the CO was, in my humble opinion a knob, and in my own 24 years regular army service, the worst Commanding Officer I ever had. On exercise, Andy was tasked to put an OP in on a village. The CO had personally sighted its location, so get on with it troops.

After a few days, the CO turns up at the location his with pet ex DERR RSM and various minions and starts giving Andy a hard time because the OP was in the wrong location and had been used before by another unit. When Andy was explaining that he was in the location the CO had personally sighted, the RSM was telling him not to mouth off, so Andy was starting to lose his temper because he was being called a lair.

When it was explained out of earshot that Andy was in the right to the CO by the Operations Officer, the CO came back to the OP and told Andy that the OP was in a suitable location. The CO in his snotty voice then told Andy that he, being a commissioned officer was never in the wrong and never apologized because he was an officer and a gentleman.

Andy's reply was classic, 'I have two young daughters and if I tell them off for being naughty, then I realize I am in the wrong, I will then apologize to my kids. You know why sir? It is because I am a man!'

CHAPTER 13

'Any idiot can fly a plane, but it takes a special kind of idiot to jump out of one.'
Anonymous.

Parachuting, Polecat, and Pancakes:
'Polecat' was our man from the RGBW at the Cyprus Joint Service Adventure Training Unit. The Polecat had his fingers in a lot of very sticky pies. He was also a bit of a 'Jack the lad' when it came to other Regiments wife's and girlfriend's - hence the nickname The Polecat. He was always on the prowl. Plus, if it was not nailed down, he would have it away!
So, off I rock up north, to Dhekelia for a week parachuting with Polecat. The first thing that happened was getting pissed up with the Polecat the night before the start of the course, and nearly getting caught out of bounds in Ayia Napa - starting the course with a monster hangover.

After a day of ground training, we started off on dummy pulls, which after my first few jumps, I was getting into it - enjoying it, even though the Polecat was being his usual disruptive self both in and out of the aircraft. We had a refusal to jump in the aircraft from some royal engineer, which was a bit of a drama because with it only being a small plane, we all had change places and unhook the static lines. It was a right pain in the arse, plus everybody was looking to see who would be next to bottle out. I am crabbing along inside the aircraft trying to sort myself out by the door when the bloody Polecat tells the pilot to bank right a fraction so he could see the DZ.

Next thing happens I am bloody Superman flying and flapping like fuck because I have unhooked my static line! Instant free fall on the job training. All I can remember was looking up at the aircraft and seeing the Polecat grinning and giving me the wanker sign! Sod this for a game of soldiers! I looked, located, and peel punched my free fall toggle to deploy my parachute - I was a happy bear. My riser came down and my parachute deployed.

My elation was short lived as I was off course by about 1 kilometre from the DZ and landed badly like a pancake in some orange grove just outside the wire, narrowly missing some wriggly tin shack followed by a bit of a walk. By that evening it was all round the Battalion that I had fallen out of a plane thanks to the Polecat.

Final Act of Revenge Against the Thieving Cypriot Pikey Car Dealers, Adios Cyprus:
As the Battalion was getting ready to leave Cyprus, there was more drama and scandal. A lot of the lads had hire purchase agreements with various local car dealerships.

Typical bloody locals - liked nothing better that to rip of the troops who were not honouring some of the agreements. Due to the political situation and the scourge of creeping political correctness the Head Shed would do anything not to upset the locals or rock the boat. So, the locals held the whip hand.

They knew the Battalion was pulling out and tried it on, so a lot of the blokes were not getting what their cars were worth or were getting ripped off. On the last night on the island before our morning departure back to blighty, several cans of 'OX8' brake and clutch lubricant were found empty in the waste compound very unusual it was normally a MT matter.

At some stage on that cold dark night, several car dealerships in Limassol were visited and some hooligans who could have possibly doused a lot of cars with a corrosive liquid caused a lot of damage to the vehicles... *I wonder who could do such a bad thing?*

Joey's World Record in Getting Kicked Out of the Training Depot:
'Joey' is a rough diamond of a bloke. When I joined the Battalion, he was a Lance-Jack PTI, and Section Second in Command in B Coy. He was proper old school - do your job and do not piss him off. In the early nineties there was still a small element of bullying and senior private soldiers trying it on with the new

lads. None of that shit happened on Joey's watch; he was like a big brother to us young lads who exercised it through tough love, help, and advice in equal measure.

'Brads' was one of the most switched-on soldiers I ever served with. A relaxed professional solider whom would go on to great things within his career. He, when teamed up with Andy the King of Comedy, would be a bloody nightmare in creating havoc within a 3-mile radius, usually drink and football orientated.

According to Joey the story is as follows: Joey was promoted to 'Full screw' Corporal and posted to the Training Depot, Infantry Training Centre, Catterick ITC. He was making a fresh start so flew back from Cyprus early to take up his new post. He had a weekend to prepare his classroom and square his admin away to make a good first impression with the recruits. At about the same time as Joey was sorting his new life out, Brads and Andy were also in Catterick doing something or other. One afternoon they decided to pay Joey a visit at ITC.

Joey was in the process of finishing off his administration ready to receive his recruit intake the following morning. After a brief discussion with Brads and Andy; Joey decided that it was not in his best interests to go on the piss due to having work in the morning. Three immortal words were muttered by Brads with Andy nodding his agreement, 'You've changed Joey.' Peer pressure had been applied. The three amigos then disappeared into town on a major piss up. Welcome back to UK lads.

Fluff had also appeared on the scene as he was on the way back from the depot to the Battalion and told Joey that staying in was for losers. Being a real pal, he provided transport downtown and arranged a bit of a RGBW reunion starting in the Colburn Lodge public house on the Garrison. Breaking strain of a Kit-Kat, Joey's fate was sealed, and the bright lights of town were calling.

The following morning Joey was suffering from a major hangover and was rather disorientated. To cut a long story short - Joey did not surface till lunchtime. He had missed first parade and starting work with his new intake of recruits. He was still feeling a bit under the weather due to Andy insisting they finish the previous evening revelry with Port shots.

That afternoon, Joey was supposed to be on a welcome to ITC interview - instead it was a "Hello and goodbye," before he was marched to the

Commanding Officer of the Depot and returned to unit with immediate effect. Fair play to Joey – he holds the world record in getting posted in and out of the depot. Peer pressure is a soldier's ultimate nightmare. In conversation in later years with Andy, Fluff, and Brads they all claim they were innocent bystanders!

CHAPTER 14

> "I don't know what effect these men will have upon the enemy, but, by God, they terrify me."
> The Duke of Wellington.

1st Battalion the Royal Gloucestershire Berkshire and Wiltshire Regiment.

Meanee Barracks Colchester Essex England April 1997 – September 1998:
Returning to the UK was a good thing because most of us were sick of Cyprus and glad to be on home soil. Plus, we were back to 24 Airmobile Brigade – wait, fly, dig, and die.

The major advantage was that the barracks were a 10-minute walk from town - a bargain for going on and off the piss! Also, my hometown of Bristol was about a 3-hour drive away, so it was within striking distance if I wanted to go home for the weekend.

The Bovey Tracey Bat, Canadian Caper, Rawston Cup; and Upsetting the Locals in South Armagh:
Post Cyprus leave for me involved a road trip. First up to Cardiff for a couple of days with Nobby and his family, followed by a weekend on the piss with 'Fluff' followed by an RV with Andy the King of Comedy down in sunny Devon.

Fluff is still one of my oldest and closest friends. Over the vast mists of time, he was also the Best Man at my wedding, which is a separate tale of woe for another chapter.

Fluff got his nickname years ago before I met him, because of him having a tuft of hair that always stood up. He was also one of the most intelligent and sharp blokes I have ever known; most of the commissioned officers were wary of his intellect and wit.

On one occasion in Northern Ireland, the Company was having a shit brief by some officious government geek, when he asked, "Any questions?" Fluff stood up in front of every man and his dog and asked, "Is it true that Mo Mowlam is going to be the Northern Ireland super-model?", which had the whole Company in fits of laughter.

The Bovey Tracey Bat:

Bovey Tracey is a picture postcard Devonshire village at the bottom of Dartmoor. It is also the hometown of Andy the King of Comedy. There is also a concentration of some of the lads from the Regiment including Embo, and another good lad 'Cyprus Eddy' due to his Mediterranean complexion and love of Ouzo. A weekend on the piss with Andy was always eventful and a good laugh, and some of Andy's civilian mates, and family friends were complete lunatics! The most welcoming and friendliest people I have ever had the privilege to meet -Proper hillbillies.

After a skin full of ale down the local football club in Bovey Tracey, we followed the bar crawl to the King of Prussia. Earlier during the evening, I had done a bit of business with 'Crafty Cliff' the local taxi driver - wheeler dealer and old friend of Andy's. Cliff had his fingers in a lot of pies and did a roaring trade out of the boot of his Taxi in various items of clothing. I was now the proud owner of a ¾ length black leather jacket - top of the range Italian; or as Andy called it the Bristol drug dealer look.

Back to the battlecruiser for more beer and banter. We were invited back to 'Troggs' gaff for a night cap and some more beers and banter. So, I'm stood on Troggs raised decking overlooking his large garden, when Andy pushes me off the top forgetting that it's a raised platform. I flew like a bat into the darkness and ended up 10 feet away, down the bottom of the garden in the bushes. Eddie the Eagle had nothing on me that night. After a bit of flapping and a drunken search party, I was returned to the decking. After a swift brandy I was renamed the Bovey Tracey Bat due to me and my leather jacket flapping silently into the night as I went flying. It still raises a laugh down with the Bovey boys.

The Five-0, 'Police' in Bovey:

The local constabulary were all chilled out and old school. Big boys' rules if you were taking the piss.

On one pleasant evening with a few beers on board, myself, Andy, Eddy, and Embo were doing a bit of business outsides Andy's dad's house. Crafty Cliff had rocked up in his cab and was selling his latest wares. In this case Ralph Lauren shirts.

Embo and Eddy were having their usual argument over who's fags they were going smoke, and I was trying on one of Cliffs shirts. Andy was taking the piss and telling jokes. Next things I know is there is a bloody huge human bear in a police uniform standing next to me! Before I could do a runner, the police officer says to me that, "The colour of the shirt don't suit you son. Try the blue on. Evening Andy - alright boy?". It turns out Lotty the local constable is a friend of Andy's dad and is proper old school. He, has a fag with Andy, buys a shirt off Crafty Cliff, and disappears into the darkness like some sort of Jedi master. Fair play, I thought I was getting my collar felt that night. Bovey Tracy is my kind of place.

CHAPTER 15

'Whoever said a horse was dumb, was dumb.'
Will Rogers.

Canadian Capers:

The Battalion deployed to Wainwright in Canada on exercise. The abuse and banter started before we left UK due to Fluff playing a practical joke on 'Big Will'.

Big Will was one of the biggest men in the Battalion, 6'7 and a front row Cheltenham rugby-head. Always up for a laugh plus he was the latest recruit to the Cookhouse breaking and entering club. Ugly rugby head was also one of his other nicknames.

'Big Tel', aka 'Colour Helpful' had been in the chair as the new support Company CQMS since the end of Cyprus. A big bloke whose bark was worse than his bite. He also picked up the nickname of Colour Helpful due to if he was in a bad mood, you got nothing from his stores. He had a dry sense of humour and used to give me grief - but also looked out for me. He is a straight talker who sometimes caused a lot of amusement and augments within the Company.

'Ricey' was a fully paid-up member of the *Do Not Give a Fuck Club*. One of the best signallers in the Battalion, he was also a legend when it came to speaking his mind and upsetting the Head Shed. He was also a major smoker and not good at running. Ricey always had a fag in his month, was sarcastic, and life was always a laugh working with Ricey. He would have a moan, then help anyone out - providing you had fags to keep him supplied with.

The Company was sorting out the kit and equipment that was going to Canada. Bergens and weapon bundles going first. A week later the Company lands in Canada, and the Company has a big sort out of kit and there is a massive stench in the hanger. On investigation, it's Big Will's bergen - it stunk like a Chinese outdoor fish market. Big Will checks his bergen and pulls out his gonk bag. A decomposing fish falls out - Cheers Fluff! Fish fingers on the menu. Big Will's kit stunk for weeks after. This then started a Companywide wind up and Jack wars. New SOP - never leave your bergen or daysack unattended because you could end up with house bricks or God knows what in your kit.

Big Tel was acting CSM for the Canada exercise, and his pet hate was people rallying the Land Rovers across the prairie - Company Headquarters being the biggest culprits, followed by the Mortar Platoon. After giving me and Ricey a right bollocking for doing a Nigel Mansell, he decides to drive himself which ends in tears. He rolls the Land Rover causing a lot of damage and giving Ricey the fright of his life. He then gets the piss taken out of him for weeks afterwards giving the Company a good laugh. Fair play: Big Tel did take it well.

FIBAR is squaddie slang for Fighting in Bars and Restaurants. Basically, this happens with troops getting pissed up and doing what troops do. Canada was no different. I was advance party to Canada, so was on the first flight with Big Tel.

On arrival in Canada, we were doing our handover/take over with the unit we were relieving, who just happened to be the Royal Irish Regiment. Happy days! I bumped into an old mate of mine from the Paddies - 'Geordie Haydon'. Let us go on the piss!

So, I am downtown in Wainwright, Alberta on the piss. To say there was a bit of a language barrier with the locals was an understatement with people trying to communicate in Bristolian, Ulster, and Canadian. It was a right good night out.

Returning to camp, we got scoff, and the biggest pizza I have ever seen - it was like a dustbin lid! Happy days! Next thing, a Canadian cop car pulls up next to us giving us the stare, so me being me, cannot help myself. I go up to this Mountie and say, "Any chance of some pepper for my pizza mate?" I was then sprayed in the boat race which was a bit of a stingy and teary deal for me.

Fair play to the Mountie he laughs as he helps himself to a piece of my pizza and says, "Don't cause a kerfuffle, you're hammered!" Then he gives us a lift back to camp.

Drama and Scandal Involving Support Company:
During a weekend stand down post-training, the lads decided to go out on the piss in the local town. As per usual it ended in tears. The first incident involved the Mortar Platoon. Due to a fuck up on the range, a certain Lance-Jack from the Platoon just couldn't take his mistake on the chin. He had to argue the toss which didn't go down well, so in the end a pool cue round his head solved his in-denial problem. When one of his mates from another Company tried to get involved, he had a slap as well.

Top tip: One does not stick one's nose in Support Company business. What happens in Support Company – stays in Support Company.

'Banger' is one of life's unique characters who is a master at DIY and fixing things. As you can imagine, he was remarkably busy in Support Company in fixing shit. He has done quite a bit of work on my house. He got his nickname because of his volatile temper and instant explosion when he gets upset. Hence the nickname *Banger* because he goes bang – Even though it's not bonfire night.

Banger and I were very merry having a good night out and a laugh with the lads, getting pissed up as one does on Canadian chemical beer. Then before sinking more beer, we decided to meet up with some of the Mortar Platoon lads at the local pizza joint, 'Tony's' for scoff.

I am stood at the counter waiting for mine and Banger's dustbin lid pizza, when in walks 'The Chin', who in my humble opinion is all that is wrong with some of ex Dukes NCOs in the Regiment. Arrogant, full of his own self-importance, and a bully. One of the younger lads, 'Foz' from Mortars who was in the queue in front of me had just got his scoff. The Chin demands that Foz hands over his scoff to him because The Chin cannot be bothered to wait in the queue. Foz is a crow, and The Chin is an NCO.

Banger then goes off – Bang! A bit of melee then kicks off with me, Banger, Foz, The Chin, and the rest of the people in Tony's. Due to the close confines of the joint, I end up on the floor trying to save my pizza. At that exact moment, Fluff and the rest of the Mortar Platoon arrive. Taking in the developing situation, the place is soon cleared out and The Chin gets a good hiding for being a prick.

By this stage there are sirens and a lot of spectators rubbernecking. The grand finale was someone picking up a plant pot and crowning The Chin on the head with it. The Chin was later found sitting on the step outside Tony's, dazed and confused with a load of soil, blood, and plants running down his head and shoulders. When the police and Andy the King of Comedy who was on duty turned up, thought it was hilarious after I had told them The Chin got what he deserved for being a bully and a clown. The Chin looked like a reject from the old kids TV show 'Bill and Ben the Flowerpot Men.'

The Chin then started to get angry with Andy and the Canadian coppers. Fair play to them, the coppers were happy for the Brits to clean their own dirty washing up. The Chin had another slap off Andy on the way back to camp and was told he would be dealt with in the morning – unlucky son! Life is unfair.

The Chin now had a new nickname- Bill and Ben the Flowerpot Men. The Support Company element involved had disappeared into the night like ghosts. When Big Tel heard about the dramas in the morning, he just laughed it off. As far as he was concerned, if Support Company lads did not get caught or arrested, he didn't give a shit. A few days later, The Chin had another slap off one of the PTIs for shouting his mouth off. Some people just cannot help themselves. This time, The Chin was the only bloke I knew that got Jap slapped in a phone box, while on the phone.

Cowboys and Indians:
Adventure training is always one of the highlights of the trip across the pond. There were various activities for the troops including white river rafting and canoeing. All the bad lads within the Company went for the supposedly easy option of horse riding – a mounted expedition in the Canadian Rockies.

The dream team assembled for a week in the saddle including me, Embo, Cyprus Eddy and Ricey. So, after a day's training to be cowboys, off we rode into the sunset – and trust me – it was not Broke-Back Mountain. It was more like, The Good, The Bad, and The Ugly, with various characters from Support and Headquarters Companies. Enter Harry Crumb and his horse 'The Devil's Spawn'.

Harry Crumb was a rather large jovial fellow, who was a mountain of a man in height and weight. He was useless at running but could carry mortar kit until the cows come home. His biggest claim to fame, was that he was the Company champion at the board game Risk. An all-round nice bloke that would always jump in for the team.

Harry's horse was the devil incarnate. The nag would attack all the other horses, and its party trick would be to wait for Harry to get one foot in the stirrups then charge off with him hanging on for grim life, much to the amusement of the lads. By day three, the horse and rider had both had enough, so the nag was replaced. It was turned around with everybody blaming Harry for breaking the horse.

'Johnny Mouth of the South' had the sharpest mind and mouth in the Company. He never missed a trick and when it came to giving abuse and banter, he was king. He was also one of the companies SNCO's who ran a happy and efficient ship. Life was never quiet when Johnny was about.

Once the days ride was over, the team would basha up for the night and shoot the shit round the campfire. Johnny was in his element with loads of banter and messing around his partner in crime, 'Veg Green' the medic.

Veg Green, the Company Medic was liked and respected within the Battalion as a whole – good at his job, a right laugh, and one proud Welshman. He and Johnny were a double act.

The Canadian guides had been working for the British Army for years and thought they had seen it all until they meet our motley crew. Apart from the language barrier and accents the Canadians just could not get their heads around the banter and messing around from Support Company. The Canadian guides were treated with respect and good humour by the lads, and by the end of the week were assimilated into the team and joining in the various banter and messing around. They also planned revenge on Johnny and Veg.

On one of the day's, it all kicked off thanks to a Territorial SNCO attached to an adventure training cell. There had already been a few incidents involving this clown, due to his inability to accept how the RGBW operated – our use of nicknames, the relaxed professional way we were with each other, and did our business. He had decided off his own back that we as a group were going to leave the horses and do a day hill walk up this bloody hill that looked like K2! "No bloody way Pedro!", was the answer he got back from all of us.

The clown was in shock and muttering about court martials and refusal to obey orders etc... I think, Johnny and Veg had a nice, pleasant little chat with him round the back and he saw the error of his ways. He disappeared back to Base Camp and kept a low profile after that little chat in the forest glade.

On a river crossing, the Canadian guides did a horse whisperer trick on Johnny and Veg, involving getting both their horses to buck and attempt to throw their riders into the river. Johnny held on whilst Veg went for a dip. Happy days. A good bit of adventure training had by Support Company.

Rumble in the Rockies:
I got this tale off some of the Reconnaissance Platoon lads. Some of the young lads from the Company were enjoying a beer downtown, when it kicked off thanks to some pissed up Canadian cowboy clown. As with every colour and creed on planet Earth, there are good and bad. The Canadian people were some of the most friendly and nice people I have ever met on my travels.

Black Roge was a good, up and coming, quiet, mixed-race young lad from Reading. Because there were quite a few Roges in the Battalion he was known as Black Roge. This was not meant as a racial slur it was a typical army nickname – plus, we all took the piss and had a laugh in the non, PC Support Company way – but if an outsider or someone wanted to go down the racist bigot road, they did so at their peril. The Company stuck together and the only colour we had was green.

This Canadian clown had race issues and because Roge was a young quiet lad, the mug thought he was an easy target! Wrong answer mate. Before the lads steamed in to batter this prick and smash the bar up, the bouncers had managed to get everybody outside where a circle was formed, and Black Roge and Cowboy Clown went one-on-one in the parking lot of dreams.

Life lesson – always watch the quiet ones.

Roge battered this Canadian clown left, right, and Chelsea in about 30 seconds. Witnesses said it was like something out of a movie, the Canadians were in shock when Clown got folded up like a deck chair on a Blackpool pleasure beach. RGBW = 1. Canadian Clown = 0. Result.

Airport Drama and Scandal with Andy and Fluff:
Airport drama and scandal thanks to Andy and Fluff. Endex – at the end of trip across the pond, we were departing from Calgary Airport when Andy and Fluff decided to wind me up. So, as we were getting ready to put our personal kit through airport security, they decided to tell Canadian law enforcement that I, as a coloured person of interest, might be carrying contraband. The first I knew of this development was getting manhandled and cuffed, kit emptied out, followed by 20 questions from Malcom the Mountie in front of the Company and civilians which caused great amusement and a photo opportunity for the lads – wankers! Fair play to Big Tel – he calmed it all down and even bought be a Burger because I was skint. I was glad to get on the plane after that morning's entertainment.

CHAPTER 16

"Terrorism is the tactic of demanding the impossible and demanding it at gunpoint."
Christopher Hitchens.

South Armagh Northern Ireland April 1998 – September 1998:
A Northern Ireland tour was on the horizon. The Battalion was off to Ulster on a six-month summer tour of duty in bandit country. I personally thought the situation in Ulster was a load of bollocks with the peace talks ongoing. The Labour Government of the day in my own humble opinion shouldn't be talking to PIRA/Sinn Fein, they should be bombing them back to the stone age! The locals in South Armagh hated us, the British Army, and the feeling was mutual. The protestants were going to get stitched up big time. As I'm writing this book in 2021, the IRA have quite frankly got away with murder, and British soldiers are getting 'Witch' hunted by their own government to appease the bloody paddy PIRA disgusting.

Before any deployment there is pre tour beat up training. In our case it was no different with the various courses and range packages. Myself had done the team medic Cadre which I found excellent. It cemented my lifetime interest in basic first aid training and confidence. 'Des' the medical SNCO was a top teacher and a top bloke.

After various courses and training, the Company was given its order of battle within the Battalion deployment. Most of Support Company were to be based at Bessbrook Mill with a mixed Platoon from ATGW Platoon and Company Headquarters attached to C Company based at the village of Fork Hill. A shit hole. Full of muppets that hated our guts. There was a .50 sniper at work plus, with the ongoing IED threat we were in for a right treat. Our Platoon brief was fight fire with fire, none of this PC bollocks and be nice to the locals - they were all wankers on this manor.

The highlight of the Battalion training was the Rawston Cup. A march and shoot competition with various Northern Ireland scenarios thrown in. I was then a member of the ATGW/DRUMS Platoon Team, and all we wanted to do was get round it and get it done. Like all march and shoot competitions it would be decided on the shoot. The falling plate shoot was run by John assisted by Andy the King of Comedy. Amazingly, the team won the shoot. All I will say is that I think I put one or two magazines down the range as did others - Andy could never add up when it came to dishing up the ammunition.

The Platoon soon settled into life in Fork Hill. The main effort being patrolling and manning the Golf and Romeo Towers overlooking the border including the town of Dundalk in the Irish Republic. A hive of scum and villainy. We knew who all the local 'Players' were - members of the PIRA or their supporters.

Patrolling and not setting patterns was the name of the game. The Paddies were good at what they did, and you never underestimated the enemy. We were in their back garden. We never let our guard down and it was a game of cat and mouse - plus we had Rules of Engagement whilst they did not. I always found the Players to big the biggest hypocrites in the universe. They were murdering cowardly scum, but as soon as they got arrested or brassed up, they would moan about their human rights and demand lawyers form the British State - the very state they were trying to overthrow.

Amazingly, if by magic, sometimes fences holding livestock would get cut or broken. What a shame the Players could not be planting bombs or up to no good if they were cashing livestock could they? Tom also managed to cut all the power to the village on one occasion, due to an accident involving the main electrical junction box at the top of the main drag through Fork Hill village - how very sad. What a crying shame.

Swamp Thing:
During one patrol as it was getting dark and the mist was coming down, I was point man for the patrol. As I did my fence mong bit and cleared the barbed wire; instead of landing safely on the other side, I hit fresh air followed by a drop straight into a bog – I was up to my neck in shit. The rest of the lads thought it was hilarious, after getting pulled out and photographed I looked like swamp thing!

As we carried on with the patrol, we had a bit of a minor aggro with the locals. I was feeling rather delicate by this stage of the patrol due to being a swamp thing and waterlogged. This rat faced crack whore woman came out of her house screaming at me, 'A wee Brit black bastard' and trying to claw her nails across my face the cheeky cow. I defended myself by using a head butt. Due to wearing a helmet I was protected. Unfortunately, the woman suffered a bit of nosebleed and some future dental work - how sad is that? As her husband tried to be a hero, he also ended up tripping and falling, sustaining some minor injuries. The kerb stones in Fork Hill really do need replacing! It was a good job Ryan King was there to help him to his feet. As always, the RGBW were there to win hearts and minds.

As we went off the helicopter, back in base there was a reception committee waiting. Apparently, there had a been a complaint from the local Sinn Fein big wig saying that local law-abiding people had been attacked! Shock horror! Violence in South Armagh! In his exact words – "The solider doing most of the damage was a short wee black fellow with a Mexican bandit mustachio, speaking like a pirate and behaving like a Tasmanian Devil. The other solider was a big fellow with a stutter." Gary the RUC Sergeant sorted out the paperwork and put the whole unfortunate business to bed with the Company Head Shed.

I still consider myself an innocent bystander and victim of an unprovoked assault that had affected my health and wellbeing.

CHAPTER 17

"The 'voice of sanity' is getting hoarse."
Seamus Heaney.

Incoming Mortar Rounds Followed by Hurry Up and Wait:
The next highlight of the tour was getting mortared in camp. We had just got back in off patrol, took my sodden boots off then boom! Incoming rounds. The cheeky bastards had fired three mortars at the base with one landing inside the wire. After a bit of a flap on, and the commanders were cutting around making sure everyone was ok, and a headcount, we were out on the cordon round the poxy village as things started happening with the follow up operation.

I will always remember 'Boycee' the C Company CSM cutting around, cool as fuck calming it down. Professional and on top of his game, he even cracked a smile at his favourite attached ATGW Platoon the miserable sod. I was then stood on Fork Hill's High Street for 48 long and very boring hours with Cyprus Eddy, some RMP, and 'Chippy' with fucking freezing feet due to a major schoolboy error on my part. I had taken off my wet patrol boots and put on my jungle boots just before we got rained on by the Mortars. After two days, the canvas sided jungle boots were no good to man nor beast in the climate of Northern Ireland. My feet were in ruin - a life lesson learnt the hard way. Don't wear bloody jungle boots in Ulster, the land of mist and bogs.

Had a good laugh on day one of the cordon, as one of the Mortar Platoon patrols stopped for a chat. Embo had inadvertently crossed the border into the Republic and had a kick-off with the local farmer who had informed him that he was in the Republic of Ireland. Embo was having none of it until the farmer pointed out a road sign in paddy talk and letters. Embo was now known as 'Colin Compass' across the Battalion.

Johnny and Banger also had a nightmare due to the helicopters dropping off their patrol in the wrong place and the mist coming down to create no visibility. The Golf Tower had to flash a firefly and hit the foghorn to give them a steer or they would be wandering around all night. Banger had taken a 'tumbledown', proper fence mong and broke his rifle and magazine. After a detailed search and look around there was a drama.

Unfortunately, he could not recover all his ammunition that had spread all over the place, because of the broken magazine, the terrain and shit weather. Goofy the new Commanding Officer, still had Banger tab the mate on Battalion orders for punishment. He had Banger charged and fined for taking a tumble - what a load of bollocks! It was an accident - shit happens. Mind you, if you like to see Banger go off, just mention tumbledown. Goofy was a knob, and Banger got his arse handed to him on a plate. The sword of Damocles, wielded by Goofy fell on Banger's head! Banger walked away with a £1000 fine and ear bending. It was 'Bang' out of order - he was married with a kid on the way.

CHAPTER 18

"Oh yeah, it's not a job, it's an adventure."
Richard Day, Recruiting Sergeant.

1RGBW Army Youth Team - Beachley Barracks, Chepstow 1998 – 2000 attached to 1CHESHIRES:

After Northern Ireland, time for a change. Fair play, the Gods were looking down on me when I managed to get posted to the Battalion Recruiting Team. The RGBW Army Youth Team. Two years away from Battalion based in Chepstow, living in Bristol. Plus, the Battalion in Chepstow at the time was 1Royal Anglian, soon to be changing over with 1Cheshires - Happy days.

I was in heaven and reunited with Nobby, who was Second in Command of the team, and Fluff was posted to the Armed Forces Recruiting office Bristol as one of the Battalions recruiting Sergeants. The job was good, but it was busy, and you lost a lot of weekends due to the team being also a Battalion and an Army asset. It was good to be back living in Bristol, in the Hood with sticky fingers doing a bit of business. Dealing with some of the civilians and the Army recruiting group was a minefield, some of the schools and teachers we had to deal with were a nightmare - limp wristed left-wing liberals.

It went on a scale of good job to shit job. Say we were working or doing an activity for Cheltenham College, or Gloucester ACF it was a good day - we were well looked after - all the staff and pupils had a good day out and they got something out of the day. On the other hand, some of the schools were just a pain in the arse due to some of the staff members being left wing moaners and would take offence at anything and fire off emails to the Recruiting Office Colonel in Bristol, so you had to be on your guard. But overall, it was a good experience and some of the students I would later see in Battalion after they had been through the system.

In later life I would deal with a lot of education professionals - I still am shocked at the depth of anti-military and snowflake undertones or bias within certain teaching sectors. On the other side of the coin, I have met and worked with some excellent teachers and mentors whose passion and commitment to the pupils has been truly humbling.

The Legend of Karaoke Kenny:
'Karaoke Kenny' is a neighbourhood legend on the manor in Horfield, Bristol. I first met Kenny and another well respected gentleman 'Scully,' when as a 14-year-old frightened youth I signed up for the Bristol Army Cadet Force. The cadets were an excellent youth organization run by either ex-forces or uniformed service volunteers with a military ethos - it was no youth club. The standing joke among us ex-cadets in later life was that Bristol ACF was the first step on the road to taking the Queen's shilling and signing up for 1Glosters.

By default, it was an insight and later a recruiting tool for the armed forces. There were quite a few lads that I went to cadets with that would join up and serve alongside me; including 'Al the Para', the 'Read Twins', 'Bunner', 'Spud', 'Shep', 'Fat Lewe', 'Matty Sheets', and The Claridge Twins. The unofficial nickname for Bristol ACF was the Hitler Youth because you were steered if you were looking at joining the Infantry into the welcoming arms of the Gloucestershire Regiment. Unless you were Al, who would start his long military career in the Grenadier Guards; bloody the wooden top, then went to the Parachute Regiment.

Kenny and Scully were our instructors within the ACF supported by 'Pep' from the Glosters, who, when I signed up to join the regular army back in the day, recruited me into the Glosters and would be my first CQMS in the Battalion. Pep was the Battalion Recruiting Sergeant during my last few years in the cadets in the Bristol Recruiting Office. Kenny taught me many military and life lessons which by default makes him my big brother. Throughout my military service and becoming a homeowner I would always crash at Kenny's place if a was in Bristol.

Karaoke Kenny was my own nickname for Kenny because he was a DJ and Karaoke King on the Manor with regular jobs in the various pubs and clubs in Bristol. Kenny was always at it with the birds, or always had some latest get rich quick scheme that I would get dragged into which would usually end in disaster.

On one occasion when crashing at Kenny's place I was trying to be clever and keep into on the downlow. I was seeing a bird who had a boyfriend, plus I was supposed to be his working roadie for him that night. Instead, I had done one and skived off to see this bird.

So, I'm having a nice quiet drink out in some country pub out of the hood in the middle of nowhere towards Thornbury. I am trying my best with a new shirt and a splash of Old Spice, when at the bar I bump into Kenny who is also at it in the pub with this bird who is not his live-in girlfriend at the time – the look on our faces must have been comical.

On another occasion, Kenny had dragged me into another drama involving the sale of Ralph Lauren shirts, which he had assured me were *the real deal*. Unfortunately, they did not survive the first tumble dry. I could have killed him for the grief that caused me after having done a bit of business in camp!

Day Care Disaster:
Nobby was in the process of renovating his house in Cardiff, as well as being the Second in Command of the RGBW Army Team. I would give him a hand doing various bits and pieces to the house, plus I was Uncle Clarence to his three boys.

The three boys where a chip off the old block. Between them, they would have a system of turning me over when I used to pull up in my car at Nobby's house. First, little Zach would come running out as a distraction tactic to give me a hug and ask to be picked up to play WWF. Then Adam would ask me if I had any kit or tools that needed to be carried in and if I had presents while Nick searched my car for any chocolate, lose change, and Gucci kit. I would always play the game and hide pound coins and chocolate in the wagon trying to be craftier at hiding stuff, but Nick was like a ferret and he and Adam would always win the game by sniffing out all the goodies.

Nobby always had dogs, which on the whole were great, apart from 'Solomon the Doberman', that would always growl and try to knock me over. Once when I had done my Dolby, the bloody fleabag took an instant liking to my US Army poncho liner - never did get it back the thieving bloody mutt.

The married lads would bring their kids into camp a lot due to the fact the AYT was fairly laid back, plus we had a lot of boys' toys including quadbikes and paintball guns. One day I am left doing the day care, because Nobby is doing admin somewhere on the Manor. The boys where their usual hyperactive selves - I swear Nobby fed them Red Bull and Mars bars for breakfast. So, I got one of the quads out for the kids to have a supervised ride round the back area.

I am trying to keep control the three lads and failing miserably as Adam, the eldest, decided to totally ignore me and do his own thing. As you can guess it ended in the first disaster of the day. Adam walks out of the woods carrying his crash helmet minus the quad bike. 'Where is the bike mate?' I ask him. Adam thinks it is hilarious, he had crashed the quad bike into a tree and bent the handlebars the muppet! Lucky for me I had a good relationship with the REME mechanics on camp, so after a quick trip to the 'LAD' Light Aid Detachment they sorted the quad out for me - fair play. When Nobby found out about it he gave me shit and held me responsible for it, blaming me for being a poor supervisor and an even worse quad bike instructor -wanker!

The day could not get any worse, or so I thought. Enter Nick, Nobby's middle son. He decided with his brothers to start the gunfight at the O.K Corral using the paintball guns. *Not on my watch boys!* As I grabbed the paintball gun out of Nick's hand, I gave his wrist a little twist because he was not giving it up without a struggle - wrong move on my part. Nick's wrist clicked. *'Christ!',* I thought as Nick was screaming in agony, thinking I had broken his arm! Drama and scandal were to follow.

After a trip to the doctors, it was a mild strain. Nobby thought it was hilarious! That'll teach Nick to be a little pain in the arse - life lesson from Uncle Clarence. Mind you I felt bad for weeks after, and trust me, Nick milked it for ages, we still joke about now. Top tip: when doing day care with Nobby's kids - avoid quad bikes and paintball guns.

CHAPTER 19

> *"I couldn't repair your brakes, so I made your horn louder."*
> *Steven Wright.*

How's My Driving? Dial 999:

Some bright spark, pen pusher in the MOD had a really good idea to have stickers put on the wagons. On these stickers were 'How's my driving?', followed by a phone number.

Talk about setting up drama and scandal. It took about a week for some of the lads to phone in from landlines and burner phones to drop me in it! Mind you, there were big RGBW signs plastered all over our wagons. I get called into the office for a bollocking after there had been complaints about my alleged driving misdemeanours, which made me a bit pissed off. So, I came up with a cunning plan!

I managed to get some lettering stickers from Karaoke Kenny, which quickly went on my wagon, adding an extra zero to the free phone number plastered on the back. It lasted months with no dramas; until it blew up in my face during a vehicle audit. I played dumb saying, 'Somebody must have been playing around!', and got away with it by the skin of my teeth. In the end we painted over the stupid signs.

St Paul's Carnival Chaos:
Being the local Regiment, we did a lot of events and functions in Bristol. The powers that be, were often in denial about the real world/Civi street.

The St Paul's Carnival is Bristol's event aimed at the Afro-Caribbean community. It also attracts the usual curtsies, hippies, and left-wing social justice warriors, so let us just say the uniformed services are not immensely popular with certain members of the crowd that attend the carnival. Let people have their fun and enjoy themselves, but if you know that your presence might cause issues, let it go. But not the Colonel in the Bristol Recruiting Office who was trying to tick all the PC Brigade boxes. Mind you, she was RLC TA so that says it all about her foolishness.

Off we go over the bridge, down the M32 to St Pauls. First drama we encounter is trying to get access to the park to set up the obstacle course. The 'Local Street Wardens' for the duration of the carnival are not happy with the Army trucks being on the Manor. Fair play to them, they were OK to me personally because I was local, so after a bit of a chat we set up and parked the trucks under the trees out of the way. To be honest the local community were sound, no dramas. The kids enjoyed the obstacle course and the local youth workers were good as gold. Plus, I caught up with some former members of the Regiment that were local and had a good day out.

The torch paper for the drama and scandal that occurred was the stupid TA colonel from the recruiting office. She had insisted that a recruiting caravan was set up next to us. I had already told her that it was not a good idea due to the local dynamics, and people were not interested in the Army on carnival day. But I was told to wind my neck in as I was only a Private solider, and lower than whale shit in her fat RLC eyes.

As the afternoon progressed and things were winding down, the pattern of life changed. One of the locals told me it was time for us to go because the kids had finished enjoying the obstacle course, and my local contacts and minders/street wardens were off down the pub. Happy days! Cheers for keeping us safe. There are some nice and genuine people in St Pauls. But it was soon going to look like a zombie apocalypse due to drink and drugs in certain sections of the carnival goers.

The team started to wind down and pack up, but this dickhead Colonel wanted to drag it out. We the AYT started preparing for a quick bug out because I knew there were going to be tears before bedtime, and could sense inbound trouble with a capital T.
First bit of drama involved 'Mick', the Recruiting Sergeant from the Guards; he had red paint thrown at him and was called a murderer by some crusty prick while he was in the recruiting caravan. Followed by some left-wing, white, Rasta who came up to me and started to give me shit. In his drug fuelled dickhead opinion, I was an Uncle Tom and sell out for being a solider of the Queen. The fool was a wigger thinking he was Jamaican. He was probably some middle-class home boy from Oxfordshire on a gap year trying to find himself.

There was a major health and safety failure at this stage due to a bit of scaffold pole contacting the gentleman's knees while we were dismantling the mobile assault course. Jimbo and I were really sorry about this – butterfingers! I accidently stood on his hands after the gentleman had unfortunately tripped and fallen over too - how sad!

The vehicles were packed up in record time. Let's get the hell out of dodge city! We had positioned the recruiting teams 4X4 and trailer between our two trucks. As we left the park, I was driving the lead wagon. Fair play, the local street wardens got us out of the park without incident. Only 400 meters to go towards freedom, past the lights and down the hill on to the M32.

Unfortunately, some curtsies and brain-dead morons were gathering on the side of the road to have a pop at us on the way out the Manor. A few missiles were thrown at the trucks and insults hurled. Some fool decided to try and open my cab door and have a go - what a crying shame that the fire extinguisher just happened to off in his face. As he fell over, his push bike fell into the path of Jimbo's truck and got crushed. What a terrible bit of bad luck that bloke was having - unlucky son. Top tip: for the day: the road to hell is paved with good intentions. Always listen to the locals.

1RGBW Army Youth Team 1999-2000
By Nobby Clarke

In mid-1999, I had signed off and was in the process of leaving the army. Returning to my hometown of Cardiff. The then RSM Burt Cook, offered me a job down at the AYT in Chepstow as the 2IC. At the time, I was a Corporal with no interest in staying in or going to the AYT. However, it was close to home – so, I decided to take it. The only bonus (besides being close to home) was that Clarence 'The Real Deal' Heal would be there. So, I knew however shit the job was, I would have a laugh every day with Clary.

I rocked up, times and dates are not important, however, the OIC was Pumpkin Head, who, shall we say, did not inspire the team or myself. A man that truly is risk averse. Something myself and Clarence are not.

Clarence was in charge of vehicles, stores, and all things valuable which made my life as a 2IC exceptionally easy because Clary could procure any item that we may be diffy, Clarence being on good terms with the REME, and the Chefs also made life a lot easier for all. The fact that we didn't have a dress code and we cut around in tracksuits or mixed dress suited Clary as the man has no concept of uniform or smartness.

An average day at the AYT involving Clary would be: Myself, and maybe my kids shooting Clarence with the paintball guns. Cruising around on the quads, pilfering whatever we could from wherever or whoever we could.

It was whilst at the AYT, I learnt a trick from Clarence that would serve me well in the future as a CQMS. In the early 00's when I was C Company CQMS, Clarence was my 2IC, and Pumpkin Head was the CSM, I carried out the exact same trick on our vehicles whilst conducting public duties in London. The trick he taught me was – on the back of every army vehicle is an '0800 How's my driving?'. Clarence taught me from the spare stickers to cut a zero off and place it over one of the other numbers. Therefore, if you ever had some wanker phone the 0800 number on you, all they got was a deadline because the number didn't exist. Clary had been driving with these numbers doctored for years and I always wondered why we never had any complaints. It served us exceptionally well at the AYT when we travelled the country and even better in London doing public duties.

Hang Gliding:
Pumpkin Head had decided that the AYT team required some adventure training to destress. Little did he know that the job we had was funny enough and we got away with murder. We didn't need any adventure training – the whole job was adventure training. Off we went, reluctantly, to Crickhowell – a place close to my heart as I did my basic training there. We rocked up for a five-day hang-gliding course where each man was assigned his own vehicle i.e.: hang glider. This vehicle does not require an 0800 number. We cracked on learning how to fly a stubby.

Firstly, we done it tethered over Merthyr Tydfil where the wind takes you 30 foot in the air tethered on all three points in a triangle. Clarence mastered this as it required little to no skill because you were held by the three blokes holding the tethers. Come day three, we set out to a concave hill overlooking South Wales to do our first solo flight.

Clarence, as usual, was bushy as fuck and giving it the big one. But those that know him, knew he was shitting is pants and really did not want to do it. I don't recall if it happened on his first attempt, second, or when. But this was the only traffic accident that Clary was not going to get away from.

I remember being stood on the hill smoking, watching Clary run of the cliff with his AYT jacket on, desert boots, and his normal *fuck you* smile. The theory of flight took over and would you fucking believe it – Clarence soared into the air like a fucking eagle! Five seconds in and he's 30 feet in the air. 20 seconds in, he's 60 foot in the air. 30 seconds in, his heads buried one foot in the dirt. To this day, I cannot explain what happened. But to watch him soaring like the eagle he was, to be suddenly head down - ass up, a foot deep in the soft Welsh mud could only be described as: 'You're not going to believe this lad... but what happened was...'

I'd like to think I was concerned and ran as fast as my legs would carry me down the steep Welsh mountain to render first aid to not only my 2IC, the Godfather to my kids, and my longest serving friend. But that was not true. I fell down the hill laughing so fucking hard, that even when I got to him and he was dazed, his mouth full of Welsh mud, winging and moaning, I could not talk or give first aid through laughing.

Even writing this today, makes me laugh my fucking ass off. When I asked him what happened, he replied, "The fucking thing's fucked!" Those that know hang gliding and the theory of flight will understand that it takes effort to crash a fucking stubby.

After speaking with the instructor, he assured us that Clarence did not crash, he steered his stubby into the ground from 90 foot. To this day, he will swear that the thing was fucked. I am glad to say he did not die or get injured for that matter.

He continues to dodge death no doubt on a daily basis. The Welsh mountains couldn't kill him, God knows how many RTA's unreported, falling from planes, drinking to excess, talking when he should be listening, firefights with the Taliban, he continues to survive, and went on to be my saviour as CQMS. Without Clarence I am sure I would never have made it to Warrant Officer.

Epilogue for Craig Apps:
During my time on the AYT I had the pleasure of working for Craig who was an old friend and mentor from the Signal Platoon. Craig was a good laugh - chilled out and all-round top bloke, who later was the 'Buzzard' - Helicopter Operations boss, Fork hill, South Armagh. Always there for a chat, a brew, a game of RISK, and banter; I will always remember his kindness. Craig lost his battle with cancer in 2008. Always remembered and respected. RIP Craig.

CHAPTER 20

"The English know how to make the best of things. Their so-called muddling through is simply skill at dealing with the inevitable."
Winston Churchill.

1RGBW Support Company, Ballykinlar County Down, Northern Ireland, September 2000 – April 2002:

Returning the Battalion was a bit of a culture shock. Fair play, strings had been pulled and I was posted back to Support Company HQ. The Battalion was eight months into a two-year posting to Ballykinlar, Northern Ireland. The ceasefire was in its infancy, so operations and patrols were still ongoing, but we had to tone it down and be more user friendly to the locals.

Due to being in Company HQ, I shared a room in Mortar Platoon lines with a Company signaller Joey C, which was a right result because he was a top bloke and old mate. Even though in later years myself and 'Mr Dead' would turn up to his wedding reception well pissed up and preforming - sorry Joey.

Mr Dead was one of the lads from Anti-tanks who got his nickname from his complexion. He was that anaemic and gaunt he looked like he was dead! He's a good lad and family man. Plus, he's from the same street as me down in Bristol so of course he's a good sort.

The Battalion also had been beefed up, literally by an influx of Fijian soldiers whom I had already met and interacted with. Due to being that far from home and still waiting for their families to come to UK, they had spent their time on leave with the RGBW AYT at Chepstow. It was an eye opener for me personally to interact and be introduced to the Fijian way of doing things, forming lifelong friendships.

The Fijian lads already had their own tribal structure and cultural sensibilities which I learnt myself by trial and error. Top tip: when they are pissed up, shut the door, let them get on with it and sort out their issues. I still have an exceptionally low tolerance level for Kava, which usually ended with me being carried to bed by either 'Papa Bear', 'Micky', 'Mikey', or 'Roko'.

I also learnt and was humbled by their old school mentality of solving problems and how everything stopped for church and rugby.

I will always be grateful to the Fijian families that when I married later in my career, how welcoming and protective they were of my wife, and how Papa Bear, who was their default preacher and church organizer, was a good friend in giving me guidance when I was struggling with married life and being a dickhead.

My shoulder still hurts after Papa Bear give it a little squeeze when I was being a rather drunk mate in a state one time and needed to be guided to my bed space and put to bed! Plus, Support Company was reinforced by a multiple from 1 Royal Welsh, led by Kev and Jaffa who were top lads.

Gonzo's Car Crime and Grand Theft Auto:
'Gonzo' was always up for going on the piss and blowing his wages as a pay day millionaire in his early years. He was already in debt from Colchester due to the fact town was walking distance from camp and Gonzo was the man about town enjoying life. In later years, the Pay Master would use Gonzo as a case study in how to become debt free in two years with a bit of tough love and budgeting.

Gonzo got his nickname due to the uncanny resemblance and mannerisms he shared with the Sesame Street character of the same name. Gonzo has hollow legs and could drink most people under the table, he was and still is a larger-than-life character who enjoys life to the full. He is always up for a laugh, a family man, and a good friend. He was also a deceptively good solider and mortarman who achieved high rank in his full army career.

As I arrived back in Battalion, Nobby had already squared me away, and Ivor the QM was keeping me on the straight and narrow. Gonzo was the talk of the Battalion thanks to his latest drunken antics. Gonzo, and his crew of scallywags including: 'Foz', 'Brummy/Decorum', 'Crowbee', 'Danny Dogshit' and 'Cook Roach'.

Foz - a Cheltenham lad with a proper Cotswolds accent, a love of cider, and always involved in various good-natured scrapes and antics.

Brummy/Decorum - a big, rugby playing, loud and uncouth larger lout who would always create chaos, hence the nickname 'Decorum'. He had none. He is also one of the most loyal and generous blokes you could ever meet and a man who always had his friends' backs. As I write this book, Brummy is still serving and one of my oldest and trusted friends. Life is never quiet when Brummy is around, especially in the pub or round his house.

Crowbee - a fresh-faced youth, just 18 years old and thrown straight to the wolves, from training into the Mortar Platoon. He had Brummy as a role model which was a disaster waiting to happen.

Danny Dogshit - acquired is nickname when he first joined the Mortar Platoon in Bosnia. He was christened by our then Platoon Sergeant 'The Hitman'.

Legend has it, that the Hitman thought that Danny was as common as dogshit! So, the nickname stuck. More of Danny in later chapters.

Cook Roach - One of the Reconnaissance Platoon lads, had the ability to survive any situation and scandal to come out the other end. Hence the nickname Cook Roach, the only things that survived a nuclear detonation were cockroaches and the Cook Roach.

For a change of scenery, the lads led by Gonzo, had decided to go over to the Royal Irish side of camp to visit the NAFFI bar, 'The Rose and Crown'. As per usual it ended in the lads getting well rowdy and pissed up.

At the end of the night, the Royal Irish Battalion Orderly Sergeant was trying to clear and close the bar without much success. Gonzo returning from having a piss, noticed the BOS had left his car running outside so decided it would be a good idea to drive back across camp to our side. He provided a drunken taxi service for the lads.

How he managed to navigate to the Battalion lines was a miracle, lucky for him that there was no internal traffic in camp at that time of night.

As Gonzo was driving through the gate with his carload of drunks, he was stopped by the RGBW Orderly Officer, Captain Eden, who thought it was a wind up until the irate Royal Irish BOS came running down the road chasing his stolen car! *Grand Theft Auto Gonzo* went straight to jail, did not pass go, or collect two hundred pounds. Also, as if by magic, his passengers had disappeared into the night.

As with any drama and scandal involving Support Company, the Battalion rumour mill went into overdrive. Squaddies were worse than fish wives when it came to gossiping. By the time Gonzo went on orders the whole sorry saga was bigger than Ben-Hur. The Company Commander, 'Bow Didley', give him seven days restriction of privileges as he was laughed out of the office. He was also given a little debriefing from 'Boycee', the RSM.

Gonzo managed to dodge most of it due to the Company being on guards and duties. But 'Banger' being the Provost Corporal was not in the best of moods due to Gonzo being a pain in the arse, so Banger had him picking up litter and cleaning up the married quarters from dawn till dust when Gonzo wasn't staging on. As with the old school army ways - you do the crime, do the time.

Gonzo took it on the chin - job done. Top tip: Don't leave your car keys in the ignition when Support Company are on the piss.

CHAPTER 21

"I may be drunk Miss, but in the morning, I will be sober, and you will still be ugly. "
Winston Churchill.

Lamp Posted:
It was my birthday, and it was a Saturday. Support Company were stood down in camp, enjoying the peace and quiet. I had arranged that evening to have a few quick beers in the NAFFI - Dunnes Bar - with Jenks and his Mrs.

School boy error on my part. I mentioned this to Crowbee, so the whole Company knew about it by lunch time including 'Our Leon', so I was going to get the birthday bumps big time by Support Company.

'Jenks' was the Battalion Bob the Builder, assault pioneer and trade pioneer full screw. He was a chilled-out bloke who never flapped, was good with his hands and any sort of tools. He was always in demand around camp building shit and looked after me when I was a crow in B Company 1Glosters. A good bloke and always good Company.

Our Leon is my little 'bigger' brother from another mother. Fellow Bristoli lad and mocha, similar interests, he is family as far as I was concerned. The only difference was height - he was 6'2. I was 5'5!

Happy Birthday Clarence Old Son – Let's Go on the Piss:
After a few beers I was feeling good and enjoying my birthday celebrations. Then I was bought a few shots and things started to get a bit blurry. Our Leon had lured me into a false sense of security. The next thing I was jumped by Brummie, Tin Head, Foz and Big Vern. I was bound, gagged, and then carried out of the NAFFI too be paraded round camp. As we went towards the block, a lamp post was selected and I was stripped off, tied up, and left there as the 1RGBW's latest tourist attraction.

Word soon spread around the Battalion and photos were taken and shared. After about an hour of ridicule, Jenko and Our Leon had a moment of weakness and cut me down. The last thing I remember about my birthday that year was Our Leon carrying me up the stairs to my room, Welsh Roge putting me in the shower, cleaning me up, and then putting me to bed.

Later it transpired that Joey C had sat up most of the night keeping an eye on me, so I didn't choke on my vomit or do something stupid in my drunken state. I was blessed to have such good friends. Plus, it was operation clean up our room and the showers - I was a mate in a state.

Man, Away Madness:
The Battalion was deployed to Drumcree to cover the various marches that were occurring during the Silly Season, which was army slang for the marching season in the province. Due to Portadown being a loyalist town and unionist stronghold, it was pretty laid back and the police took the lead on the public disorder. We still had some jobs on and low-key patrolling ongoing.

As Support Company deployed on its various tasks there was the worst radio call that everybody didn't want to hear; 'Man Away'. The call means that we were missing a man, possibly kidnapped by the various warring and criminal factions. Major flap on, big drama!

'Richie' was a Company character; he had served in the Bosnian war as an international volunteer - a medical orderly with Croatian HVO. He had suffered a head injury courtesy of the Serbs. Upon his return to the UK, he took the Queen's shilling. Richie was known for being a bit scatty, going off into his own little world, disappearing, and speaking to complete strangers. During a rest period he had taught himself to speak Spanish thanks to a DIY book and CD set. He was nice bloke; just scatty.

Man, away had been called and Richie was the missing man. As the Company was in the process of conducting a search, checking every nook and cranny, the OC was having a major sense of humour failure. 'Hyperactive Bobby' the Company Sergeant Major was going more hyperactive and mental than usual. It didn't help matters that Mortars were making light of the situation, taking the piss, and blaming Brummy for not being particularly good at his job in babysitting Richie. One job Brummy had, and he fucked it up.

Fortunately, Richie was located to everyone's relief. The lunatic had nodded off and was found sleeping under one of the Saxons armoured personal carriers. This caused great embarrassment to the Company and Richie was about a popular as a rattlesnake in a lucky dip for the rest of the deployment. To add insult to injury, it was Brummy that found him. To say that Richie had grass burns was an understatement when Brummy dragged him out from underneath the Saxon, much to everybody's amusement.

ATGW Platoon was responsible for the Obins Street Interface in Portadown. This was a shit job because the small nationalist enclave at the end of the row, went out of their way to wind up the majority unionists in the rest of the street during Silly Season. Our troops were there to keep the peace and by a perverse twist of fate, we were protecting the nationalists that hated our guts. There had already been a few niggles on the interface.

On one occasion when Company Headquarters were out and about doing the rounds, some drunken fool came up to me, got in my face, and started giving me loads of racial abuse. Bow Diddley the OC gave it back to him in pure Jamaican patois due to the fact he was from The British Virgin Islands. The look of incomprehension on the bloke's face was a picture. Plus, the Fijian lads were having none of it and by some miracle of science, the pissed-up twat ended up headfirst in a wheelie bin. Shocking how drunks end up in bother. It was also amazing how the police at that location were having a smoke break when this alleged assault happened.

'Eddie the Chinky' - a great bear of a man with some oriental bloodline. He was the sarge running ATGW Platoon, a main stay of the Battalion rugby team with a great booming laugh, and a thick Geordie accent that few of us West Country boys could understand.

One night Company Headquarters was mobilised acting as another multiple out on the ground. The OC had arranged to RV with Eddie and the ATGW boys in a quiet area of town that they were patrolling at some stage in the evening.

As we stopped short there was no sign of Eddie. Next thing we saw was a Chinese delivery driver stood outside some random house in the cul-de-sac with a big bag of scoff. Eddies 4-man patrol popped up out of the darkness, scaring the life out of the poor delivery driver, paid him, and picked up the Chinky scoff for the ATGW boys.

The look on Eddie's face five minutes later when Company Headquarters rocked up at the ATGW wagons just as they were enjoying ribs and prawn crackers was priceless. The OC saw the funny side of it, and Eddie got grief after that for his nocturnal eating activities from the lads.

CHAPTER 22

'Never argue with a drunk or a fool.'
Aaron Sorkin.

NAFFI Brawl:
Due to being undermanned, we had Number Seven Company; Coldstream Guards attached to the Battalion. This led to a few problems and drama's involving Support Company. The Guards had a different way of doing business than the RGBW and ways and means which led to misunderstandings and friction which led to all-out war.

The Guards loved their drill and bullshit, which did not go down well with us and our relaxed way of doing things; our first names terms and nicknames when we addressed each other. I had to laugh one day as some Guardsman, 'Wooden Top' passed one of his officers in camp, stopped, slammed his tabs in, and produced a textbook salute before asking Rupert for his, 'Permission to carry on Sir?'. *WTF was all that about?* With the RGBW, it was a quick salute and a, 'Morning Sir', or boss. In those days, our Battalion was multi-racial with a relaxed way of working. The Guards to us were weird, alien, and all white without any of the usual RGBW banter which led to drama and scandal.

Saturday night in the NAFFI was always a Support Company and Headquarters piss up if the Company was not deployed or on guards and duties. Things had been building up with the Wooden Tops Guards due to a few comments being made to the Fijians and some queue jumping in the cookhouse. The match that finally ignited the battle of the Ballykinlar NAFFI - Dunnes Bar, was provided by Gonzo, who was taking the piss out of the guards as he does.

Due to Gonzo being chief instigator and wind-up merchant, he was the first member of 1RGBW to have a slap off some Wooden Top! The thing I will always remember about that night was Gonzo's rather large bleeding nose, followed by Brummy and Big Vern from Mortars throwing tables at the opposition - then it all went nuclear. Enter 'Cortina Ken', from the MT Platoon.

Pride of place that night goes to an old time MT Lance-Jack - Cortina Ken, who was a mild-mannered old timer who taught most of us in the Battalion to drive and maintain the various vehicles, starting on Land Rovers. He got his nickname Cortina Ken after the old style 1970's Ford Cortina. He wasn't a big bloke and had a reputation for being quiet and mild mannered who wore bottle top glasses.

That night, he was a Battalion legend - transformed into a Ford Granada. He became The Incredible Hulk that night banging out guardsman left, right, and Chelsea. He was like Chuck Norris; people couldn't believe it. Ken took care of business.

The guard was called out, quickly followed by the Dog Section and the Battalion Orderly Officer. Meanwhile back in the NAFFI, the Guards were conducting a fighting withdrawal back to their accommodation, while every member of the RGBW and REME joined in to give them a slap. The Guards had not done themselves any favours and the clash of cultures had now gone nuclear.

Big Will, Crowbee, and Foz had decided to carry on a Support Company tradition of stealing signs and anything else that wasn't nailed down. The NAFFI 'Dunnes Bar' sign was next on their wish list. As with everything that Crowbee got involved with, it ended in disaster with the final screw refusing to come loose and Crowbee doing a Humpty Dumpty and falling off the NAFFI wall causing a lot of damage. Lucky for the lads there was no CCTV in the NAFFI because by this stage it was looking like Hiroshima after it had been nuked by the USAF.

The Dogs of War were then unleashed into the NAFFI. Big Clint's Battalion Dog Section. It was biblical how quickly it all went quiet as peace and harmony returned to the Dunnes Bar after the dogs went in.

Unfortunately, not quick enough for 'Dean' from the MT who was given a nasty bite on his tattooed arse from one of the dogs - much to everyone's amusement. After the storm had passed and things had quietened down the NAFFI resembled the city of Dresden after a visit from RAF bomber command during the last war.

There was a lot of bar brawl damage, including beer bottles stuck in walls and broken windows. Another good night in the Dunnes bar. Congratulations SP and HQ companies 1RGBW - in the shit yet again. The powers that be weren't happy about the whole drama.

Monday morning, the Mortar Platoon plus attachments were parading with A Company ready to start pre-deployment training in preparation for a six-week exercise in Belize. The Battalion bush telegraph had already done the rounds and tapped out the various messages, reference: The Dunnes Bar Destruction; there was quite a bit of cookhouse gossip going round and apprehension at the fate of the guilty parties. Everybody knew the shit was going to hit the fan over it.

'Danger Mouse', then appeared with a big grin on his face. He informed us that the following blokes were required to go for a little chat with 'Boycee' the RSM! Gonzo, Brummy, Foz, and I were wanted down the Support Company office for a little chat with the OC Bow Didley, and Support Company CSM 'Hyperactive Bobby' ASAP. The shit was just about to hit the fan reference the battle of the Dunnes Bar.

DM (Danger Mouse) was a nightmare SNCO who was one of the most professional soldiers I have ever known. He was also a sarcastic bastard! He looked like the cartoon character, and along with his brother 'Bomb Head' they were known throughout the Battalion for their dry sense of humour and ability to produce results through tough love. More from DM and Bomb Head in later chapters.

To cut a long story short, the outcome of the various *chats* was that the Dunnes Bar was to be squared away and repaired by the lads involved in the brawl, assisted by 'Jenko', and 'Si', the Battalion Assault Pioneers. And there was to be no repetition of the violence. No more ongoing dramas with the Wooden Tops under pain of the hurt locker coming down on all our collective heads. Belize was an ideal opportunity for everything to calm the fuck down.

The following day, the now reinforced A Company group was on parade for Belize Administration. DM had a big shit eating grin on his face, which was very unnerving. He told me he had a *treat* for the Mortar Platoon which set off our alarm bells.

When DM was smiling and preparing *treats* it ended in tears before bedtime. 'Big Dave OC' from A Company then told us the Company was being bolstered up for Belize with four Guardsmen from Number Seven Company. As the four

Wooden Tops fell in with the Company there was a deathly silence. They were only the same blokes we were scrapping with in the NAFFI! Here we go - Round Two.

They later confided in me in the jungle, that as they walked up to the A Company parade and saw the Mortar Platoon, they thought their lives were over and could feel the hatred in the air. It turned out they were good lads and peace returned to the RGBW happy valley and everybody got on. Let bygones be bygones - life is far too short to hold a grudge.

CHAPTER 23

"The jungle is neutral."
Freddie Spencer Chapman.

Belize Bedlam:

This segment of the book is filled with bittersweet memories for me. It has been difficult to write. It is written in honour and respect to Danny Dogshit and Tin Head. Two of the biggest jokers, sword brothers, and good friends to all those that served with them. Good lads who both made the ultimate sacrifice whilst on later operations in Afghanistan. Rest in peace my friends - see you both in Valhalla where we will all share a horn of ale in the warrior's Hall of Heroes.

After the usual RAF flight chaos of hurry up and wait, the 1RGBW A Company group arrived at Airport Camp Belize for a week of acclimatizing and low-level training, before going up country to Guacamalo bridge to crack on with jungle warfare training. Most of the blokes were jet lagged and chin strapped after the flight. But Mortars decided to go on the piss and head down to Raul's Rose Garden - the world-famous brothel for the three B's: Boozing. Buffoonery. Banging birds.

Rose Gardening:

Raul's Rose Garden was a rite of passage for most blokes that did Belize. It was a concrete block warehouse/B and Q shed, that was a $20 Belize dollar taxi ride from camp. 'Russ the Yank' was the usual cabby who looked like the actor John Candy and drove a 'Ghostbusters' style wagon.

The Rose Garden was a spit and sawdust brothel/bar with the stars in their eye's corridor out the back, where the blokes would bang whores. As per usual it ended in a mass piss up and blokes dipping their wicks. The funniest things being: Brummie running round the place putting the large land crabs that lived in the urinals on people's heads, Gonzo being hung like a Donkey running around and scaring the whores with the size of his pork sword, Scottish Tommo the medic sat by the stage quietly supping his beer and making sure the lads were using condoms 'BFAs'; and then running a small clinic taking care of the ladies of the night. With his medical bergen and his general quiet and friendly manner, he was a genuinely nice bloke who went out of his way to help people.

'Big Vern' was a gentle giant of a man, who looked like the hitman from the comic Viz, but had the unfortunate habit of gobbing off and opening his big trap at the wrong time and place. This made him unpopular with the Head Shed. Poor old Big Vern, he meant well, but every time he did would end in disaster and ridicule. However, he did redeem himself during the Dunnes NAFFI bar brawl.

Tin Head was an educated, slightly older lad who had been traveling and teaching in Southeast Asia before he took the Queen's Shilling. He had acquired his nickname due to his love of biscuits which he kept under his bed in an old school, large Victorian style tin. He was always the voice of reason and a calm and collected lad that was always up for a laugh.

Enter Tatiana - an extremely attractive lady of the night who had, had more pricks than a pin cushion. Big Vern being the lunatic that he was, soon found himself smitten and up for getting mugged off by this old trout. He was like a lamb to the slaughter; word soon spread around the Platoon. To sort out this drama and scandal within the Platoon, the problem was soon solved with the help of some of the A Company lad. Tatiana was terribly busy for a couple of days servicing the needs of the single, red-blooded lads from Mortar Platoon. Big Vern soon saw the light about his love interest after an adult conversation with Tin Head, who was always the voice of reason.

The morning after, a rather hung over and dishevelled Platoon paraded for beat up training before we entered the jungle. The first bit of drama and scandal had involved Crowbee stealing a push bike in camp because he couldn't be arsed to walk back to the block - so here we go - Mortars in the shit again. 'Dalek', the CSM was not a happy teddy bear, and the whole Platoon smelled like Weston's Cider Factory and were still well pissed up. Later that day, Crowbee was given a 30 seconder by the Platoon as a punishment for being a prick! Top tip: of the day: Don't get caught when out on the rob.

Dalek was the A Company CSM. Not a bad bloke; he took things a bit too seriously and due to being Welsh, he sounded like Davros the Dalek off the tv show Dr Who - hence the nickname.

DM pulled me to one side, to give me the heads up. Thanks to an unnamed gossip and a fucking grass, the shit had hit the fan back in NI on the 'Pads' married quarters estate due to Mortars trip downtown to the Rose Garden.

Uncle Dave the OC wanted a word in my shell like to get the Mortars side of this developing story and major fuck up. *'Why me lord?',* I thought to myself as I went to the Company office. The OC explained that the rumour back in NI was that the Mortar Platoon had taken the married blokes and young lads downtown, got them all drunk, and then took them to the Rose Garden banging whores! It had created a load of drama and scandal that the OC didn't need on his plate. I explained that the only people involved were the usual Mortar Platoon scrotes, and at no stage were the married blokes doing the dirty. Reference the young lads from A Company: Tommo made sure that they had taken precautions.

The OC then gave me a gypsy warning to pass on! Play the game - enough said. Big boys' rules. The last thing Mortars needed was to be on the OC's radar. Gary and Cyprus Eddy who were running the Platoon wouldn't be happy, and shit would roll downhill at a rapid rate of knots. Nobby just threatened to beat us all up if he had his beauty sleep disturbed again with us being rowdy and fucking up.

Due to beat up training and battle prep ready for the jungle, the trips down to Rose Garden were put on hold to let the dust settle. We never did find out who gossiped, but we have unproven suspicions.

River Rat:
As soon as the Platoon went up country things got serious with jungle school and survival training. Cyprus Eddy and Roge had pulled a flanker and were running the ranges as part of the Permanent Range Team thus, avoiding most of the jungle school. This left the Platoon in the hands of the jungle warfare instructors or 'Jungle Jedi's'. In the case of the Mortar Platoon, Nobby, Big Will

and DM were responsible for keeping the Company resupplied and were used as an extra Jedi if needed.

The first bit of a laugh was provided by Tin Head. Rule number one in the jungle was keep your machete oiled and sharp. He was chopping some bamboo when he fucked it up and chopped his left hand. We were all expecting to see claret and severed fingers and were disappointed that due to the lack of maintenance on his machete, he escaped with massive bruising on his hand and fingers! He was renamed ET hand. The Jungle Jedi's were not impressed.

During one of the exercises, we were using the river to navigate and practice our jungle patrol skills. As Big Will was taking the exercise, he was lead man followed by Brummie, Charlie the boss, and then me as the signaller.

Radio communications in the jungle were a nightmare, especially when on the move due to all the comms being done in High Frequency. You didn't have time to put up slopping wire antennas or copper wire, so you had to rely on the 1-meter whip antenna, which even when shortened or coiled got caught in the foliage. So off we go having to use the river as a jungle highway.

After a while, my spider sense was starting to shake due to the river water reaching up to Big Wills chest! I mentioned this to Will, and he told me to stop flapping; he had already recced the route and it was all sorted. As I lost sight of Will due to the bend in the river, I took my next step.

The next thing I remember, I was fully submerged like a bloody U-boat. With the sun shining on the water above me, I had tripped on an underwater obstruction. *'Dump your bergen'*, was my first thought. It was pulling me down, but unlucky for me, my handset was curled round my shoulder and stuck on my webbing; and due to the weight of my bergen I couldn't swim up or free myself up to the surface - Flap on!

Meanwhile, back on the surface, Brummy looked round just in time to see my jungle bush hat floating down the river, and bubbles where I was supposed to be. Brummy thought it was hilarious - until I didn't surface. Brummy and Nobby managed to locate me via my radio antenna, they then found my webbing straps and pulled me up and out of the river in tears of laughter onto the riverbank, then all hell broke loose.

I resembled a drowned rat with Nobby rolling me on my side and getting my webbing off to access my lungs to apply pressure to get the water out of my system. Brummy was laughing his head off while I was still trying to breathe and process what was going on. Crowbee was arguing with Big Will and blaming him for me nearly drowning, the boss was trying to calm it all down, Gonzo and the rest of the boys were laughing about the whole pantomime, and to cap it all off as I'm trying to breathe, Big Vern comes up to me and says he had recovered my bush hat from the river! I could have killed him! Another fun filled day in the Mortar Platoon. I was now known as Floater! Blackman in the pool.

CHAPTER 24

"The jungle is dark, but full of diamonds"
Arthur Miller.

Snakes and Ladders:
The jungle environment has an abundance of wildlife and various sights and sounds. One morning, at first light, myself and Brummy were in our stand to position waiting for the Platoon to go into their routine. About 10 meters in front of me, I noticed a movement. At first, I thought it was a rather large snake, but it happened to be an exceptionally large tail of a Jaguar that crossed in front of our position. The look of disbelief on Brummy's face was a thing of beauty; it's the only time in history I have known Brummie to be lost for words. I thought I was David Attenborough having seen one of the rarest big cats in the world.

Gonzo has a phobia of snakes. One morning, Gonzo was doing his personal admin when he was told to stand completely still. There was a snake - a rather large, bright, Fer de Lance was enjoying the sun on the top of his bergen. Gonzo went white as a sheet, then did a runner down to where Platoon HQ was set up with the radios. He was going metal about snakes and flapping like a two stroke, having a complete nuclear meltdown! Then there was a massive burst of laughter in the harbour area. The killer snake was a plastic one Danny Dog Shit had bought from UK! Fair play, it was a bloody good wind up and Gonzo got ripped for days after.

On a serious note, DM found a Fer de Lance down by Company HQ a few days later, which concentrated minds wonderfully.

Baldy Beacon Blaze:

The Platoon had withdrawn from the jungle and was re-located to the native village at New Maria near Baldy Beacon. The lads were looking forward to getting the Mortars out, getting rounds down the range and letting it rain 81mm high explosive showers.

Before the live firing we all had to learn how to adjust fire by sound because in the jungle you couldn't see the fall of the shot. The Platoon was late getting to the RV with the New Zealand SAS old timer that was giving the lessons, plus we couldn't leave the vehicles unattended. I had to remain with the trucks because I had comms up with A Company and needed to send the Platoon nighty sit-rep.

Welsh Roge was keeping me Company, and we promptly got our heads down as the Platoon disappeared down the track! On the blokes return Gonzo reckoned it was, 'The most boring lesson of his life'. We, the elite Mortar Platoon 1RGBW deployed to the village and sorted out our shit for the up-and-coming Mortar shoot.

As dusk was falling, we were preparing to go into night routine; and because we were semi non tactical a ging gang goolie around the campfire seemed like a great idea. So, I asked 'Charlie' the boss if it was alright to have a campfire. Charlie being an officer and a gentleman said, "Yes, but don't take the piss. Keep it small and controlled!" "Sure, thing boss, no problem." *What could possibly go wrong?* We were all responsible adults - plus we were dry, no boozing.

About an hour later as the boss and myself were sending the nightly SITREP to zero on the radio, I glanced up, and to my total shock and surprise saw daylight and a massive sheet of flame. Brummy and Crowbee had only let the small, controlled fire spread and engulf a small native hut. It looked like something out of Lord of the bloody Rings. Plus, the rest of the blokes were dancing round the fire half naked like Lord of the Flies! Charlie the boss went full on ballistic. Mortar Platoon went straight into London's burning mode and put the flames out.

The old saying goes, don't let children play with matches. The updated version reads, don't leave Brummy and Crowbee without adult supervision. How Charlie kept his temper that night was beyond me. When DM and Nobby got wind of it, there were going to be tears before bedtime. As per usual the Platoon was in the shit yet again.

Smoke Grenades:
During live firing, the rest of A Company would trickle through the location, conduct training, and come and say hello with the usual banter when visiting the mortar line.

On one occasion, I had taken my radio kit down to were 'Johnno' and the boys from Company Headquarters Signals Detachment were set up to do some signals administration and shoot the shit. Then on the net, a *No Duff Casualty* was called. This means it's a real man down. Johnno was all over it, calling in the medivac helicopter.

I was speaking to the medics and getting things sorted for the chopper and manning the Company net. The casualty was one of the young lads from the Company Stevie T. I think it was a snake bite or heatstroke; anyway, there was a flap on. Stevie was in turbo bobbins - a lot of pain. Tommo the medic was doing a great job, and DM and Nobby were sorting out the stretcher on the back of the meat wagon/Ambulance.

Brummy and Crowbee were also 'helping' and being there usual sympathetic selves by taking the piss out of poor Stevie T for being weak and feeble.

As the chopper was inbound, I was popping smoke, so the pilot had our exact location for the medivac. As the smoke grenade popped, to my absolute horror, I had committed a schoolboy error! I had forgotten to take wind and direction into account. The ambulance, Johnno, and Stevie T were all now engulfed in purple smoke looking like a Paul Daniels magic show. I was ripped for weeks after that little failure at Sioux smoke signals. I was fined a crate of beer by DM for being a mong.

One night a few days later, the Platoon had finished live firing and were located in another semi decent village/base camp Augustine, with Company Headquarters. DM was set up there also administrating the Company. Life was pretty chilled, sorting out the Mortar Kit ready for the FTX, then R and R. There had been some random Yank blogger/reporter sniffing around doing a story on the British Army in Belize. So far, Uncle Dave had kept him away from the madness of the Mortar Platoon. DM then appeared and told me to have a whip round; we were off on a little adventure!

The Platoon had been tasked to look after the Yank reporter and let him experience the Mortar Platoon banter for his last night up country with A Company. This was an order from Uncle Dave - but don't take the piss or fuck it up. So off DM and I go in his Land Rover to do a bit of business with the locals to get some beers and rum. Between DM's bartering skills, my Billy basic Spanish, and as the locals called it my pirate talk, we got it all sorted. Fair play to Anthony, he was a good bloke and got the banter and joined in with the beers and buffoonery. Mind you; Brummy did threaten to come and visit him in the states if he mugged us off online. The article is still on the net: 'A Yank in the British Army', by Anthony C. Lozado@WND

CHAPTER 25

"Con dinero baila el perro. With money the dog dances."
Mexican Proverb.

Mexican Madness:
R and R - Cancun Mexico here we come! After 10 hours on a chicken/Freddy Kruger style, Yank, happy bus from Belize to Mexico, a mixed bag of Mortars and Assault Pioneers from 1RGBW, and our attached Guardsmen the 'Wooden Tops' arrived.

You're a real Munson:
The fun and games began on the bus five minutes after leaving Airport Camp, with the first beer down the range. The happy bus had a VCR set up playing the film 'Kingpin' with the main character of the movie being 'Roy Munson' who had everything: money, women, a bowling champion etc; then he blew it all! A real Munson i.e., a fool and a loser. So Gonzo coined the phrase, 'You're a real Munson,' for anybody that made a fool of themselves or dropped a bollock within the Platoon. It soon spread all over the Battalion and is still a favourite banter bomb to this day.

Big Vern gets sent to Coventry:
On arrival in the legendry resort of Cancun in Mexico, there was the usual drama and scandal. For once it wasn't our fault.

The Rupert who had booked the hotel for the lads had fucked up. There was only accommodation for 20, not the 22 that were on the bus. Not a problem.

Myself and 'Willie' from the Assault Pioneers had Visa cards, we would sort it out with the friendly hotel staff using my basic Spanish. Enter Big Vern, as we are trying to square away the hotel drama.

Vern is gobbing off in my ear saying how he wants an ocean view and a jacuzzi in his room; it's doing my head in. I turned round to Vern and told him to go and grab a beer with the rest of the boys over in the Slices Bar across the road while Willie and myself sort out the hotel; the last thing we need to do is upset the hotel staff. Not Big Vern. He was like a hyperactive kid and typical, he didn't know when to keep his big mouth shut! So, I lost my temper. 'Vern, there you go son, you're in a single room, here's your fucking key, and for the next three days don't come anywhere near the Platoon. You're being sent to Coventry. To quote Sir Alan Sugar, you're fired! Jog on son! Don't speak to us - not even at scoff!' Unbeknownst to any of us, later in the trip Big Vern would have the last laugh.

Crowbee's Bad Day:

After the first night of fun and frivolity Crowbee, at breakfast the following morning, was having a bad day! When I say a bad day, I mean a Chernobyl nuclear meltdown. He had lost his wallet, had a handover from hell, and to add insult to injury he had bumped into Big Vern in the lift earlier. Vern had pulled two yank birds and was on the way up to his room for some beast with two backs action - fair play to Big Vern getting laid - he had a result the wanker.

Brummy, being his usual sympathetic self, came up with a solution for Crowbee's lack of cash; he would lend him $1000 bucks for the rest of the trip, but there was a catch! Crowbee could only spend the money on booze. He had also managed to break a chair in the hotel lounge due to being pissed up, so more expense.

The hotel only did us breakfast, that was it on the food front for Crowbee, so he was going to be a little Hank Marvin (Starving). It was quite amusing seeing Crowbee sat on the kerb like an orphan while the rest scoffed Macke Dees and proper Tacos. Richie was caught sneaking him food which did result in Richie getting throw in the pool for showing weakness and mercy. The only positive to come out of this for life changing moment, by a twist of fate we had bumped into a couple of British birds who were travelling and seeing the world. It was their last night in Mexico. We had a good bit of banter and took them clubbing with us because they were skint. Crowbee and Claire have now been married for nearly twenty years.

Shit Shorts Excuse:

By day three I was on my chinstrap with the boozing and madness. All I wanted was a morning off to chill out by the pool, read my book, and give my liver a rest. Danny Dogshit my roommate was having none of it, so I needed a good excuse to skive off for the morning.

I told him I would meet up with the boys later when my shorts had dried. Wrong answer son! Danny was straight on it. My lame bullshit excuse was destroyed in seconds - it's the bloody tropics, your shorts dry in extra quick time, plus I had borrowed them from Danny in the first place. Gonzo soon got wind of my pathetic attempt to avoid going on the piss. I was then summoned to the swimming pool and was given grief and told to man up, and was thrown in. Who were said peer pressure was dead and buried?

Medic:

One night on R and R, I was rudely awoken from a rum induced stupor with a call for the med kit. I always carried a med pack on our various jolly boys outing and adventures due to the fact there were always minor injuries, bumps, and bruises mainly caused by drunken antics.

Tin Head was knocking on the door half cut and unsteady on his feet. His right upper arm had a couple of sheets of kitchen roll folded over and stuck on with electrical tape. As I am cutting the pathetic attempt at a dressing away, he was going on about Yaqui Indians. I was thinking had he been stabbed or glassed by some smackhead?

The explanation was brilliant. On his arm was a brand new native American Yaqui dream catcher tattoo. It was pucka. Some of the best ink I have ever seen. One small problem was that Tin Head was from Reading in Berkshire, not the reservation. He had ended up in some local bar got chatting to some Yaqui blokes and got inked up. That was typical of Tin Head due to his ability to travel far and wide and make friends with the locals. Bit of Vaseline, and a fresh dressing; Tin Head was good to go.

Big Vern Nearly Gets Marooned in Mexico:

On the day of departure at first light, a sorry sight greeted the Mexican hotel staff. The 'Les Hooligans' as we British were know as in Mexico were pulling out of town back to Belize. Fair play: we were a mess. Hungover in a mixture of swapped football shirts, "I've got drunk in Cancun" t-shirts, Sombrero's, stinking of booze and worn out.

Most of us had given or traded our football and rugby shirts with the hotel staff because the Mexicans were mad for the Premiere League and English football/soccer. The hospitality and general friendliness of the Mexican hotel staff was brilliant. I will always be grateful for their time and effort, not like the average yank who looked down upon them and were rude and ignorant to the local Mexicans.

Richie was ill and we had a slight problem. Big Vern was a no show as we were getting on the bus. After a quick search and ask about there was still no sign of the clown. Unlucky Vern. We can't stick around; the bus is waiting. I'm having visions of a massive shit storm coming our way when we get back to camp.

About two hundred meters down the road, the lads on the back seat see Vern running after the bus. After making the driver drive on another hundred meters, Vern is banging on the back of the bus. We stopped and let him on - he was nearly in tears; that got Vern ripped by the lads. He had gone to get his tattoo finished and had got his timings wrong. He was one lucky teddy, plus the tattoo was wank.

Richie in Ruin:
As we departed Cancun on the happy bus back to Belize, it was like the retreat from Moscow with everybody in turbo bobbins and on their chinstraps. Richie was the worst, and I was genuinely worried for his health. I think he had alcohol poisoning, so the priority was to get him rehydrated, keep his temperature down, and get back to camp in one piece. He was in ruin, so he was bedded down on the back seat of the bus, being babysat and sipping water mixed with Dioralyte under the aircon. As per usual the blokes couldn't resist taking the piss out of poor Ritchie. I think it was Gonzo who wrote Munson on his forehead with a sharpie marker pen. Richie survived the bus trip and got sorted by Tommo the medic when we crawled back into camp the following day.

Border Balls Up:
We rolled into the border town of Chetumal on the Freddy Krueger bus. It was getting dark, and we were all keen to do the last leg and get back to camp, but as always, there was a drama!

The connecting bus to Belize had already left or broken down with no replacement available so we were stranded; for 12 hours, AWOL on the Belize/Mexican border. The place was a shithole and looked like somewhere out of a scene for Narcos. As always it ended up in a good almighty row. With a bus load of tired and pissed off squaddies pointing the fingers of blame and suspicion, having an argument for the sake of having an argument was on the cards.

We were having a few beers to calm down as Willie was trying to phone the camp from some Tardis type phone box, when we noticed that Tin Head was missing. For fucks sake! That's all we needed to cap off a really shit day!

Next thing we know, there's a beep of a horn and some airconditioned bus rocks up. Off jumps Tin Head, 'It's all sorted lads! He's taking us all the way back to camp for $30 dollars each, plus tips.' How Tin Head managed this I will never know, but he had squared it all away the legend! We were on our way back home to A Company 1RGBW.

CHAPTER 26

"Wen cak-roach mek dance, e'no invite fowl" When cockroach makes a dance, it doesn't invite the fowl"
Belizean Proverb.

Meanwhile, back in Belize!
Some of the lads had gone to San Pedro Island for R and R, and for once it wasn't the Mortar Platoon that had fucked up - that honour went to 'Signals George'. The whole tale of woe was told to me by Nobby and DM.

Signals George:
A member of the A Company Signals Detachment and was not a big bloke. But boy did Signals George like a drink! Fair play he had hollow legs. Always messing about he was the original happy drunk. He had already dropped a bollock on the exercise due to his love of beer. He was manning the VHF communications relay rebroadcasting link when we didn't get his hourly radio check. So, after several attempts to raise him on the net, myself and Gary had a bit of a bimble into the jungle to go and check on him. We had to walk up this massive bloody hill where George had set up his radio kit, both breathing out

of our arses and getting more and more pissed off with him when we got to the top of the feature.

My first thought was, *'Fucking hell, he's dead!'* George was sprawled out on a couple ammo tins, his radio kit was all over the place, and he looked like Tango man. Then Gary started laughing. As we got closer, I could hear George snoring and could also see a few beer cans littering the area. Fair play to George, he had got hold of a six pack in the middle of the jungle off the natives and had himself an afternoon drink up. He had got a few beers down range, fallen asleep, got sun burnt, and forgot about his hourly radio check. It was kept on the down low because it was typical Signals George behaviour bless him. He looked like Tango man for a few days after which gave everybody a good laugh. George was a good sport when it came to giving and receiving banter.

On St Georges Key, George went for a few quiet beers and in his own chilled out way nearly got the whole group kicked off the island since George, golf buggies, and beer don't mix very well.

According to eyewitnesses, George took the buggy for a spin, did a Dukes of Hazzard style river jump and rolled it causing a few bobs worth of damage; upsetting the local business owners in the process. DM had to bail George out from Company funds to pay for the damage and placate the irate locals. Nobby reckons you couldn't have made up that little comedy show.

I end this amusing tale in remembrance and in respect to my friend and our fellow brother in arms George. Sadly, George was suffering from P.T.S.D. and passed away in 2017. Rest in peace my friend - there is a bar stall up in the clouds with your name on it: 'Signals George'.

Scrote Boat to Key Caulker:
A Company 1RGBW, were due to depart Belize on Tuesday 11th September 2001. All the kit was packed up; and the lads were looking forward to going back to Blighty. That morning, we were sitting on our bergens ready to get on the transport down to the airport to do a John Denver and go home back to Blighty. Then it all went quiet, and the officers disappeared. It was if time stood still.

DM then gathered the Company together a said that the Yanks were under terrorist attacks and there had been a massive loss of life. The Head Shed was having a brief over at British Army Training Support Unit, Belize; and the

Company wasn't flying anywhere. Stand by: Dalek was busy with the Head Shed.

There was a small American presence on camp, so the Padre gathered us all together for a quick prayer. We all squeezed into the NAFFI, and it was on the big screen. DM's words will always stay with me. Forever. 'Blokes, at some stage this will affect us all, square your shit away because we will be going to war after this.'

Due to the ongoing situation and no fly zone in the States, we were sitting on our bergens in Belize till further notice. So, Mortars did what Mortars do best - went on the piss! Dalek the CSM went mental the morning after because at the morning muster parade, Gonzo had attempted a pre-parade drunken shave and ended up looking like Pinhead from Hellraiser. The CSM asked Gonzo if he had shaven. Gonzo's answer was, 'Yes', but he was feeling a bit delicate from the night before. This got a good laugh from the Company - not the CSM. Of all people stood next to Gonzo, it was Brummy and Danny Dogshit who were both stinking of booze and the worse for wear. The CSM just lost the plot with the whole Platoon.

Mortars were then put on a drinking ban, and Uncle Dave then came up with a cunning plan after a chat with the CSM, Nobby, and DM to get the whole Platoon banished from camp. All the kit was packed away ready for the flight home, so extra military training was off the table.

'Pack your Adventure training kit and shorts. You lot are getting fucked off to St Georges Key for enforced adventure training', was the brief from a pissed off Cyprus Eddy. Plus, there was a dirty rumour doing the rounds that there was a Para Regiment PTI there with orders to beast us.

As we arrived on the Key, the fun and games started immediately with this Para Regiment Physical Training Instructor gobbing off; getting all keen as he was swinging on the overhang showing off his muscles and physical prowess. Unfortunately for this clown, he lost his grip and fell on the wooden jetty then into the water! It must have hurt, but we were too busy laughing to care. After an hour of getting fucked around and getting beasted on a swim test, morale was low.

Enter Nobby with a solution! The Scrote Boat to Key Caulker. The brief from Nobby was, 'Grab your daysacks, the Scrote Boat is leaving in five minutes! You lot are getting banished from Uncle Dave's kingdom'. So, we all piled on the RIB, minimum kit. I will always remember I had Franny the PTI's T-shirt on because Nobby had thrown most of my bag in the water earlier that day when unloading the boat. Of course, he claimed it was an accident!

After about an hour on the boat we hit party central, back packers' style on Key Caulker. It was like D-Day when we came ashore. All the gap year people, and back packers didn't know what hit them. Two days, and two nights on the piss with Nobby as the responsible adult in command of the crew of the HMS Scrote Boat.

First thing is first - get the accommodation sorted, get some cash, get on the piss, and hopefully pull some hippie, gap year birds. Accommodation not a problem, Tin Head assured us it was sorted. He had squared us some beach huts - Happy days.

Now for some cash, even though most of us had a fold up in our skyrockets, Tin Head had squared the huts away on his Visa card and got it on drip. First major fucking problem was that the one and only cash point/hole in the wall on the island was broke. Plus, only a few of the bars took plastic.

A quick council of war was called on the beach. 'Empty your pockets lads of all your cash, put it all the hat.' It was like a Paul Daniels magic trip when all these Belize dollars started to appear in the hat, considering a few blokes were pleading poverty. Nobby took control of the funds for the duration.

The few off us with plastic would stand a few rounds and scoff for the lads because it was cheap as chips: something ridiculous like a pound for two pantie rippers = White rum and pineapple juice. Scoff wasn't a big deal because we had Army issue horror bags/packed lunches on the boat. Let the fun and games begin! 1RGBW Pirates of the Caribbean. More like the Pirates of Penzance!

Gonzo Gets Caught Short:
We were all enjoying a well-deserved drink up in some beach bar, when Gonzo was desperate for a call of nature - number twos. Unfortunately, the bogs were the other end of the island, so Nobby told him to go for a swim, wink, nudge. So, off Gonzo goes for a swim to cool off and attend to the call of nature. Happy days.

Unfortunately for Gonzo, the local tides and currents took his chocolate brownies back to the shallows where the lads were swimming and enjoying the beach bar. This then created chaos with a scene straight out of Jaws the movie, as people abandoned the water from the onslaught of the chocolate brownies that Gonzo had produced.

Gonzo policed up his arse in the water and went back to having a drink in the bar without a care in the world; because the unfolding chaos was none of his business as far as he was concerned.

Dutch Birds:
You couldn't have made this one up.

We were on the piss on this remote desert island, sharing clothes and toothbrushes, and having a good old lads on the piss time of our lives. We were in another native hut type beach bar, and in walk a load of fit as fuck Dutch birds. After we had got our chins off the deck, human nature took over and introductions were made. It turned out that they were a university fraternity on a break from studying. Most were either rowers or netball players. All I will say, is that a good time was had by all for Anglo-Dutch relations.

Fair play, there was this one Dutch bird who about 6'4, blonde and well built, physically fit, and attractive like some Viking Valkyrie. Drinking like a pirate, she was explaining to me she was a rower. Happy days! I was being the perfect gentleman when she said, "You're a little hobbit," and then picks me up like I'm a baby and throws me in the sea! Fair play, I got ripped for that one off the lads!

B and Q Shed:
The morning after in our deluxe accommodation looked like a scene from hell. I awoke with a burning hang over, naked on a pissed stained mattress sweating like mad next to Nobby. In the bed opposite us were Gonzo and Danny Dogshit, and on the floor between the beds was one of the assault pioneers getting eaten alive by various insects.

The whole place stunk and was humid as hell. Worst of all its was like a large B and Q shed with a single light bulb hanging down from the ceiling and cockroaches and moths all over the place - well done Tin Head! Take a failure on trip advisor for this Club Med hotel son!

We were all gagging for a brew and Gonzo was tasked with sorting it out. It turned into a bit of a drama due to there being no kettle - just a microwave oven. How Gonzo produced cups of tea was a modern-day miracle.

Twelve days later, we were permitted an air corridor via Florida to fly back home to the UK, due to September the 11th and the States being on lock down. It was surreal transiting through Fort Lauderdale Airport. Security was through the roof and a lot of the Yanks were shellshocked due to the terrorist attacks. The Americans were their usual generous selves and even gave us Brits a clap on our way through the Airport. The terrorist attacks were a tragic act of pure evil. It would have life changing consequences for all of us from 1RGBW A Company, later down the line.

Don't Trust Officers with Knives:
On return from Belize, it was back to normal jogging in Ulster. Support Company were deployed in some shit town covering some march or other, doing the 'public disorder' thing. It was boring and tedious; hurry up and wait in our snatch Land Rovers. Company HQ were co-located with the police parked up in some side street.

Joey C and I were chilling out with 'Hyper-active' the CSM, when we all heard this commotion from the back of the wagon. 'Bow Didley' the OC was calling the 2IC a bloody fool in his posh, refined, officer home counties accent. Then the OC shouted for me to grab the med pack because the 2IC had cut himself. The 2IC had decided to cut some maps up to size ready for lamination and had rested them across his knees and used a scalpel instead of scissors. The result was cut maps and upper legs, doing himself a mischief in the process; much to the OC's scorn and the amusement of Company HQ. The CSM and I had to walk down to Anti-Tanks wagons before bursting into fits of laughter in the back of Eddie the Chinky's wagon like naughty schoolboys!

Top tip: Don't trust officers with knives.

Master Stitch:
As the Battalion was preparing to leave Ulster, we all had to go and get fitted for our ceremonial uniform 'Blues', ready for public duties and drill. Most of the Company were deployed, based out of Portadown.

One morning, some random bloke just rocked up at our portacabins in a tracksuit, hungover to fuck, stinking of booze, with a daysack and a briefcase. He said, 'Alright mate?', to me and Leo, the Company CQMS. Then the cheeky bastard went out the back, flopped on my bed, wrapped himself up in my USMC poncho liner, got his head down, and began snoring like a hibernating bear. Welcome to the wacky world of the 'Master Stitch.'

When I returned a few hours later after sorting out some wagons, James Bond - 007, was sat in Leo's desk in a pin stripe suit with a tailors measuring tape looking like something out of Saville Row sober as a judge and measuring people up for their number ones. It was the bloke in a track suit from earlier. Master Stitch was a right character.

CHAPTER 27

"There are two places in the world where men can most effectively disappear –
the city of London and the South Seas."
Herman Melville.

1RGBW C 'Criminal' Company Cavalry Barracks, Hounslow, West London. Public Duties. April 2002 – September 2005:

Return to the UK mainland, London Town. The Battalion moved lock, stock, and barrel to Cavalry Barracks, Hounslow, West London for public duties. I was not overly impressed with this turn of events, because I was a drill mong and scruffy. I had no interest in standing outside Buck House or the Tower in my blues, getting happy snapped by Timmy the tourist. Mind you some of the ex-Dukes were in heaven because it was there thing! Drill, Bulling boots, and bullshit. Nobby had been promoted to C Company CQMS and I went with him into C Company stores and the HQ set up.

Pirates of the Caribbean:

The only good news was that the Company was off on a 6-week exercise to Jamaica, on Exercise Red Stripe before the boots, belts, and bullshit of wooden top central. What a bloody result! I've always wanted to go to Jamaica, and there were some good lads going with us.

The Company flew into Kingston on a British Airways commercial flight, which was fantastic. It beat RAF/Crab Air hands down. The bonus was the aircraft didn't break down.

Due to the political situation, we flew over the pond and moved up country in civvy's which was cool. The Jamaica Defence Force put us up on a tented camp with a few wriggly tin 'Tenko' style shacks on the site of an old hotel in Port Antonio. That's when the fun and games began.

Before anything on the morning of day one, we had the dos and don'ts brief off the Head Shed. Plus, Bo Didley the OC was well versed on Caribbean culture because he was born and raised in the British Virgin Islands, he gave us the cultural brief and the certain words *not* to use.

'Panzer Leader' one of the officers, had also arranged for the local Police Chief to brief us all up on the local dynamics, and crime and punishment Jamaican style. It was quite surreal when this rotund Jamaican bloke in a polyester uniform rocked up and gave us a brief not on crime, but his brother's jerk chicken joint, and his cousins bar and grill. Mind you we were tuned in and fully educated on the marijuana/smoking the herb mugs game - Don't do it or it will end in tears before bedtime.

Language Difficulties:
The Company started sorting itself out to get on exercise, but there were a few problems starting on day one. As I was trying to sort out transport and get the lay of the land, there was a communication breakdown. Being Bristol born and bred, I speak pirate! But when in Rome do as the Romans do, and in Jamaica they speak Patois/Patwa. After trying to speak to the locals in my Bristolian, there was no comms, and the look I was getting from the locals was *what planet was this man from?*

Salvation came from an unlikely source the OC Bo Didley. I'm stood there in front of the locals looking like a right clown, then along comes the OC and speaks the lingo like a local; hand signals and all, and sorts it all out like a pro. The OC was born and raised in The British Virgin Islands a child of Empire. So fair play, he was all over it. Enter the 'Examiner'.

Examiner was our local guide and Mr Fix it! I have been incredibly lucky in life to meet some truly extraordinary people, and Examiner was one such person. The man was a Jedi master in the jungle and a great teacher. He was also a good laugh, and at nights always good for a bit of banter and telling tall tales around the campfire. After a brief conversion with some of the Jamaican Defence Force lads, I knew that I needed a crash course in the local lingo, thank

God for Examiner. After a few days I could speak to the locals. Every day is a school day.

'Kane the Train' was a mild-mannered Clark Kent kinda bloke, until he lost his temper. Then he was chief jap slapper. He was a bloody good squaddie, a right laugh, and he was Evo's partner in crime when it came to windups. I call him Kane the Train because he is a bloody good model railway builder and enthusiast, making top of the range models and a good living out of it.

Treasure Island:
Due to the nature of the Jamaican jungle, navigating and tabbing around the Ulu was a nightmare. It was all hills and rivers, and for the lads in Reconnaissance Platoon it was hard going. Kane the Platoon Colour man was having a bit of a drama with a new, keen as mustard officer.

I was tasked one day to resupply Recce with water and rations, but there was an ongoing drama with one of the local farmers due to a possible theft of coconuts involving the Brits as I rocked up on the RV point waiting for Kane and the boys to appear.

I first had to deal with the great coconut theft. The three JDF lads manning the check point were looking a bit sheepish when Examiner and myself where speaking to the local farmer who was eyeing some of the goodies in the wagon including my DPM Gore-Tex jacket.

As I was surveying the crime scene, I couldn't help but notice a load of coconut shells thrown in the bushes behind the JDF lads little set up, and one of them wiping milk from his lips trying not to burp. I don't consider myself to be Sherlock Holmes, but even I could work this crime of the century out. It all ended without incident - the JDF lads did a few hours work for the farmer who was now the proud owner of a DPM Gore-Tex jacket and enjoying a British Army ration lunch. There were also some fresh coconuts and bananas in the back of my wagon for the lads out on the ground.

When Kane and the Recce turned up it was red hot, and the humidity was through the roof. They were glad of the water resupply, plus Nobby had thrown some cool cans of pop in the Norwegian container which was a life saver for the boys.

After a quick conflab, it was decided I would squeeze the lads and their kit on the wagon and do several lifts to get them to the next RV improvisation; and adaptability was the name of the game! Why bloody walk when you could drive? Slight problem - Mr Keen Officer decided to get involved in the discussions, and he was determined to keep on tabbing up the Ulu.

It's amazing how hard of hearing and busy you can get, especially when Kane the Train had gently taken this young officer to one side to have an adult conversion with him. I swear to God that at no stage did Kane threaten of use violence during this frank and honest discussion on the merits of using Clarence's taxi service. It was a long afternoon, but in the end Kane's boys covered the 10 miles to their night-time harbour area in record time.

Later that week, Nobby, the boys from Company HQ and I went on a treasure hunt in the river. There was a bit of drama and scandal while the Company were conducting a river crossing. One of the blokes took a tumble, became a human U Boat, and lost his LSW rifle to the depths of the river. It was then our job to recover the LSW. As per usual it ended up as an exceedingly long and wet afternoon of Company HQ becoming human seals that eventually recovered the LSW.

Kane the Train Goes Off the Rails:
Some of the Recce lads went on local R and R to a posh little yuppie hotel down the road. We knew it was going to end in tears because Kane was planning to go on one his legendry benders. But hey ho, it was nothing to do with us. Kane and his lads were out of camp for a few days, so Company HQ were looking forward to some peace and quiet.

About two o'clock in the morning, the peace and quiet was shattered by a bench crashing over the wall and into Company Headquarters like a tomahawk cruise missile narrowly missing the lads who were getting their heads down, creating a load of noise and waking the camp.

After a lot of running around and noise, things calmed down. The JDF guard didn't see or hear anything, and nobody was sure who was responsible. The finger was pointed at some of the local youths who were seen earlier in the evening, loitering with intent. In the morning camp security was improved, and the blokes were briefed to be more vigilant.

When Kane the Train crawled back into camp after his weekend on the piss, he looked like death warmed up. Nobby was in disbelief that Kane the Train hadn't gone off the rails and there was no drama and scandal.

It was only on the plane home that the truth of that night finally came out. Kane was the guilty party. He had snuck back into camp and created chaos just to wind Nobby up!

Typhoons:

Towards the end of the exercise, it started to rain, and the wind started to blow. The JDF informed the Head Shed that a typhoon was on the way and the local advice was to pack up and move down to Kingston a few days early. The last thing we needed was to be caught up country and get delayed.

Bonus, as one of the chefs had been at it with a local whore and was showing signs of picking up an STD - as you can imagine, this news spread like wildfire through the Company. Some blokes were not happy that this chef was cooking the scoff after possibly picking up a dose from banging some local whore.

As the weather was turning bad, everybody and everything was getting pissed wet through and generally pissed off.

Due to the rural location of Port Antonio and the Company sending a lot of money in the local community, the locals were gutted that we were leaving. The last few days before departing, the lads spent a lot of time swapping, trading, and giving away various bits of personal kit etc. Before long, Examiner and his merry band of helpers were cutting about in DPM Gore-Tex and wearing Bristol Rovers football shirts.

As with everywhere the British Army goes, it's always the kids that get looked after. On the day of departure down to Kingston, Bo Didley gave the local kids and school all the Company sports kit, and a lot of the blokes chipped in as well with bits and pieces.

Nobby being a knob donated all my civilian clothes to Examiner out of the kindness of his heart. I looked a right dickhead on the plane home wearing Archie's Cheltenham Saracens RFC shorts, flip flops, and an Ochos Rios hotel staff t-shirt that one of the lads had acquired! Kane and Nobby sniggered, took the piss, and gave me grief all the way back to Blighty.

As the coaches left Port Antonio, all the locals came out to wave us off. Some of the local birds were trying to locate some certain members of the Company whom they had, had month long relations with. All joking aside, I have to say that the people of Port Antonio were some of the nicest and the most welcoming people I have had the pleasure to meet in all my travels on this lonely planet Earth. Examiner and the JDF lads were spot on.

CHAPTER 28

"It's not whether you get knocked down, it's whether you get up."
Vince Lombardi.

NCO Cadre:
The Infantry doesn't fuck around when it comes to you getting your first stripe, or in DM's mad little world, and words of wisdom, 'It's the hardest to get; the easiest to lose'. Unlike other formations or Corps in the British Army, in the Infantry you must earn your first Lance Corporal's stripe. It is not a freebee, or a time served pat on the back, it's a pass or fail course. It's all voluntary - tell the DS that you what to ring the bell meaning bin it, voluntarily withdraw - you can quit any time. Or the DS can fail you and fuck you off at any time if you're not up to standard! It's brutal.

'Norm Bates' had joined the Battalion at the back end of Ballykinlar, and because he was a bit older and an ex-fireman with a lot of life experience he was posted straight to Mortars. He fitted straight in and was always up for a laugh, being the life and soul of the party. Norms biggest downfall was when he dropped himself in it, it affected everybody in a 30-mile radius. Every man and his dog knew about it when the jungle drums started beating.

I was playing catch up on the NCO's Cadre. I had fucked around, had a laugh, and cruised along for the last 12 years. I was the oldest bloke on the Cadre by at least seven years, and it was the last chance saloon for me to kick my career into gear and get first my stripe up. I was told by Bo Didley I was on the Cadre - tough shit! Dry your eyes mate. I was then marched down to the training wing for a pre-Cadre brief by none other than DM the Chief DS, with his brother Bomb-Head who was then the RQMS hovering in the background giving me the benefit of his dry sarcasm and wit.

In life sometimes you need to be told straight and to the point where you have gone wrong and face facts. Trust me. After a reality check by DM, grow up Clarence you're on the pain train sonny to 1RGBW NCO Cadre. The Cadre DS were the pick of the NCOs from the Battalion; firm but fair and ruthless in weeding out the dead wood. There were some good lads going for promotion with a strong contingent for Support and Headquarters companies, so we would stick together and help each other out. DM was master and commander of our ship of fate for the foreseeable future.

I was in camp sorting my shit out when I was summoned to report down the QMs complex. Bomb-Head wanted a word in my ear at 1900 hours sharp. Don't be late. That's the last thing I needed... I was lit up like a bloody Christmas tree on Bomb-Heads radar - not a good place to be. I reported to Bomb-Head's den at 1850 hrs flapping like fuck, not remembering how I had managed to incur his wrath. Fair play, as I walked in, Bomb-Head started laughing at me saying I looked like a naughty little schoolboy waiting outside the headmaster's office.

'Relax,' he said and put the kettle on. 'OK mate, what kit do you need for the Cadre? I'm going to issue you a brand-new set of combats for the Cadre muster parades so you don't look like a bag of shit. Don't forget I was you first section commander in 1Glosters, when you were a day one, week one fucking crow'. After a brew and those words of wisdom, I had the run of the clothing store and some other bits and pieces from the G1098 stores fully kitted and ready for the NCO Cadre. After an hour I was well squared away by Bomb-Head, and later he helped me with some of my lesson plans and teaching practices. The especially important and humbling life lesson I took away from the evening was, *always look after your blokes and help and support comes from unusual places.* The lads on the Cadre were in shock at how well turned out I was. Cheers Bomb-Head.

Brummy's Shorts:
Day one was fitness testing, starting with the three mile 'BFT' Battle Fitness Test run in the morning, and the eight mile 'CFT' Combat Fitness Test in the afternoon. If you fail day one, fuck off back to the lines - stand up fail.

The trick was not to get noticed, pass the tests, and survive day one. Being on the NCO Cadre meant that you had to be well turned out and as smart as a carrot. The RGBW being a bit more relaxed on the dress code state that the dress for the BFT was trainers, black shorts, and RGBW Company t-shirt ironed. 'Jed' was the PTI, so we knew we were going to suffer.

Enter Brummy's muddy trainers. Fair play, he did have an ironed Support Company t-shirt, but he had fucked up big time by wearing a pair of scruffy blue shorts. The look of disbelief, followed by an explosion of rage from DM was epic! Day one of the Cadre and Support Company were in the shit as per usual. Norm and I just couldn't help but laugh at Brummy which started the ripple effect on the rest of the Support Company lads.

Top tip: Don't wear blue shorts on PT.

Brummy was that punished by Jed the PTI, he was sweating through the floorboards of the gym. To make matters worse for the Support Company lads, most of us were laughing at Brummy's fuck up which didn't go down well with the DS who blamed us for not working together as a team in checking each other over before the parade. Also, how dare we laugh on parade! So, we were also shown the errors of our ways via a beasting.

On the eight miler, I was slightly off the pace of the main pack when I was noticed by DM who was on the prowl! He tabs back to me, sparks up a fag, blows smoke in my face, and asks me if I'm having a nice time and how were my knees holding up since I was an old git? Fair play to DM, he knows how to motivate me. I was breathing out my arse, but there was no way I was going to be last man knowing that DM would ruin my life if I was. I caught up and slotted in the back of the squad with Our Leon and Norm dropping back to make sure I was still jogging on. Coursemanship was the name of the game.

Ring the Bell:
A genius idea that DM and the DS had borrowed from the US Navy SEALs. The Cadre was a pass or fail course, but the DS weren't going to fail any man Jack of us! We could ring the bell and bin it at any time we wanted. It was all down to us to quit. Plus, the DS wanted to teach us and improve our military and leadership skills. If we didn't like it, go, and see the DS who would make us complete the days training, before arranging a chat with DM and the Boss. Finishing in, turn to the right, gain some height, and fuck off back to camp! A big fat Freddy fails.

Mind Games:
The DS lead by DM were masters at breaking people. This was done so they knew if we were successful and passed the Cadre, we would be physically and mentally strong NCOs ready to lead men on operations.

On one exercise we were on section attacks - we were doing one section attack after another. It was as hard as nails. We were on our chin straps, the weather at Brecon was awful, and some people were already having sense of humours failures; but as a course everybody was helping each other out - nobody was going to ring the bell today.

It was dusk on cold, dark, Brecon evening when the Cadre had finished its latest set of attacks. As the reorg was happening, 'Robbo' one of the DS' had a big shit eating grin on his face as he called me and Ben over to his Land Rover. "Listen up dickheads. Change of command appointments. Ben you're Platoon Commander, Heal you're Platoon Sergeant. Use the road semi tac tab down to Farm Four; you're leaving in five minutes so brief up the Section Commanders, now jog on toads".

We checked the map, and to our horror we were at an eight-mile tab. Under pressure, we got the lads sorted semi tactically. 1 Section and Ben at the front, me last man behind 4 Section with Our Leon as my signaller - plus it started snowing - bollocks!

As we started to move, DM appeared out of the mist like the prince of darkness wearing an Arctic parker holding a brew. I had to laugh; the pain train had arrived. "Listen blokes, it's fucking freezing and there's a nice minibus going back to camp tonight. Any takers? I'm doing you a favour, so who wants to ring the bell to make the bad man go away kiddies?"

About eight blokes jacked it in then and there creating chaos with the order of battle, the DS quickly separated the lads that had binned it and DM waved the rest of us on our merry way as he sparked up another fag.

About a mile down the range road as we tabbed round the corner, Veg Green and Robbo were stood with white light on, smoking and drinking brews next to a couple of four tonners. Jedi mind trick wankers! "Get on the trucks," was the only comment passed to us. Fair play, they suckered every man Jack of us. Every bloke that went on and passed this Cadre had definitely earned their stripes and dug deep. Our Leon and I still have nightmares about DM appearing out of the mist and darkness - an excellent teacher and solider. He along with his brother Bomb-Head were two of the driest most sarcastic bastards on planet RGBW, but I will always be grateful to those two pushing and working me hard whilst kicking my army career back on track - wankers.

CHAPTER 29

"In life when you get tested, when you get rejected by everyone and when you get pushed aside, you actually get the best out of it. That has been a learning curve for me."
Sourav Ganguli.

Four Ton Truck Drama and Scandal:
Because of the ongoing fire strikes, and the Battalion covering Northern Ireland, the Cadre was on and off, which was a nightmare. One minute you were back with your Platoon or Company, the next minute you were on the four tonners traveling up the M4 to sunny Brecon from London town.

As we would parade outside the Training Wing in camp, quite a few blokes just wouldn't turn up - they had binned the Cadre for various reasons. I wasn't going to judge or gob off because on the previous NCO Cadre I had binned it after getting picked up on muster parade and throwing my teddy out of the pram - even though I had a brand-new jacket on. People in glass houses shouldn't throw stones. Plus, the less numbers there were it made the whole Cadre easier to administrate for the DS, and for us remaining 'toads' it was still a nightmare, but there was no dead wood. Everybody wanted to be there and hopefully do enough to pass the bloody thing.

On this evolution of the Cadre, we were told to parade at Training Wing on a Friday afternoon, and as per usual there was drama and scandal provided by the Support Company call signs. Norm had been on piss the night before at 'Dinger Bells' leaving do. I stayed sober due to the fact I was duty student and responsible for sorting out the trucks, getting the blokes loaded up on the coach, and was one of a few of us driving the four tonners down to Brecon.

I didn't realize that Norm was half cut. Typical Norm, he had been on a weekend bender. Luckily, 'Moley' for Reconnaissance Platoon relieved Norm of driving duties via a hot seat driver change as we were driving out the camp gates. Thankfully for all involved, Norm didn't manage to cause too much drama on his little DUI round camp.

DM led the green vehicle convoy from his Land Rover. As we crossed the old Severn Bridge, Moley's wagon started having problems, so the convoy pulled over. On investigation the wagon was out of fuel. How we managed that was anyone's guess - I put it down to a dodgy fuel gauge, blockage, or a leak.

DM was not a happy man, but fair play to him, he was blaming the MT Platoon for giving the NCO Cadre shit wagons. I was then told to sort it out as a command appointment! So, I dapped DM off to the local ESSO to get some diesel which he did with a big grin on his face; that didn't bode well for me. His exact words were: 'If the truck doesn't work, you are on for a failure. A big, stand up, fucking failure'.

Lucky for me, 'Dave the Silver Fox' from the REME had shown me how to fix various DAF problems in my role as the Company MT Rep, including lack of fuel to the injectors. After tilting the cab, loosening the injector leads on the top of the engine, and pumping the accelerator pedal to get fuel into the system retightening the leads, success! We were on our way, much to my relief and the passing of my command appointment.

Norm had then woken up and was giving me the benefit of his wisdom the mug.
Top tip: On the four-ton DAF, always dip the fuel tank visually.

DM on Covert Ops:
With everything in the Army, the troops would always find something to moan, bitch, and whinge about. On the NCO's Cadre there was a lot of moaning and whinging. People, including myself, were losing their temper and throwing there teddies out of the pram. As on any promotional course, there were saints and sinners.

When the weather is terrible and people are tired, there are always some top lads and team players that will dig out and help - selfless commitment. Unfortunately, there are also 'Jack Cunts'; certain people that will always look after their own interests and not work for the good of the team.

One night in the harbour area it was nails, the ground was frozen solid with snow and people were under pressure with various tasks and jobs to do. I was in a command appointment and busy cutting around making sure the shell scraps were dug, and that my sections area of the harbour was up to the DS's high standard.

Coursemanship was all about working together as a team and helping whoever was in a command appointment to pass their test and get a tick in the box. Everybody has strengths and weaknesses - mine was my fitness and carrying a knee injury, so I was struggling. My body was falling apart, so the lads in my section would make sure I never got dicked to carry the 94mm LAW or the GPMG.

My strength was that I was a signaller and a senior bloke, so I knew most of the lads on the course as well as the DS. I could use this to keep everybody's communications working, cut about and be all over the section administration - this was what coursemanship was all about.

Unfortunately, there were also 'DS Watchers'. These certain individuals would watch out for the DS, and suddenly become all keen and squared away super soldiers. Once the DS had disappeared, they would revert to type and become lazy and Jack.

On this particular night, as I finished digging the last shell scrap with the lads, I went to check on the sentries. To my absolute horror it transpired that 'Gingersnap', one of the lads from C Company had been manning the sentry position for three hours and was in shit state due to the weather and fatigue. He should have been relieved hours ago. Our Leon took over the sentry position. We got Gingersnap under a poncho, brewed up, and squared away. With most of the work routine completed it was agreed that Gingersnap could do with an hour in his gonk-bang.

After doing a bit of a detective work, I found out who the Jack selfish bastard was that had that left Gingersnap on Stag for 3 hours. The cheeky cunt was in his basha getting his head down when I woke him up and asked what the score was. He started to get gobby and give it the big un', so I lost my temper, dragged him out of his basha, and encouraged him to change his ways. Everybody agreed that he got what he deserved - Happy days!

We cracked on with the harbour routine. There had been similar incidents of Jack-ness in the other sections, and a lot of whinging with a few other lads binning the Cadre after the night from hell.

In the morning DM appeared from the darkness and mist, and as if by some Jedi mind trick, knew what had happened during the night with the whinging and certain people being Jack. At first the Cadre thought someone had grassed, but that was impossible! How he fucking knew was a bloody mystery.

At the end of the Cadre when those left were waiting in the corridor for the pass or fail grading board, DM made a confession. He said some people were going to be disappointed because at night DM would insert himself into the harbour area and cut around with his helmet and belt kit on, weapon in hand, and observe the comings and goings. Because it was pitch dark and light discipline was enforced, he blended in, and nobody knew he was there. Fair play, he had the DS watchers pinged. DM didn't miss a trick.

'Dapper' was a PTI and one of the other senior blokes on the Cadre. We had been Crows together in 1Glosters, and like me he was playing catch up in the Last Chance Saloon. He had got his nickname due to his size 14 feet and his ability to run marathons. He was always dapping about and could run for miles - a natural runner.

Dapper Mr Freeze:
First week in the field, and map and compass navigation was our bread and butter. It was an essential skill for a Junior Non-Commissioned Officer. It started off in the classroom, then progressed to navigation exercises day and night. If you failed it, you were binned.

On this nights Navex, it was an individual effort. You started off at staggered times going clockwise and anticlockwise around a 6-mile night navigation course at Brecon, starting and finishing at Dixie's Corner. As per usual the weather was terrible; it was sleet and ice plus the dreaded mist clang.

As I was tabbing around, hitting the various check points, and trying not to get lost, I bumped into Our Leon who was going the opposite way round. As we approached one of the unmanned check points to find the ammo tin with the next set of directions, we saw someone flashing white light about 200 meters away.
A safety point drummed into us by the DS, a flashing white light means a no-duff casualty. As we headed down to the light source, we found Dapper up to his chest in a bog. He was in shit state and looked like Mr Freeze from Batman. He was going white, and the top half of his body was starting to freeze.

At first, we were laughing and taking the piss - He looked a right mess, and it was funny as fuck. But as we got him out the bog and onto firm ground, we knew that he was in serious trouble with the onset of hypothermia, or a serious non-freezing cold injury.

The nearest manned safety point was Dixie's Corner, so after a bit of emergency first aid and getting some of our dry and warm kit on Dapper, we half carried and dragged him to Dixie's Corner to get help.

As we got onto the metal road and up to Dixie's Corner, I located the Land Rover Ambulance, and the medic got to work on Dapper. DM then rocked up and in his unique way asked me, 'What's up Clarence? You lost toad?' As I explained what had happed to Dapper, he laughed, sparked up a fag, and asked us what we are hanging around for we had a Navex to finish - jog on toads and don't be late or lost.

It was a long night under the Welsh stars. Poor old Dapper was taken in to Sennebridge Camp, NCO Cadre over - fair play to Dapper, he completed and successfully passed the Cadre the following year.

Top tip: Don't fall in the Brecon Beacon's bogs.

Boot Theft:
As the Cadre progressed and got harder, it took its toll on my body. I was really struggling with the fitness, was in shit state with my knees, and hanging on via pain killers. I had acquired the nickname the 'Hobbling Hobbit'.

After another Brecon soaking, my knees were swelling up and I was in trouble. Luckily, Norm had some decent pain killers. As I was sorting out my admin under my Basha at stupid o'clock in the morning, I took my boots off to strap up my knees and have a quick 30 minutes under my Basha - *Big* mistake on my part.

About half an hour later as I'm getting my shit together - no boots! The DS had been on the prowl, and I had fucked up big time. My boots had been robbed by the DS.

That was it. I lost my temper and threw my teddy out of the pram much to the great delight of the DS. After a quick and ill-advised rant from me, I was put on a warning and summoned to report to DM. However, that was quickly put on hold since my knees swelled up to three times their normal size and I could barely walk.

I was half carried to the ambulance by Brummy, where the medic took one look at my knees and was flapping like a two stroke and told DM that I was being withdrawn on medical grounds. My knees were swelled up and facing off centre.

DM sparked up a fag, looked at the Medic and I, and said the Cadre is now in Static Defence Phase, no tabbing. We were going into trenches, so I had time to recover. The medic agreed and I was given some top of the range pain killers, had my knees strapped up, and thrown a radio. I was given Platoon Signaller Command appointment. I was also on a warning and would be on the Platoon Commander's interviews upon my return to Sennebridge Camp. As I hobbled down to the office in camp, I knew that I had fucked up big time with my rant. My knees were killing me, and I felt like a right mong. Time to face my fate like a man - it was out of my hands.

The Boss gave me fuck all and told me he expected better from me as a senior bloke who knew the score. The look of disappointment on his face was worse for me than getting binned. It was pure embarrassment on my part. I went next door expecting to get fucked off back to London by DM. I was made to wait, then DM told me my fate. I was put on a final warning. One more fuck up, and I'd be binned. End of chat - now fuck off.

Later that day as we were weapon cleaning before returning to camp, I was summoned again to DM's office. This time on entry he started laughing, saying that he and the DS were surprised that it had taken that look for them to wind me up and get a reaction. They thought it was funny as fuck me losing my boots.

On a more serious note, next week was the teaching phase with only limited PT, so my knees would hopefully recover. I was still on a final warning, and the DS were expecting my lessons to be the best on the Cadre due to my age and experience. He then produced a roll of tube grip elastic bandage for my knees and told me to keep going. I was in the Twilight Zone for a pass or fail - I had entered the Last Chance Saloon. 'Don't piss me off again you mong, you should have known better you fucking clown, now fuck off!'

In life we all get that road to Damascus moment of soul searching. I had mine that cold dark night in Brecon.

CHAPTER 30

"The mark of a wise person isn't never making mistakes - everyone makes plenty of them. Rather, it's the ability to quickly admit - and fix - them!"
Whitney Tilson

Brummy Playing the Numbers Game:
As the Cadre progressed, the command appointments got harder, and the pressure was on all of us to perform. We were all dead on our feet and the weather was getting worse.

One night in the Harbour Area we were all given a wanker's brief and told to produce a set of orders for a Platoon attack in the morning. At first light the DS would then nominate one bloke from each of the three remaining sections to produce the set of orders, crack on and brief the Platoon. Each Section produced a model, as well as maintaining our harbour routine in defence. It meant nobody got *any* time in their gonk bags, because we individually had to write a set of orders.

Brummy being Brummy, had just had a command appointment and played the numbers game, convinced his number wouldn't get called he had a few hours in his gonk bag after staging not bothering with doing his written orders or anything else.

It was a tired and beat up Platoon that gathered round the model pit the following crisp, winter's morning in Brecon. The numbers were then called by the DS - shock and awe – Brummy's number was called. The look of total disbelief on his face will always be part of 1RGBW PJNCO Cadre 2003 legend and folklore.

Brummy approached the model and started to give his set of orders from a piece of damp A5 paper with words to the effect of: 'We were getting picked up by 4 tonners, going there - pointing at spot on the map, getting dropped off, then doing an attack. That's it. Any questions?' You could have heard a pin drop. The tension in the air could be felt.

One of the DS' asked Brummy if he had actually written a set of orders. Brummy said, 'Yeah'; he had them on a piece of A5 paper which now had become sodden bog roll! This got a good laugh from the rest of the course, me and Our Leon were sniggering round the back. Typical Brummy, in the shit and not giving a shit.

The DS' were in total disbelief at Brummy's pathetic attempt at orders and trying to bluff his way out of it. DM hit the roof, and what was left of the A5 paper was promptly ripped up. DM then smashed up the model pit like a raging bull in a China shop.

Brummy had a full five minutes of the wrath of DM, who went proper mental because Brummy was taking the piss. DM was not repeating the same swear words for the whole tirade. By this stage, the whole Cadre was rolling around in hysterics due to Brummy looking like a naughty schoolboy getting caught smoking round the back of the bike sheds. Stand up fail on Brummy's latest command appointment!

I have seen some bollockings in my time, but that was the worst I had ever seen! Top tip: Don't play the numbers game and try to mug DM off. I was surprised he didn't get a slap round the back for taking the piss.

Chase the 4 Tonner on Route 66 Norm:
As a result of Brummy taking the piss and some of the Cadre monging it, the DS then came up with a character-building exercise called 'Chase the 4 Tonner' on the Route 66 along the range road. The aim of the game was quite simple; if you caught the truck and managed to get on board over the raised tailgate you had completed the exercise and passed the run.

The troops patrolled to the RV on Route 66. Upon arrival we could see the trucks out in the distance. On the whistle blast, we ran off and the trucks drove off. We ended running a couple of miles before the fitter lads on the Cadre climbed aboard the trucks. I was towards the back of a group of runners, my little legs were going like pistons, and I was breathing out of my arse when I got level with the tail gate of the 4 tonner.

Not being the tallest of blokes, I had major difficulty in trying to climb aboard the 4 tonner. Lucky for me, Norm and Moley were already aboard and could see I was I shit state. Being experienced mortarmen, they just reached down from the truck, grabbed me by my helmet, and pulled me onto the truck. I felt like a human giraffe. I landed in the back like a tortoise with my moustache covered in snot, still breathing out my ass!

Cheers lads! I had passed the run. The lads were too busy laughing at me being in ruin, that's coursemanship for you - my neck was sore for days after.

Norm the Telegraph Tole Kid:
One of the last PT sessions on the Cadre was a boot run round the Black Hut Loop at Brecon. This was an individual effort, but as with most runs on the Cadre, you usually ended up running in small groups with your mates to keep each other going.

Norm had already incurred the wrath of the DS before the run had even started for getting caught making sarcastic comments. So, the DS pointed to a telegraph pole in the dead ground - no words were needed because this was a regular occurrence - Norm running up and down to various telegraph poles. Hence the nickname, 'The Telegraph Pole Kid'.

As we started this run, some light relief was provided by none other than DM. I was running along with Norm and Ginger Snap, when I heard DM's booming tones coming from the rear of the pack of runners. I had to laugh because he was sat on the roof of the Land Rover battlefield ambulance, feet on the bonnet, 4-way light flashing, loud hailer in hand whilst giving out words of wisdom and encouragement.

All I heard was, 'Oi! Toads from mortars, don't make me drive up there to ruin your day!' I had to laugh, I thought it was bloody hilarious. Later, the DS played a Jedi mind trip on a few of the blokes behind us at the rear, who had got on and rode the Jack wagon and binned the run.

The DS had got together all the blokes that had Jacked it in earlier and had ridden the Jack wagon. There was then a big belly laugh from one of the DS' who then set about briefing up the lads. 'Listen up! You lot are like Lazarus, suddenly rising from the dead to complete the run after having a nice ride on the fucking Jack-wagon! Wankers. You have all fucking failed for lack of spine and integrity'. Top tip: Keep going and don't get on the Jack wagon.

On return to Barracks in London we had a weekend off, and a nervous wait to find out who had passed the Cadre. All of us were dog tired and battered. I could hardly walk; my knees were in shit state. Everybody was glad it was over and most of us were glad to be away from Brecon.

The DS' were still playing their cards close to their chests on Monday morning, and we were told that Wednesday was D-Day - either you had done it, or you didn't make the grade. I was going in first as I was the senior bloke on the Cadre. Fucking great! More sleepless nights for all of us.

We all had to practice drill for the Pass Off Parade on the Battalion Drill Square, ready to parade in front of every man and his dog next week, as well as post exercise admin and classroom work before the final week on the Cadre.

I was a drill mong, plus the shortest bloke on the Cadre, so I ended up smack in the middle of the front rank. The look of disbelief on DM's face was a picture and his exact words were, 'No fucking way you drill mong, get in the middle rank! Out of the way toad!' This was more pressure on my already frayed nerves whilst waiting to see if I had passed or failed.

Wednesday morning. 0800hrs sharp. I was in the corridor of doom, at the Last Chance Saloon of 1RGBW's Training Wing. I was marched in to face the DS and learn my fate. The boss then turned around and gave me fuck all for my outburst, reference the DS stealing my boots. Fuck me! That was it? I felt like a right fool.

Then DM sparked up a fag, looked me straight in the eye, and gave me that judge, jury, and executioner look of his. 'Listen up Clarence old son, what would you do now if I gave you a stand-up fail?' That was it. I thought I had failed. *For fucks sake!*

I told him, 'Fair play, I knew I had fucked up a couple of times and my whole body was falling apart, but I was never doing a PJNCO Cadre ever again. Far too old for it, and it was my own fault for leaving it till I was 30 plus. I had tried my best, I respected all the DS, so see you down the pub some time.'
Nobby was going to kill me.

I saluted and marched out with my head held high, not giving them the satisfaction, but gutted deep down inside and feeling like a right fool and grade A failure. The other blokes in the corridor looked shocked as I walked out the office looking like a failure. Then from the office one of the DS shouted, 'Oi Clarence! Get back in here toad. Nobody told you to fucking leave, dickhead!'

I marched back in the office. DM and all the DS' were laughing at me and taking the piss. DM told me I had passed 13th out of the 19 men left on the Cadre, in the overall standing. I was on cloud nine - Happy days!

I was then bought down to Earth with a bang when I was told some home truths. I had struggled with the fitness, had to watch my mouth because I had a habit of not engaging the brain before opening my big trap, so I had to watch my step. I was given a major shot across the bows. On the plus side, I had done well in my role as the senior bloke on the Cadre, being a team player, using my experience and helping people out. 'Any questions?'

No.

'Jog on then toad. Go and enjoy doing some drill you mong!'

That morning tally was that Our Leon, Norm, Ginger Snap and Moley had passed. Unfortunately, Brummy had failed. I was gutted for him, but he passed the next PNJCO in 2004.

In hindsight, it was a fucking beast. I have to say we had all, definitely earned our stripes and learned a hell of a lot. I will always have the upmost respect for DM and all the DS' from the Cadre of Hell. They had run a hard course. All the lads that passed the Cadre went out to achieve good things in their army careers. Me - I was glad it was over, and I had passed. Never again - it took my body a month to recover.

CHAPTER 31

> *"I don't know what London's coming to — the higher the buildings the lower the morals."*
> *Noël Coward.*

Cardiff Cluster Fuck:

The NCO Cadre finally completed, we had the weekend off to recover and sort out our personal administration. For the peasants amongst us, myself included, a suit was required attire now we were Lance Corporals come next Friday. We had to be ready for a Corporal's Mess function. I needed a new suit as well as a Corporal's Mess tie - time to seek counsel from Nobby and Bomb-Head.

The tie was an easy fix thanks to Bomb-Head, the suit was a different matter. After a Friday night drive to Bristol RV at Karaoke Kenny's, it was a drive across the bridge to Cardiff to go suit shopping with Nobby and his wife because I didn't have a bloody clue about suits and Mess etiquette. I was a flip flops and puffer jacket type of bloke.

On arrival at a rather posh Welsh tailors, we encountered our first drama. The bloke running the gaff thought I was casing the joint ready to rob it - cheeky bastard! Then after that, because of my Hobbit sized body I was special measure which started to push the price up. Not to mention the extra shoes and several shirts. Nobby was his usual disruptive self - it was a long tedious and expensive afternoon.

My first night in the Mess was always going to be eventful due to having a few lunch time beers with 'LBD' and Our Leon, so I was half cut before I even entered the Mess. This followed by a row with some bloody wife giving the big un because she was married to corporal such and such was told to jog on, and some other jumped-up Mister Nobody was trying to pull rank on the piss. Most of the Cadre was in front of the Mess SNCO the morning after for various crimes against Mess etiquette.

Ringer - For Whom the Bell Tolls:
Life after the JNCO Cadre carried on as usual with public duties, or as I called it, bulling boots, and bullshit. The highlight being London District Major-General's inspection. This was a nightmare - a throwback to the days of the Empire where the whole Battalion would be formed up on the square to be inspected by some toffee-nosed officer, looking down on to the peasants.

Outside the Guardroom, the Battalion had a ships bell that was sounded three times a day, due to the Battalion serving as marines back in the Napoleonic wars. On the day of inspection, a fresh-faced crow straight from depot was told at midday to go and ring the bell a few times by the guard 2IC who thought that the young lad knew what he was doing with the ships time and sounding the bell. The young lad didn't have a clue, and when he asked the Senior Private what he was supposed to do, he was told to, "Just ring the bell crow. Fuck off!", as he was busy smoking.

The whole Battalion was formed up getting inspected by the great and the good from the Wooden Tops/Brigade of Guards, when the bell was rung and was kept ringing. It wasn't closing time at the pub either. After a few minutes, a senior officer from the guards comes running up to the Guardroom going ape shit because of the ringing of the bell by this young lad. The officer was foaming at the mouth trying to get his words out. The Guard Commander was away doing something, and the 2IC was out the back sorting out some issues, the senior team and the rest of the guard were stood around laughing and smoking which didn't go down well at all with the great and the good.

In the end this senior officer pushed the lad away from the bell and stopped the noise. He managed to lose his temper and the only words he could get out was, 'Stop ringing the bloody bell you, you ringer!' Henceforth, on that day Ringer was given his nickname, much to the amusement of all present. Ringer was now christened; the nickname has survived the test of time.

Ringer is still serving at the time of writing this book.

C Company Evel Knievel Stunt Riders:
'Village,' a young lad from some hamlet deep in the Cotswolds, recently joined the Company from depot. Due to his accent and young age, he was given the nickname Village - i.e., village idiot. He took it in good humour, and also fancied himself as some sort of motor-cross/motorbike stunt god.

On this fateful afternoon, he and his mates had built a ramp on the side of the football pitch and were having a motor-cross meet. Due to Village giving it the big 'un, a bit of a crowd of off duty lads had gathered to watch the man himself preform some expert motor-bike riding. As the excitement built up, Village revved up his bike and like a bat out of hell approached his take off point for the jump. Fair play to Village, he did take of well, but the landing didn't go according to plan! He became a human crash test dummy with a broken leg and smashed up motorbike to everybody's amusement. That was the end of his stunt career, and the Head Shed of the Company put an end to the biker meets on the football pitch.

The next day, I was guard 2IC when one of the other budding C Company stunt riders was returning to camp via the front gate. The sentry on the front gate, manning the barrier started to drop it as the 'Stunt-man' arrived in camp. Thinking he could beat the barrier; the rider was clothes lined off his bike and ended up in a heap on the concrete much to the amusement of the guard. It created loads of paperwork for me, but it was funny as fuck. Result being barrier one, motorbike rider nil. Top tip: Leave bikes to the experts.

Tower Trouble:
Due to the fact I was hobbit sized, I was special fit for my blues. Unfortunately, they were never completed, so I was kit and capes man for the Company which suited me down to the ground. No drill for this call sign!

After doing the weekly checks and finishing the Company administration on Friday afternoon, Nobby had disappeared up the M4 to Cardiff. I was the Company HQ admin guru for the weekend - time to chill out and take it easy. The Company was on duty at the tower. I was chilling out in camp. Then my mobile bleeped.

To cut a long story short, I had to do an admin run in the Company FFR Land Rover to the Tower of London. The OC needed his laptop from the Company Office, plus the Platoon on duty at the tower needed a few bits and pieces from the Stores and the Armoury.

I had to get going. Due to it being Friday afternoon and I was heading into London traffic, Pete, Coops, and Roger the Dodger from the South African contingent came along for the ride. So off we went in the Wagon. Stickman was driving, and I was navigating.

As we arrived at the Tower of London, I was in a hurry to get the job done and get out of Dodge. At the bottom of the steps to the Guardroom I had my hands full and was dressed in my usual scruffy windproof smock when this Beefeater appeared. He looked at me like I was breaking into the vault and asked me what I was doing and why I was parked by the steps? I replied, 'Alright mate, won't be long. Just dropping of some kit for the OC and the lads. I'm keen to get trucking coz I don't want to get caught and locked in because of Keys Ceremony thing mate.'

The bloke looked like he was going to have a heart attack! 'How dare you speak to me like that Corporal! I was a senior Non-Commissioned Officer in the Royal Corps of transport'. As I had already explained to him, I was only dropping off a laptop and few bits - I won't be long alright mate, chill out, calm down, nobody has died chief.

It then escalated pretty quicky. The Beefeater was having none of it and was giving it the big un. I then upset the clown by taking the piss out of him. 'Listen mate you're not in the Army any more you're a bloody tour guide you bloody REMF, you look like Jack Duckworth off Coronation Street'. That was it. I cracked on with the job in hand. Stickman was laughing his head off and told me the Beefeater had a right monk on and was going to file a complaint! Yeah, cheers for that mate. Off we drove back to camp, I'm on the piss with the Boks son.

Monday morning the shit hit the fan big time. Terrible Tony the RSM wanted a word - oh dear. As I entered the big man's lair, he was giving me his old Platoon Sergeant look that says, he is going to ruin my life. 'For fucks sake Clarence! I've just had the GSM on the phone, giving me grief. What the fuck did you do at the Tower Friday night nugget?'. As I explained the whole sorry story, he started laughing his head off. Fair play to the RSM he did see the funny side of the Beefeater being called a tour guide.

I was then banned from the Tower of London for life. Never to darken its door ever again. Plus, I got loads of grief off Nobby for being on Terrible Tony the RSM's radar.

CHAPTER 32

"The night has ears"
Masai Proverb

Kenya Exercise Grand Prix - Kenyan Kerfuffle:
The Battalion deployed on exercise to Kenya with the usual *hurry up and wait*, and the dreaded AIDS brief. Top tip: Do not bang the local birds bareback. Nail your kit down, because the local were known as the 'borrowers' or to quote 'Peggers', 'Thieving Pikey scum.'

As the Company MT Rep and Assault Pioneer, it was a great exercise for me, especially building a Company location from scratch under the direction of Peggers, the new C Company CSM.

Peggers was a small dynamo of a bloke with big heart and would always look after his lads. He was keen as mustard, and sometimes he was a little *too* keen resulting in Company HQ winding him up which would make him mister grumpy.

'REME Dave the Silver Fox,' the best mechanic I have ever known. I was always bumping into him throughout my Army career. He got his nickname through his silver-tongued success with the women. More kids than the old lady in the shoe, and more fan mail than the average boy band.

Top Gear African Special:
Driving in Kenya was a nightmare due to the state of the roads and the local drivers being bloody dangerous. Some of the roads were no better than farm tracks, and when it rained, they became black cotton and lethal to the unwary.

Getting bogged in was a daily occurrence, extra cross-country driving training for the Company was down to me. So, after a few weeks out in the bush we as a Company were doing ok with the driving and getting from A to B.

On this day, I was out and about in the FFR doing a deal with the local white landowner for an Impala ready for a Company BBQ before live firing. The OC had also jumped on the trip to do some officer things, throw back from the Empire stuff with the local gentry.

It had rained so the tracks were a bit of a mess, but I thought we would be OK due to my Jedi driving skills. As we returned to the Company camp location, about 200 meters in disaster struck and I got the Land Rover bogged in, which Evo clocked so the whole Company was summoned to watch my driving disaster. The OC laughed, shrugged his shoulders, and walked into camp wishing me well in digging out the FFR. Fair play, I was ripped by the lads for weeks after. Respect to Peggers, he jumped in another wagon and pulled me out. I went from Jedi to stuck I.

Medic for the Medic:
The final exercise started with a monster 2-day tab over 20 miles of the African bush. The CSM was having reservations about our attached female medic from the RAMC who was overweight and who's fitness was not up to the Company standard.

Due to political correctness and equality creeping into the Army at this stage in history he was overruled. So, off the Company walked. Several hours later there was a drama. Peggers and I who were to the rear of the Company snake tabbing with Evo's Platoon were called up front. We were both breathing out of our arses carrying extra ammo and the 51mm Mortar when we arrived at the centre of the Company snake. The Company Medic was in shit state. I thought she was going to have a bloody heart attack! She was proper going down due to the heat, being fat, and unfit. The CSM had to call in a medical CASAVAC for the Medic, embarrassing for the Company, plus 'Ratty' on the other end of the radio net in Battalion Headquarters got us to repeat the radio call so every man and his dog knew what was going on. It did not help matters that Evo was taking the piss while all this was going on. Peggers was then Mr Grumpy for the rest of the day.

I'm all up for equality and diversity. During Herrick 14 in Afghanistan, a female medic 'Hayley' earned everybody's respect by doing all the pre-deployment training and fitness tests. She struggled on some of the tabs but completed them and during the tour earned a MID for her heroic actions. Massive respect for her. It's a pity that some of the other females attached to infantry Regiments are not up to her high standards.

Hookers, Doctors, and Platoon Sergeants Behaving Badly:
The best adventure training package, and R and R in Kenya was the water sports and sailing package which was held down the coast at Malindi. This was run by another Battalion character, 'Bosun Bob'. C Company had got lucky - Three days AT followed by four days R and R down at Malindi.

Bosun Bob was the sort of bloke that whatever happened, he would always land on his feet and come out smelling of roses. He was also my old Section Commander from Mortars. If you were in Bob's section you knew that you were going to get a good deal, because Bob always got lucky. He was old school; always up for a laugh and was Mr Teflon.

'Happy Nights Disco' was the local watering hole which was your typical squaddie dive. The lads loved it. Bosun Bob was strict when it came to looking after the blokes. He insisted that a duty NCO was on every day and night, he briefed the blokes up about being careful with the locals, especially the woman i.e., don't bang birds bareback because of AIDS and STD's. Always stay in pairs when returning to the hotel after a night on the piss due to the possibility of getting mugged or ripped off. A right caring bloke.

I was advance party down the coast with Evo, and when we arrived, we were glad that some of the Support Company lads had finished the AT package and were now on R and R including Johnny Mouth of the South, Gonzo, and Harry Crumb.

After a quick ground brief and familiarization with Bosun Bob we got on the piss big time with the Support Company lads. The Italian bloke that owned the complex, including Happy Nights Disco, was a bit of a rogue and was happy to take the coin the British Army was spending, but was worried about some of the lads on the piss, creating some drama and scandal. Because I picked up some of the lingo and had Dennis as my translator, I made sure we all made the effort not to upset the locals and play the game. He was happy plus; we came up with a cunning plan for Happy Nights Disco. There was a duty NCO in the hotel, but not in the Happy Nights Disco.

Enter Harry Crumb who was now the duty doorman and employee of the week in conjunction with the local bouncer. Harry was now our man in Happy Nights Disco, and he got free food and drink when on 'Duty' during the R and R package.

One afternoon around the swimming pool, it was the usual boozing and banter with the blokes chilling out, throwing people in, and generally fucking around. Some of the lads were still pissed up from the night before and were topping up.

I was minding my own business and trying to do a deal with the local Mr Fixit reference wood carvings when I had a tap on the shoulder. Some Rupert from the Gun Bunnies attached to the battlegroup started giving me grief. He was bumping his gums saying that I as the Duty NCO was letting the lads run riot in the pool.

A loud-mouthed yob from 1RGBW was bombing people, being a drunken uncouth larger lout, and had told him to jog on! He was going to report me to my Platoon Sergeant for not doing my job properly. I told him, 'No problem. Report me!' I would introduce him, because the drunken larger lout in the pool was my Platoon Sergent Evo! Typical bloody Evo, a nightmare on the piss and dropping me right in it as always.

Later that week, I'm having a quiet, early evening beer in Happy Nights with one of the Bones Brothers when this well-dressed local woman comes up and goes mental at us. She tells me in perfect Queen's English that it's a bloody disgrace and major health hazard that some of the soldiers were having unprotected sex. They were also lying and promising the world to some of the local girls, only for the women to be forgotten about when we pulled out and returned to the U.K. It was not on. Bones started laughing and told her that this was what soldiers did - unlucky.

She started giving *me* grief, saying that 'Being older, I should set a good example to the young men in my charge'. I replied, 'I had the Medic giving out free condoms and I'm not going to stand in the way of boys being boys, and girl being girls. They are all adults and you as the madam should look after the girls in your charge - not coming over here giving me grief! Jog on Cinderella, you're ruining my night!' Cheeky cow, mugging me off and taking the piss.

The next day, after a morning of water sports with Bosun Bob, I had to grab the Land Rover and take one of the lads down to the local clinic - not for having a dose of an STD - he had cut his foot quite badly on coral. Our Medic had patched him up but reckoned the lad might need a stitch and a check-up from the doctor.

On arrival at the clinic, which was quite smart and catered for tourists, the lad went off to get sorted. I'm in reception doing the paperwork when I was told to wait; the Doctor would like to speak to me. No worries. The female doctor then appeared from the surgery, and before I could blink, asked me if I enjoyed my beer last night and if had I found her slipper? It was my turn to get mugged off. It was only Cinderella from last night.

She wasn't the local Madam, but the local doctor who had trained in London before returning to work in Kenya. I looked and felt like a right dickhead. Top tip: Engage the brain before opening mouth and gobbing off! Never - I repeat - never judge a book by its cover. It was a start of a beautiful friendship. RIP Dr Susan Mumba who died after becoming ill while working up country in the central highlands later that year.

Scrap Metal:
For the ranges and live firing in Kenya, Company Headquarters put a lot of time and effort into producing and building a Company battle run range. We made bunkers, decent targets, and used the ground well. Peggers was a happy teddy bear. It was a good set up and the Platoons were looking forward to a good day of live firing. It was all tided up and checked the night before, ready to go live in the morning. 'Tis' the CQMS was enjoying himself and was happy for the training to begin.

It was a nice morning on the Savannah. Everybody was set to put some rounds down the range. Peggers went out to do the final walk-through and talk with the safety staff - happy days. Slight problem – most the metal targets and half the barbed wire was missing. It was like Area 51. The aliens had been and abducted all the shiny stuff. It was like a Scooby Doo mystery.

Peggers went mental and after a talk with our locally employed civilians, a visit to the local village was launched and put into action. It was amazing what the locals had done, there were figure 11 and 12 metal targets used as roofing, and lining fire pits. All the livestock was now penned off in barbed wire enclosures, and sandbags were used by the village well. The locals had been on the rob last night, with C Company range, and defence stores being their golden egg. Fair play, it bought a new meaning to the phrase of: *You must nail everything down in Africa.*

A Few Words of Wisdom from 'Evo'. Reference - Kenyan Kerfuffle:
A couple of amusing incidents in Kenya revolved around Peggers. Peggers was a top guy who always had the benefit of the troops foremost in his mind. While in Kenya, Peggers was constantly concerned about snakes and was forever drilling into the guys to ensure that there was no rubbish that may attract rodents as this in turn would attract snakes!

Enter Evo. As previously mentioned in "Jolly Boys Outing", Evo was now a Platoon Sergeant and was still a huge practical joker and wind-up merchant. One bin bag, some green cloth tape, and a roll of black cotton and the snake was prepared and secreted near a bin bag. A quick test on the roving sentries proved fruitful when Floyd Morgan nearly had a heart attack.

Hearing the commotion, Peggers came to investigate. 'Robbo' had laid the groundwork telling Peggers that the guard had seen a snake. Peggers shone his torch and saw the bin bag and started informing anyone nearby about rubbish discipline. This is when Evo struck - pulling the snake from under the bag toward Peggers.

Peggers span around and started to sprint away. As he did, the cotton attached to the snake tangled on his boot, the snake was now chasing Peggers. As he sprinted away while looking over his shoulder, he was shouting, "There it is! There it is!" He managed about 50 metres before the fact that half the

Company were pissing themselves before he realised it was a joke! The CSM was now known as Snake Plissken.

A few weeks later, the Company were at Archer's Post and conducting a night patrol to a FUP. As the Company were moving, the sound of running water was getting louder and louder, the Company went firm whilst a recce party went forward to identify a suitable crossing for what sounded like Niagara Falls.

While the Company were stationary, Peggers decided to remove his socks for the crossing. As soon as he had his socks off, the Company started to move. The whole Company were expecting some raging torrent to cross, but when we got there it was hardly a stream and less than ankle deep! Due to the delay, the OC was keen to make up lost time and continued with speed. When we eventually stopped you can imagine that Peggers regretted removing his socks - Blisters 'R' Us. Peggers: a top bloke, an excellent CSM with a sense of humour and who always looked after his lads.

Doomed Romance - Mills and Boom!
The final bit of drama and scandal involving the Company was provided by 'Mayonnaise', one of the young Privates in the Company. Due to the local dynamics and economy, the local single women always went for a British Army squaddie. Money talks in Africa. Young Mayonnaise fell in love with a local bird.

Apparently, she was a 'singer' and that was that. He disappeared into the Kenyan night like some love-struck teenager. He went AWOL and was now running away to join the circus. This then created a mountain of paperwork for Peggers, and a lot of shit for everyone else due to the security and diplomatic situation in Kenya at that time.

He turned up a few weeks later; heartbroken and skint. 'Tee', the Company Clerk said that he had been taken to the cleaners, ironed and dry cleaned out by the Kenyan bird.

Who says romance is dead? Then he had to see the Doctor ready for the full MOT AIDS test the clown.

CHAPTER 33

'If we turn to the war in Kosovo, what do we find? We find the manipulation of the audience's emotions by the mass media.'
Paul Virillo

1RGBW Kosovo Spearhead Deployment 2004:

The Battalion was put on Advanced Readiness Spearhead, which meant ready to deploy anywhere in the world at short notice. We had to do some beat up training and ranges before the Battalion went live. A march and shoot competition were conducted at Brecon. One of the new SNCO's in the Company was Kev who was a good friend who had recently come back from a posting away from the Battalion.

Kev was a diligent and helpful bloke that always went out of his way to help people out. He was one of the kindest and nicest people you could ever meet. He would never lose his temper; I mean he was Mister composure and calm. Kev made the ultimate sacrifice in the line of duty, leading and looking after his lads from the front on operations in Afghanistan 2011. RIP my friend. Always remembered and respected.

I was tabbing along quite happily with Peggers. We had bolted on to the back of Evo's Platoon and were shooting the shit and jogging on, when word came down that there was a drama up front with Kev's Platoon, and that Kev had lost his temper! 'Fucking bollocks!' was Peggers first words. I thought it was a windup, Kev was the mildest mannered man in the Battalion. As we walked round the corner it was like a scene out of WWF smackdown! Seeing was believing! Kev was full on doing a damn good impression of Stone-Cold Steve Austin. He was raging, folding this this young lad all over the training area, smackdown style. Fucking hell!

Peggers grabbed Kev and pulled him off and calmed it down. Evo and I were just looking at each other in disbelief, trying not to laugh.

In life you will always meet parasites and wrong uns. This little prick Kev had ragged was in that category. He had been caught stealing and was generally being a wanker. He had taken Kev for a mug, mistaking Kev's kindness for weakness - wrong choice son.

When it had all calmed down, I spoke to Kev laughing, saying that in 14 years friendship that was the first time I had seen him lose his temper. He sparked up a fag and said that was the first and last time he would lose his temper with one of his lads. He was pissed off with himself, but some men you just can't help; 'You just have to clothesline them', was his final word on the situation. I don't do bullying and abusing people, but sometimes a bit of rough justice is needed to educate and advise certain wrong uns.

The Battalion was then put on standby on 24 hours, notice to move. As we had finished the beat-up training, 'Panzer Leader', one of the officers from Battalion HQ jumped into the passenger seat of my Land Rover FFR for the drive back to London. My civilian radio was on, and the news with the big story being the ongoing situation in Kosovo with the Kosovan Muslims burning the Kosovan Serbs out was read. It was all kicking off big time. Panzer Leader said he hoped I had packed my kit! I thought *bollocks to that boss, I'm out on the piss with Our Leon this weekend!* Wrong answer son - me and my big mouth.

'Panzer Leader' was not your typical officer, he was a comprehensive school lad, that had done well. Took the back streets to university, then on to Sandhurst. He looks like a poster boy for the Waffen SS. Blonde haired, blue-eyed, Teutonic! He is at the time of writing a Half Colonel. One of the best officers I have had the pleasure to serve with. He got the banter and was firm but fair, and no bloody hurray Henry.

Word came down that the Battalion was off to Kosovo at 0800 the next day Friday morning, and two hours later, C Company trucks rolled out of the gates of Hounslow to RAF South Cerney.

A few hours later me and Skurp's were in a hold of a C130 Land Rover FFR with a trailer and a shit load of ammunition including 81mm mortar rounds, flying high across the Med. Big fireworks if we were to take incoming enemy rounds on landing. Not a very reassuring point, and I was getting messed around by the RAF, reference radio batteries in my trailer. How did they expect us to communicate without juice for the radios? Typical RAF jobsworths.

As we landed, we got our helmets and body armour on, ready for a drama with our rifles ready just in case. What an anti-climax as we drove across the airstrip to the international base and were told to hurry up and wait.

Panzer Leader was already having a row with some Irish Army Officer because the bog-skipper was whinging about the Mortar Platoon wagons having St George Cross stickers on their trucks instead of the Union Jack. Typical Mortars.

Later, during the deployment on a cold dark night, some scallywags nicked the flags from outside the Multi-National HQ building. Not wishing to point the finger of blame and suspicion, but Mortarmen were reported out and about that night! For once, Brummie was noticeably quiet and looking very guilty and suspicious.

My first patrol was a bit of a mixed bag, off the cuff job, with the Battalion arriving in drips and drabs due to Crab Air and the Russian Antonov An-225 bringing in the vehicles. A mixed bag of 1RGBW Patrol was thrown together with 'Sniper Dan' in command, me as tail-end Charlie, with a few B Company lads and some officers doing a ground orientation.

Sniper Dan, one of my oldest and trusted friends all the way back to us being crows together in 1Glosters. As it says on the tin, he was a sniper, a Jedi, and a switched-on gun nut. His hobby was militaria, especially Soviet kit, so to him, Kosovo were Tesco and Walmart rolled into one shopping Army sponsored shopping trip.
As we were patrolling in downtown Pristina that first day, things had calmed down a bit. The locals didn't like having issues with 'Shoot Back' British troops because we were known not to fuck about - unlike the Swedish troops who the locals classed as easy meat.

The Serbs were getting burnt out by the Muslims, even though they were all classed as Kosovans. A few days before there had been major public disorder. It was now quiet, and it had been shouted from the roof tops that a British Battalion had been flown in to inject some muscle into the mainly Scandinavian peacekeeping troops that had little real experience in dealing with public order. Whereas the Brits were surprisingly good at creating disorder.

I got talking to some of the local kids as we were on patrol who were calling me chocolate face, while Sniper Dan was on the sniff for some militaria - time to do a bit of business. Dan stopped the patrol short and put us in all round defence.

When one of the officers inquired what was happening, I just shrugged my shoulders and told him to watch and learn. Dan then went to the cash point got some local cash out. The look of disbelief on the officer's face was awesome. Dan's answer was that he needed some cash to get some Russian kit! Welcome to Kosovo lads!

Peggers got all keen as C Company deployed out on the ground, as certain members of Company Headquarters were still hung over - this was not replicated by 'Clint' and 'Archie'. Clint and Archie where a double act pair of jokers, both Forest of Dean lads.

Clint had recently taken up boxing, and was a big, strong lad. I was being a bit cocky one day during some low-level boxing training in the gym with Nobby and was showing Clint how to counter punch. I was giving it the Apollo Creed being cocky, when Clint threw an excellent counter punch straight into my ribs resulting in me being put on my arse, having two cracked ribs, bruising, and a week on light duties! His sarcastic comment was "How was that for a counter punch Clarence? Did I do good?" I had to laugh even though it hurt like hell. Life lesson for me - don't show off!

Archie was a rugby-head who was always in the shit for various misdemeanours and was a fully paid-up member of the doing my own rugby thing club. He was punching out, leaving the Army, and in the process was on a wind down and not really giving a shit.

We were out on patrol one day in the C Company HQ Land Rovers when Peggers called a halt. He was in his element doing his CSM thing. He got out his map and proceeded to give C Company HQ a bonnet brief, finishing with, 'Is there any questions lads?'

Archie piped up, pointed at the map, and asked what that big blue squiggly thing was? Peggers looked at him in total anger and disbelief, 'It's the fucking river dickhead!' Archie then said 'Waa! No shit Sherlock!' The whole of Company Headquarters started laughing, which resulted in Peggers losing his temper and threatening to kill Archie and Clint for not taking things seriously.

Peggers had a monk on for the rest of the day. The OC pulled me to one side and told me to get a grip of the lads and not wind up the CSM.

CHAPTER 34

'My guitar survived Kosovo, then I went to visit a record Company back in London and fell off my motorbike with it on my back, smashing it to bits. I was travelling at two miles per hour.'
James Blunt.

Wombling:

Arms searches and finds were the name of the game. C Company weren't having much success, and the Company Head Shed weren't happy because of the bragging rights within the Battalion. We were out and about one day on a Company search operation. C Company HQ were in an abandoned school trying to keep out of the rain. Clint had already pissed the CSM off by getting one of the Land Rovers bogged in, so it was turning into a long and boring day. As the Platoons were doing their various tasks, Company HQ were having a brew up, while the OC was on the net talking to Battalion HQ.

Archie was bored so was having a sniff around the school when he and Clint decided to see how effective our helmets and body armour were. Clint then got me in a bearhug, while Archie and Peggers picked me up, turned me over, put me on my front, and then made sure my helmet was secure.

The wankers then proceeded to throw me through a plywood dividing wall headfirst. As my head went through the other side of the wall, the lads thought it was great fun. I was then used as a human battering ram for a couple of human spear runs.

On one of the runs through the wall, Peggers called a halt to the fun and games, my head was ringing, but the Company had its arms fined! At the semi destroyed base of the wall, or what was left of it, there were AK magazines and RPG rounds! The Company had hit the jackpot! The OC and the CSM were incredibly happy teddy-bears that night. I had a sore neck and a headache, thanks to bloody Clint and Archie, the pair of wankers.

'Roger the Dodger' was a highly intelligent, articulate South African lad who was built like a brick shithouse, and a Commonwealth Games judo champion. He was a product of the white South African boarding schools. He was a good lad who was one of life's quietly confident, mild-mannered, destroyer of worlds.

He along with another big South African lad 'PJ', were my cover men during the search operation. Something happened with some local wannabe gangster, who started to get lemon with me and thought I was on my own. Enter Roger the Dodger. He was like some ninja! The local 50 pence gangster was tucked up like a kipper in a blink of an eye and educated in the error of his ways.

Word soon spread in the Kosovan village that the hobbit sized British black bloke who was always flanked by two huge white South Africans was not to be approached. I was the hardest man in Kosovo for a day. A warrior king thanks to Roger and PJ - and yes - I did milk it with the locals. Next day I was back down from hero to zero behind the wheel of my FFR with the OC taking the piss and giving me grief for my driving.

Roger the Dodger is a top bloke, and I would make use of his calm and intelligent manner. He would always help me out if I struggled with paperwork and was also one man I would never like to upset because he could drop the hammer in a brutal, fast, and efficient way, without making a noise or breaking into a sweat. He was one scary bloke if he went into the destroyer of worlds mode.

He was always protective of his friends. One night out in London, I was out with Roger, Coops, and some of the other South Africans when there was a bit of a drama with the bouncers in the Springbok Bar. The bouncers didn't like squaddies and as it spilled out onto the street, Roger took care of business in about 30 seconds. No more dramas with bouncers, they were human starfish.

A Few Words of Wisdom from Roger the Dodger - Life in London-Town, Cavalry Barracks, London, 2004:
My mate came into my room on camp with his new posh girlfriend who had this Shih Tzu called Bailey. They were going away for the weekend and asked whether I could look after it. I agreed. Bailey was clearly a house dog, a lap dog, who only ever went outside when his owner picked him up, placed him on some grass for him to do his business, and brought back inside again. So, there we were: a very posh Bailey staring at me, a ruffian from his fluffy little pink pillow wondering who the heck I was.

The next morning, I decided to go for a long mountain bike ride like I did most Saturday mornings. It was a cold and rainy day, so it was going to be a muddy one. I propped Bailey up in my daysack on some warm kit, so his head was well clear for him to look out on what was to surely be his first real adventure. And off we went round the streets and parks of West London. Every so often I checked on him, but after a while I kind of forgot about him. When I got back to camp, I unslung my daysack to find a scene of mud, bile, and shit. The stress of my bike riding skills had left a very dead Bailey!

Panic!! I ran into the utility room and put the dog and daysack into a washing machine, closed the door and in my haste pressed 'Quick wash'! Ssshhhhiiiittt!! It was the longest half an hour of my life as I watched Bailey going round and round in a sea of brown bubbles.

Occasionally his head would press against the clear door, and I had to shield it from other squads using the drums. Eventually the cycle ended, and the door clicked. I pulled Bailey out, looking nothing like a dog anymore; his stomach had filled with water, bloating him into a warthog looking creature. So, I began a period of Heimlich manoeuvre panic pumping until Bailey resembled a large, smooth looking drowned rat. I noticed one of his eyes was protruding from its socket, so I pushed it back in with a bit of a squelch.

I feared faced with this disaster, my mate's misses might produce the second heart attack of the weekend. I took the dead animal upstairs and put him under a hand dryer, ruffing him up with my fingers to try and bring him back to something looking like the animal he was. And there I was on a Saturday morning, bent over a hair dryer, hand going full pelt with a dead dog half hidden under my jumper.

What an escalation. After a while, Bailey's hair was fluffing up uncontrollably. His face had disappeared behind a perm, and he looked like a brown candy floss. I ran to my room with Bailey tucked under my arm like a rugby ball.

When I got there, I placed him on his cushion but couldn't tell by looking at him, which was his front or what end was his posterior! What a fuck up. I knew I had to make the call with some huge lie soon, but before then I still had a makeover to achieve, I got out my hair putty and cam cream out and began smoothing down his hair, eventually getting him to a dog looking state.

I picked up the phone to my mate and explained that I woke up to find a dead Bailey. He hung up and a few minutes later, called back saying his misses was terribly upset and that they were both sorry I had to be dealing with that. I wrapped up Bailey in a towel, which covered most of him except his little face and a tearful couple eventually came and took him away. Phew! I had got away with it!

Kazakhstan, 2016:

After a six-week training package in Almaty, we were told by Kazakhstan High Command to sing our "Regimental song of glorious pride" at a Kazakhstan cultural concert on our penultimate night in the country. We couldn't think of one so we rehearsed, once, "We Will Rock You" in the showers. Good to go.

On arrival to the venue, hundreds of people swamped us with flowers and a full Army parade sounded the rock stars into the arena with a two-minute standing ovation as we took our seats. So, it starts - pumped up patriotic speeches by Generals with footage of missiles going off on the big screen behind, and Kazak soldiers doing ninja moves as tanks piled through walls.

Then, what can only be described as performances directed by North Korean choreographers, dancers appeared while simultaneously hectic looking soldiers boomed out like Soviet tenors and a complete cultural ejaculation onto our faces ensued. But then the moment everyone in Kazakhstan had been waiting for, with cameras rolling and loud applause, we were called to the stage for our reach around. In chords between that of screaming cats and mating whales, we crucified a Freddie Mercury classic.

Astonished onlookers with faces like yours when your girlfriend suggests changing the home theatre into a baby room, we chorused out sounds never been heard since the great massacre of Abujen in 1976. We could have been singing "The Wheels of the Bus Go Round and Round" for all they knew. Precious stuff. Once the car crash was over and we quick marched our way off stage, it was left to one soldier of the audience who was laughing hysterically to give us high fives as we returned and crouched deeply into our seats. I then realised my right sleeve was now over my shoulder where I had been awkwardly rolling it up during our performance and that I had now literally seen everything. A minute's silence followed which could have been for any number of reasons.

*****

The Company spent the rest of the deployment on Airborne Reaction Force standby at the huge American base at Camp Bondsteel working with Black Hawk helicopters and eating decent scoff in the Yank D-fact. The Yanks did get a little concerned when some of the Company rugby-heads started throwing the ball around next to the million-dollar Black Hawk helicopters!

CHAPTER 35

"This is Malaya. Everything takes a long, a very long time, in Malaya. Things get done, occasionally, but more often they don't, and the more in a hurry you are, the quicker you break down."
Han Suyin.

Exercise Suman Warrior Malaysia:
Battalion HQ plus some odds and sods deployed to Malaysia on exercise, this was a joint Commonwealth exercise throw back from the days of the British Empire. Singapore, UK, Malaysia, Australian and New Zealand provided troops for the joint exercise and defence pact. The first drama was that it took the RAF/Crab Air three days to get there via Cyprus, and Sri Lanka finally landed at the RAF/RAAF base at Butterworth, Georgetown, Malaysia.

Free Swimming Lessons for the RAF:
During the stopover in Colombo, Sri Lanka, there was a bit of friction between the Army and the RAF. This was due to a certain female member of the 'Flight Crew'. This RAF trolly dolly/scoff box technician was having a meltdown with 'Ivor' the QM over the accommodation, she was whinging like fuck and complaining about having to, shock horror, share a two-person hotel room with one of the female Army clerks. I thought, *what a muppet typical bloody RAF trolly dolly delusion of grandeur.*

'Jed' a fit as fuck PTI, good at his job in the gym, but a bloody nightmare on the piss, could do a weekend bender and on Monday morning run a marathon. His party trick was doing drunken press-ups and the plank. Life was never dull with Jed on a night out.

This RAF bird just couldn't get her head around the accommodation issue, and it was starting to piss people off. Especially the way she was speaking to Ivor. At some stage during the proceedings she bumped into Jed, who being a good PTI 'helped' her into the hotel swimming pool for a free-swimming lesson. She did end up sharing a room with the Army female clerk and was incredibly quiet and subdued for the rest of the stop over. It always amazes me that BA and Singapore Airlines fly people around the world every day, and can fly Heathrow to Singapore in 12 hours, but it takes the RAF three bloody days.

Ivor's Reconnaissance Patrol:

The exercise was pretty laid back because there we no radios or command posts to set up or man. It was all done on computers and was at aimed at Strategic Officer level, so it was a right skive for the lower ranks. Ivor had extraordinarily little to do as the QM because the Malaysians were hosting us, so Ivor was organising cultural exchanges, some low-level training, and most importantly sorting out the R and R package.

One day I was told to pack my kit. I was off on a reconnaissance patrol with Ivor, Jock, some New Zealanders, and Ivor's Malaysian counterpart. Fair play, it was the best patrol I ever did in my Army career! Basically, it consisted of having a look at which hotel we were going to stay in for R and R and wait for the RAF to fly us back home due to the Malaysians not having enough accommodation for all the SUMAN troops.

Ivor and Jock enjoyed a drink and a bit of a cultural exchange with the locals and Kiwis, it was a right result for me and plus a nice little earner for because I was under orders from Master Stitch to bring back some berets and bits of uniform for the tailors shop back in camp. I had bought some trading badges etc ready for this eventuality. Looking back now, I would have to put down Suman Warrior as the best experience of my Army career. I always look back with a smile when I think of Ivor's Malaysian recon patrol.

The only drama occurred when I was mistaken for a hotel employee one night, much to the amusement of Panzer Leader and the Pole Cat. The Kiwis were also a good bunch that were easy going and friendly - real nice people and sweet as a nut.

Officers and Gentlemen - Not!

Before we settled into the four-star hotel for R and R and hurry up and wait for the flight home via the RAF, Ivor had the whole unit together for a dad chat. The meat on the bones being that we as the RGBW had got a good result with the hotel and basically having a paid week off in the tropics courtesy of Her Majesty's Government. 'Enjoy it lads these little earners are few and far between but behave! The civilian tourists have paid a lot of money for their holiday in the sun. We are representing the British Army and the country. Any laddish behaviour and lager lout antics will not be tolerated. Be under no illusions, if you fuck up here you will be on the pain train back in the UK.'

Whilst having a quiet beer one night, in a bar across from the hotel with Panzer Leader and the Pole Cat, it nearly kicked off. For once it was nothing to do with me or the Pole Cat. It was Panzer Leader.

We had got chatting to some middle-aged doctor and his wife who were on their honeymoon. The wife was also a doctor and a good laugh, up for the banter and telling us a few yarns about her time working in casualty in some South London shit hole hospital. The bloke doctor was a bit of a dick and took himself far too seriously.

He was a bit of a Ken Barlow 'Boring'. I was thinking to myself, *you and your new wife are chalk and cheese*. At some stage, the male doctor and Panzer Leader got into a conversation about military history. I thought this was pretty random, and I knew Panzer Leader was all over the subject, a real history buff.

The RAF bombing of Dresden was the subject of the rather animated discussion when the doctor said it was a war crime and the RAF bomber command crews should have been put on war crime trials. He stated that they were no better than murderers.

Panzer Leader then promptly went full on Tiger Tank mode. He started moving tables out of the way and clearing space, and when I asked him was going on, he said that he was going to jap slap this doctor all over the manor.

As luck would have it, while Panzer Leader was preparing for battle, the two doctors were having their first domestic over the ongoing situation. Pole Cat and I managed to drag Panzer Leader out of the bar and calm him down because I was thinking, we're fucked if it kicks off either way! Get involved in Panzer Leader jap slapping this doctor clown or having to face Ivor for having a row with civilian's downtown! Talk about drama and scandal. We withdrew in good order to the next bar. Enough said. Officers and Gentlemen could wait for another night.

CHAPTER 36

"The people of the Falkland Islands, like the people of the United Kingdom, are an island race. They are few in number, but they have the right to live in peace, to choose their own way of life and to determine their own allegiance. Their way of life is British; their allegiance is to the Crown. It is the wish of the British people and the duty of Her Majesty's Government to do everything that we can to uphold that right. That will be our hope and our endeavour, and, I believe, the resolve, of every Member of this House."

Falklands Islands 1RGBW Resident Infantry Company, June – December 2004:
A Company and Mortar Platoon 1RGBW deployed down the South Atlantic on a four-month tour. All good with Johnny as SNCO Mortars. We also had some new bodies/characters in the Platoon for the tour borrowed from ATGW Platoon.

The Falklands were cold wet and miserable, like Brecon without the trees. The local Benny's were a strange lot. It was explained to me by the Settlement Manager at Teal Inlet that most of the original population and their descendants lived on East Falkland, and that the 'Newbies' lived on West Falkland.

Most of the locals that had lived through the 1982 conflict lived in the East and were happy and helpful with the British military, whereas certain elements on East Falkland were introverted and not very trusting of outsiders.

'The Laminator' CQMS for the deployment, was an experienced SNCO who went on to be commissioned. A top bloke who had a reputation for always doing his best for the Riflemen. His OCD trait was that he laminated everything. Any paperwork or notices in the Company store were fully printed out with cap badges and laminated, hence the nickname, The Laminator.

'Glue-Head' one of the most chilled out and laid-back blokes you could ever meet. He got his nickname because of his reading accent and laid-back demeanour, because when he talked, he sounded like he had just come from B&Q, with a tub of solvent, and had glue sniffed the lot up his hooter down the bus shelter with his scumbag mates.

'Trigger' the carbon cockney copy of the famous character from Only Fools and Horses. Trigger was always up for a laugh, and when he did have a bad day or dropped himself in the shit, the whole Platoon would know about it much to the amusement of all concerned.

The Cruel Sea:
One of the first five-day settlements patrols the Platoon did was a Naval one, with a day on the ship followed by a RIB drop off at Teal Inlet, then a three-day patrol and a helicopter pick up on the Friday morning; back to MPA for tea and crumpets. The patrol consisted of the Boss, me, and six of the toms. HMS

Dumbarton Castle was a fishery protection vessel. The Matlow's were good as gold, and we were well looked after until the next day when it all went horribly wrong.

We sorted our shit out on the flight deck and boarded the RIBS that were going to drop us at Teal Inlet. The weather was fucking freezing and the wind was up, Gore-Tex till Endex. After about 10 minutes at sea, disaster struck. The bloody engine on the boat stopped turning over, so we started drifting into the middle of the bloody South Atlantic and to make matters worse, the weather turned bad. It started sleeting, and the wind was up; it was like a scene from your grandad's favourite black and white war film with blokes stuck on a life raft after getting torpedoed by a U-boat.

After a few minutes flapping from the Jolly Jacks, it was still a no go on getting the engine started. As time dragged on, we started to get cold and very wet. I was starting to get pissed off with the lack of action from the Navy. The bird driving the boat started crying, and the Navy bloke couldn't get comms to HMS Dumbarton Castle. To my horror, I looked round and TC, one of the St Vincent lads in my Section looked like Mr Freeze from Batman. Fair play, TC was manning up, but I could tell he was going down big time. Flap on!

I got out the patrol sat phone because there was no way I was going to fuck around with a PRC320 HF set with numb hands. I got comms up with the RIC Ops room and gave a sitrep and a grid off my Garmin 101 forerunner wrist GPS. TM, the Sigs Det Commander, had to ask me to repeat the grid due to the grid being in the middle of the drink. After about an hour of the rerun of the 'Cruel Sea 2004', the RAF Search and Rescue Sea King 'Yellow bird of shame' was hovering over us, and the welcome grey shape of HMS Dumbarton Castle was steaming to our rescue.

Slight problem the RIB broke along with the crane for lifting it back on board the Dumbarton Castle. This being the case, we were too heavy for the davits with us in the RIB, so we had to climb up the scramble net on the side of the ship. Due to mild hyperthermia and exhaustion, it was one of the hardest things I have ever done getting up that scramble net, back on board the warship.

Once back on board, the shit hit the Royal Navy fan. We were literary stripped of our sodden uniforms and taken to the wardroom that had been turned into a temporary medical receiving station. I was then taken to the Bridge because the captain wanted a word as I was being vocal in my enquires regarding the other RIB that contained the other half of the section and the Boss.

Old Captain Pugwash himself was a top bloke that assured me that they had eyes on the other RIB, and they were in the process of recovering it. All I said was that I was concerned that in the infantry we never split up and left lads behind. The captain told me than in the Royal Navy they never left anyone adrift or split their boats up. Fair play to the captain, he was all over it.

After a while the other RIB with the rest of the patrol was recovered, and the blokes were squared away and warmed up onboard the Battleship. The next day we were landed at Teal Inlet and started patrolling. I was glad to be back on land. Captain Pugwash was finally over, Endex. Fair play, the Royal Navy were a good bunch of lads, but playing battleships wasn't for me. The boss was well pissed off his new Gucci digital camera didn't like the South Atlantic Sea water and was well and truly broken beyond repair.

Fancy Dress Drama:
The RGBW 'RIC' Resident Infantry Company got settled into life in the Falklands. The Company Head Shed decided we would open our own bar, which was warmly received by all the lads, our new mates from the Royal Engineers, and the RAF Search and Rescue Ground Crews. Johnny Mouth of the South decided it would be fancy dress, and Mortar Platoon was expected to perform.

The Friday night came round, and before the bar even opened there was a drama involving the RAF Police. The lads were making their way through the maze of corridors to the RIC Bar when we were stopped by the 'Five 0.' A report had been received detailing racist behaviour involving the RGBW RIC.

Due to the fact, that we were dressed up in fancy dress it was a rather amusing situation. I was dressed as a Cadbury's miniature hero's chocolate bar and was being escorted by two members of the Ku Klux Klan.

When were stopped by law enforcement, the two members of the Platoon that were dressed as Klansman were ordered to remove the white hoods. The look on the policemen's faces were of total disbelief, because the two accused racist Klansmen were in fact AJ and TC, two coloured lads from the Islands of St Vincent in the Caribbean Sea.

Benny the Bell End!

During one of the weeklong settlement patrols, we had a drama with one of the locals. Brummy and I were leading a patrol. First stop was a Helicopter Monday morning drop off at Pebble Island for a two-day patrol round that manor, then another airborne pick up and drop off to Goose Green, patrol to another settlement, ending in a final helicopter pick up on the Friday lunchtime to get back to MPA for tea and crumpets.

As per usual, things didn't go exactly according to plan. As we got off the chopper at Pebble Island on day one, the weather was terrible - wind and sleet - it was awful, and there was extraordinarily little cover. The place was a barren windswept wriggly tin rubbish tip! The only good thing was we got some good happy snaps next to some destroyed Argentine aircraft left over from the war.

As we patrolled, we were met by the settlement manager. The first thing he said to me was that we couldn't sleep in any of the buildings. As I was trying to reason with the bloke and explain that there was no cover and that sleeping under ponchos in this weather wound be a nightmare, he was having none of it. So, Brummy being his usual diplomatic self, called him a bit of a bell end.

In the end we patrolled out of the settlement and luckily located a small cow shed on the outskirts which we used for cover and our bivouac area for the night. It was covered and dry, and we all squeezed in. As I zipped up my gonk bang that night, I thought what a bunch of dickheads some of these people were, Benny the Bell End would be speaking Spanish if it weren't for the British forces - what a wanker.

The following morning, we were up early, and walked the short distance to the grass airstrip ready for the helicopter pick up. As I was on the radio speaking to our Ops Room, there was another incident with Benny the Bell End. He had come up to the airstrip and was bumping his gums to Brummy and Micky the Fijian, about how he wanted the Patrol Commanders name as he was going to complain about us using his shed to sleep in.

As I was packing up the radio I thought, *here we go the usual drama and scandal thanks to Brummy the diplomat!* But fair play, for once it didn't end up in a Brummy drama. It was Micky the Man Mountain Fijian that resolved the problem. He just turned around and told Benny the Bell End, 'Go home mate, or I will fold you up like a deck chair bro,' in his gentle voice. As Micky stood up and towered over Benny the Bell End, the bloke crumbled and couldn't drive off on his quad bike quick enough. Problem solved. About twenty minutes later the helicopter came in and flew the Patrol off into the sunset.

On arrival at Goose Green, we de-bused from the chopper and there was a welcoming committee. I thought, here we go again more drama and scandal. Complete reversal of fortunes. The manager at Goose Green was spot on, a top bloke. He had already opened the community centre/hut for us and put the heating on. 'Stay as long as you want lads, plus we've got a few people coming over tonight so the bar will be open. We'll give you a lift part of the way tomorrow to save you walking'. The icing on the cake was that we had lamb chops for tea - no rations for us that night.

After a few beers that night, he told me that word had already spread about our little run in with Benny the Bell End. Word on the Islander's grapevine was that he was a very unpopular man and had a bad reputation for being rude and difficult with the Patrols. Micky was now a legend for being the 'fold up like a deckchair man'. I was also in shock that night as Brummy behaved himself after a few beers. I always look back fondly on the Patrol at Goose Green – nice, genuine Falkland Island locals at that settlement.

Mortar Platoon - Saving Private Crowbee:
The final exercise on the Falklands was a full Company attack supported by the Mortars making it rain live firing, 81mm rounds. Due to the Mortar Line being located at Cape Petal it was decided by the Head Shed that the Navy would transport our ammunition and drop it off for us, due to the lack of helicopters and distances involved.

The Platoon had tabbed in the night before, and we were busy preparing our base plate positions. I was getting the radios checked and all up and running, ready for live firing the next day. All we had left to do that afternoon was go down to the beach and wait for 'Captain Pugwash' and the ammo.

HMS Dumbarton Castle arrived offshore, and the two RIBs were soon spotted approaching the single beach where we had gathered to receive our ammunition. Then the boats stopped short and were just bobbing about! Typical - we all knew that drama and scandal were soon to follow.

Due to a combination of tides, currents, shingle, weather, and draught, the RIBs couldn't make it into shore to unload the ammunition, and time was running out for the Dumbarton Castle because of the tides. The last thing the Navy needed was the Battleship getting stuck on a sandbank.

So, after a quick discussion, Johnny decided that the quickest and easiest way to get our ammunition was to form a human chain on the beach, with some of the blokes wadding out to the RIBs to get the tins. Fair play, 'Trigger' and 'Glue-Head' were the first to volunteer for the task.

'Crowbee' was also volun-told, much to everyone's amusement. The sea was bloody freezing, but the wind was not too bad, so the Platoon cracked on with 'Saving Private Crowbee' ammunition hump and dump. The highlight being Crowbee looking like a drowned rat at the end of an exceptionally long day.

Mortar Platoon Artic and Mountain Warfare Cadre:
Earlier on the deployment the weather was awful and there were no helicopters flying, so the Platoon had to tab back from Onion Range to MPA. It was like a scene from Ice Station Zebra when we started walking, it was nearly a complete white out and blowing a gale.

The first couple of miles were a nightmare. At one stage, the snow was nearly up to Harry Crumb's waist on top of one of the features, so it was up to my shoulders, and I had to tab behind him. He was now a human snow plough.

As we came down of the hill the weather cleared a bit, so Johnny called a halt for some warming up exercises and Platoon child's play which involved sledging on roll mats, and ice skating. How nobody got injured was a bloody miracle!

A few hours later we stumbled into MPA looking like we had just broken out of Stalingrad.

That particular tab back from Onion Range was a beast, and fair play; Johnny had kept us all going which reinforced our team and Platoon ethos.

CHAPTER 37

"The desert is so vast that no one can know it all. Men go out into the desert, and they are like ships at sea; no one knows when they will return."
Jean-Marie Gustave Le Clezio.

JSUB, Iraq, January – July 2005:
After a bit of leave I found myself in Iraq as part of the Joint Support Unit, Basra. I had volunteered to go to Iraq because I was getting married and was saving up for that. Plus, my soon to be wife was keen for us to buy house and settle down away from the Regiment, ready for when I left the Army. The Battalion was moving to Chester in September 2006, and my future wife was looking forward to living and working in the City of Chester within the UK. She had contacts within the strong Filipino NHS community, so I was on 'Operation Save Up Some Pound Notes,' ready for becoming an adult with responsibilities.

My job in JSUB was a Vehicle Commander, and multiple Second in Command whilst running convoys from the Basra Airport to Camp Navistar just over the border in neighbouring Kuwait. We were a mixed bag of regulars and reservists, multi cap badges, cutting about the TAOR in soft skin unarmoured Land Rovers, terrific! Typical - British Army war on the back of a fag packet, done on the cheap.

'Cockney Airborne Wanker' was a wiry bloke who sounded like a typical Cockney wanker – a top bloke. He was also from the Airborne Community, maroon beret, wings, and all. He was the typically loud Cockney, but with a heart of gold. He was given the nickname 'Cockney Airborne Wanker 'or CAW for short. I would always give him grief because he was RLC. He was loud and always laughing - the life and soul of the party.

The Parachute Drop!
Due to the German made roads of Southern Iraq, the Main Supply Route – MSR, had extraordinarily little cross-country driving, and the road layout and visibility was usually quite good. The biggest threat at that time being VBIED's 'Vehicle Borne Improvised Explosive Devices' due to the fact it was difficult to plant stuff in several layers of well-made German concrete and asphalt. Plus, there was another major threat to life - the local ragheads didn't drive their vehicles, they aimed them! No DVLA driving tests out in Iraq, so RTA's were a major, and daily occurrence.

To counter all these problems, we would do dismount drills on the junctions to stop and control traffic, and hopefully deter any dramas. During one such task we were leapfrogging and keeping the RAF Fuel Tankers rolling that we were escorting on that particular day, when Cockney Airborne Wanker jumped out of the back of the wagon to do his dismount drill. He did his blocking task and jumped back on the Land Rover. The drill was then for him to get back up on the top cover, standing up and telling the driver to, 'Go!' Unfortunately, it all went horribly wrong, and I had a ring side seat to the clown show.

As the CAW was getting back on top to cover position, he shouted 'Go' to the young inexperienced driver who did exactly what he was told and hit the accelerator pedal! The wagon shot forward at warp factor nine, and CAW shot out of the back of the wagon going the other way because he wasn't holding on and getting a grip.

There was no parachute roll or feet together that day for CAW. His landing was a special needs 'Eddy the Eagle' crash landing without a parachute! It was hilarious! With CAW being Airborne, it was banter and piss taking gold dust. He was recovered by my vehicle and later cross decked to his original vehicle to the great delight of all the lads. Fair play, CAW took his ribbing with good grace, and on a serious note we amended our mount/dismount drills, and I was glad that he wasn't injured or hurt. Every day is a school day when out on Operations.

Weightlifting and Hobbit Throwing:
The coalition forces in Southern Iraq were a mixed bag of nationalities. We were living in Allenby Lines of the A-pod on the Army side. We were moved from the RAF side due to a slight difference of opinion with the RAF Regiment.

Because 'Mowgli' and I had the audacity to sit on the 'Reg' table in the RAF Cookhouse, some RAF Regiment plastic para bloke was giving billy big bollocks to us in front of everybody, so we stood our ground. We had told him to wind his airfield defence force neck in, the fat prick.

'Mowgli' was a fellow Lance-Jack, who was from the Devon and Dorset Regiment on attachment to JSUB same as me, whom I became great friends with during our time together in Iraq. He was from Exeter, but had some mixed blood in him from somewhere, and he looked like the spitting image of Mowgli from Rudyard Kipling's The Jungle book. Hence the nickname Mowgli.

When we would up to roll into the Yank Desert Camp just over the border in Kuwait at Navistar, it was hurry up and wait, chill out, and ponchos up to create some shade and try to keep cool. It was also good because the Yanks had a massive ISO container ice box where you could help yourself to bags of ice, and bottles of ice-cold water.

I used to live next door to the Czech Special Forces PSD in Allenby Lines and would have a laugh and good banter with them. Plus, we used to do a bit of business together. When I was off duty, the drill after evening scoff would be to get the camp chairs out, chill out, and shoot the shit with the Czech lad's that were built like cyborgs.

I would teach the Czech's language skills, or as they used to call it, 'Pirate English talk' and have a good bit of banter. They would laugh at my Borat impressions. The Czech lads were serious hard, some were ex-Spetsnaz and they loved to push weights. They were permanently on Op Massive - built like oak trees and always training hard.

One day at the border, the Czech lads rocked up as we were chilling out waiting for the return convoy, and they popped over for a chat by our Land Rovers. I'm having a bit of banter with 'Mocha' the Czech boss when he decided to wind up the Yanks. A big American convoy had lined up next to our Land Rovers and had come over to swap some kit, have a chat, and compare our kit for an hour. Some of the Yanks were doing improvised weights to pass the time.

The Czechs called some Yanks over for a bit of an alpha male, weightlifting, Operation Massive competition. Then to demonstrate the Czech prowess, Mocha grabbed hold of me. In one fluid motion, he had promptly lifted me above his head and started bench pressing me above his head like I was a 30kg human curl bar. The looks on the faces of the Yanks were a picture.

Then Mowgli got involved. After a whispered discussion with Mocha the Czech was followed by a burst of laughter, the Yanks were introduced to 'Hobbit Throwing'. I donned my helmet and body armour, and the Czechs would take it in turns to try and throw me over a huge, soft sand-berm. Mocha was declared the winner when I was human catapulted over the top of the berm, to the great amusement of a quite a large crowd of international spectators. Mowgli was now top of my revenge list.

Nobby's Parcel:

One day I received a parcel from Nobby who was then based in Germany with the ARRC. Fantastic! I was over the moon and in need of a good bit of morale.

That night, I was sat out the front of the huts with the Czech lads all excited because it was a big deal to get a parcel from home and we would all share and swap our goodies. I was all excited giving it billy big lips to Mocha and the boys that I was expecting some good shit from Germany. Wrong fucking answer!

Nobby and his minions had filled the 'Parcel' up with empty KFC fast-food wrappers and crushed boxes and had also sent some chocolate over in the parcel because they knew it would melt. The final insult to injury was the parcel also contained some British Army rations - the shit ones, like brown biscuits that nobody would eat! Mocha just looked at me like I was a complete knob, then they all burst into laughter. I was now known as 'Oscar' from Sesame Street because he also lived in a trash can, and my parcels were trash.

Locked Out:

On my return from Iraq, I flew into RAF Brize Norton. Our Leon picked me up, and it was late when I finally got back into camp. My weapons etc, went into the guard room with the rest of my serial numbered kit ready for the next day where I would go down the QM's department and de-kit from tour, as well as get six months, worth of abuse from 'Bomb Head'.

'Charlie' was my roommate in London. We had done the same PJNCO Cadre, so were tight. Charlie was a bloody huge ex policeman from St Vincent and the Grenadines. He had a great big booming laugh and was a man about town when it came to chasing women, which was always a laugh because Charlie couldn't speak Bristolian and I couldn't speak Vinci Creole!

It's late at night and I've just came back from Iraq. I'm chin strapped. My body clock is on shutdown and the only thing I want to do is get my head down. So, I make my way up to the middle floor of the Support Company accommodation in the old Victorian barracks. As I put my key into the door it doesn't work! Why won't the bloody door open?

After several attempts, I'm starting to get a bit pissed off with the bloody door. All of a sudden, the door to our shared room creeks open and Charlie appears looking a bit sheepish - he's just standing there in is boxer shorts looking like some 1970's porn star. 'Thought you were back next week mate,' was all he said to me as I entered the room. As I approached my bedspace, my spider senses started tingling! Something was not right.

There was some bird in my bed trying to hide under the covers! Typical Charlie! He was only banging some bird in my bed, and to add insult to injury, she had one of my t-shirts on. Looking over to my locker and admin area, it was all open - Charlie had been 'borrowing' some of my kit.

'For fucks sake Charlie, you're taking the piss mate!', was my only comment as I was trying to take it all this in. Charlie just laughed and said, 'Chill out mate, you're back early - you got any milk?' I had to laugh. Life was never dull sharing a room with Charlie. The bird was all embarrassed as me and Charlie started to laugh and have a bit of banter. I ended up crashing around at Our Leon's at the Pads Estate after that.

CHAPTER 38

"Bombing Afghanistan back into the Stone Age' was quite a favourite headline for some wobbly liberals. The slogan does all the work. But an instant's thought shows that Afghanistan is being, if anything, bombed out of the Stone Age."
Christopher Hitchens

1RGBW Dale Barracks City of Chester, Ready to Redeploy to Afghanistan - September 2005 – April 2006:

When I returned to London, the Battalion was in the process of moving lock, stock, and barrel to Dale Barracks, Chester. I had loads of leave, and a flight out to Singapore and the Philippines to see my fiancée to catch, so I was keen to do a John Denver and leave on a jet plane.

'Uncle Charlie' in my humble opinion, was the last of his kind. He had come all the way up from a Junior Leader Solider with the Glosters, to SNCO, and was then posted out to become RSM of 1Cheshires and gained a commission. He was a mountain of a man, and a strict father figure to us all. I nicknamed him Walrus due to his moustache, but never said this to his face because he would have killed me.

The following morning, I was in shit state and was summoned to 'Uncle Charlies' Office. I was marched in like a prisoner and had a full five minutes of

Charlie's wrath for being pissed up and not reporting to him directly. I was going straight to jail, not passing go, or picking up £200. I was in complete shock and awed mong mode. Then there was a massive burst of laughter from Uncle Charlie! He had got me on a wind up, hook, line, and sinker. To cut a long story short, I was cut away till 3rd of September on leave, reporting back to Headquarters Company 1RGBW in Dale Barracks, Chester.

A few days later after packing my room up and putting all my shit in the stores, I was on a plane to Singapore with a connecting flight to Manila, after getting a load of abuse and banter from Bomb Head when I de-kitted.

1 RGBW Afghanistan September – April 2006
Yanks a lot!

After a nice leave period in Southeast Asia, I returned to the Battalion straight into pre-deployment training ready for Afghanistan. The plus side was that after ranges at Warcop in Catterick I had to take the wagons 'Saxon APCs' the Battalion had borrowed back to the D and D at Alma Barracks, Catterick. So, I had a quick catch up with Mowgli and a walk round camp reminiscing about my first posting from depot to 1GLOSTERS.

I was soon on another RAF Flight to Kabul on the advance party to Afghanistan. On arrival in Kabul Afghanistan, I was again posted out from Battalion. I was given a couple of beat-up Land-Cruisers, some bits of ECM and other kit, three blokes, and told to get myself down to the American Base at Camp Eggers, Headquarters of the Combined Coalition, and report to the British Liaison Officer for a briefing and ground orientations.

Colonel 'Mad Max' was my new boss. He was a Senior Officer from the Fusiliers - totally fearless with a lot of operational experience - and for an officer and gentleman, he was well up for the banter and piss taking. Plus, he was on exceptionally good terms with the Yanks, which made my life a lot easier.

He protected the team from office politics, unnecessary tasks, and bullshit. We unofficially nicknamed him 'Mad Max', because he was a lone wolf that took no shit from anybody and was always calm and collected when the shit hit the fan. Officially, he was the 'Boss'. He was up for a bit of business at the Yank swap meets, and up for the banter and piss taking - a bloody good bloke for a Rupert!

Back in the day, 'Toobs' was the first Fijian recruit to the RGBW that I met. A rugby mad, fit as fuck, flying Fijian. He was never quiet, had a loud laugh and a wicked sense of humour, and was good man to have backing you up if it kicked off. He was a bloody pain in the arse when it came rugby. Everything in his world stopped if the rugby was on. I would wind him up constantly on my pre-patrol briefs, saying that unfortunately we would be out on task for the match! He would go mental. Life was always a laugh with Toobs driving my wagon and being on the team.

'Big Country' was a big, good old boy, US Marine from the backwoods of South Carolina. Strong as an ox, but never a bully or bullshitter. He was genuinely a nice bloke that would do anything for his US/UK teammates. He was straight on the banter and 'buffoonery' as our American cousins called it. And he was one of the few Yanks on base that could understand my Bristolian accent, or as he used to call it to wind me up, that 'London limey talk,' the bloody Hillbilly.

'The Von' was our team's Second in Command, and also from the USMC. To look at him, he looked like a Teutonic warrior straight out of a Wagner Opera. With a Von in his surname, he was soon nicknamed Major 'Von' of the SS. Another professional, motivated marine, who would always be competitive on our joint PT and range sessions. His upper body strength was impressive, and he would always try and beat us Brits on the tab back from the range sessions at the ANATT. So, to win, me and 'Mad Max' would cheat!

The brief I got from Colonel Mad Max on day one, was that my new job was commanding the British PSD-Delta Team as part of the US/UK DIAG program – Disarmament of Illegally Armed Groups.

Personal Security Detail, 'PSD', was the American term for a close protection team. Or as Mad Dog called it, a glorified taxi service with guns. I called it 'Toyota Taxi Service Land-Cruisers, not Land Rovers R us'. There weren't many Brits on camp apart from some senior officers and a RMP Close Protection Team and some odds and sods. So, my brief from the boss was play the game in camp, get on with the Yanks, and don't take the piss.

Flying Fijians:
After an excellent handover from the outgoing Gurkhas, and a few days to square away the team admin and get some in country training organized by the boss, 'PSD-Delta' went live.

Driving around Kabul was a fucking nightmare. It was a cross between Blade Runner and Black Hawk Down. So, one of our first jobs out and about was a trip to the main British Base at Camp Sutor, followed by a run to the airport to pick up some VIPs, then back to Camp Eggers for some tea and crumpets.

It was all going rather well until we hit the usual Afghan traffic around the Masoud Circle Roundabout. I was commanding the lead vehicle with Toobs driving when disaster struck. Some crazy locals had decided to weave in front of us on a push bike. Toobs ended up giving the bloke a gentle nudge that resulted in the bloke and his bike flying over the top of the wagon like a crash test dummy.

A quick emergency stop followed by a quick IED scout around on the side of the road resulted in one broken bike, a large crowd, and a crash-landed broken local who had the presence of mind to give me the international sign of, *you give me compensation/cash,* in his broken state, the cheeky bastard. However, I was more worried about the cracked windscreen on the wagon.

Due to a large crowd gathering, and a US Military police unit getting involved in the five minutes of fame, we did the usual British trick of shrugging our shoulders, giving the Yanks our call-sign, and driving off laughing. Toobs was given shit for being a shit driver and sending an Afghan flying via Toobs the Flying Fijian. Mad Max was in the back of the wagon chilled out taking the piss and saying, 'Welcome to Kabul boys.'

This incident would bite me on the arse later in the tour. Toobs calmed down and drove us back to camp rather subdued because we were all taking the piss, and I told him if his driving was shit again, I would plant his face in the dashboard which became the standing PSD Delta joke 'dash-boarded'. Mind you, Toobs would have killed me if a tried to plant his face in the dashboard! He was hard as nails and would give me a good hiding. Another fun filled day for PSD-Delta in the delightful capital of Afghanistan.

CHAPTER 39

"When you're wounded and left on Afghanistan's plains, and the women come out to cut up what remains, just roll to your rifle and blow out your brains and go to your gawd like a soldier."

Rudyard Kipling.

The Colonel's Dragon tooth:

For some of the jobs we would do, me and the boss would fly solo in the beat-up Land-Cruiser with civilian tops on trying to blend in with the locals or look like civilian contractors. It was all rather hush, hush. I can remember going to some nice compounds with swimming pools, and other times restaurants with one hand on my pistol trying to look relaxed.

This particular night was dusty as hell, with poor visibility. The Boss had done his business and decided he wanted to drive for a change. Due to a mixture of Afghan inner city roads, dust, and Officer driving skills (or lack thereof) the Boss had a bit of a driving drama!

We were on our way back to camp when he missed the turning and decided to do a U-turn in the Embassy Quarter, which resulted in the wagon having an argument with a concrete anti vehicle obstruction - i.e., a great big four-foot-high dragon's tooth, straight out of some World War II Battle of Berlin movie. I swear the bang was heard in Kandahar!

It resulted in the front of the wagon being in a bit of a mess. I was trying not to laugh - bloody Officers and driving. On further examination, the front of the wagon was proper fucked. How it still drove was a testament to the ruggedness and reliability of Toyota Land-Cruisers. The Boss was having a bad night and threatened to fill me in if I started taking the piss or I didn't stop sniggering, he would Jap slap there and then. He was not a happy teddy bear.

As we got back to camp at zero dark thirty, I parked the wagon in our PSD parking area and threw a thermal sheet over both wagons because I wanted to keep it on the downlow. It would be the talk of camp if it became common knowledge. Drama and scandal would follow because it was a truck off the Yanks, and Officers weren't supposed to drive; plus, it was a hush, hush, task that didn't need advertising or nosey parkers getting involved.

At first light I went down to see the American Civilian Contractor 'Tex' who was responsible for the vehicles. I thought, here we go, loads of paperwork and dramas, I'm in trouble now. He smiled at me, took a mouthful of chewing tobacco, and said, 'Let's go up the parking lot so I can have a look see, there partner.' So, off we went I was like some naughty schoolboy getting marched down to the headmaster's office. As I uncovered the wagon and Tex had a walk round, he called me a 'Limey Jerk.' 'No problem, you will have you a replacement vehicle in two days', he would take care of it - no paperwork - no questions.

I was just stood there in the parking lot looking like a rabbit in the headlights in total shock. Tex just laughed at me and then explained that he had a massive State Department Budget, so money wasn't a problem, and it kept the Afghans employed. He winked at me and said there were whispers about the Boss and his Black Ops round camp. As PSD Delta, we had priority. The only thing he wanted to acquire was a bottle of Jack-Daniels for him on the quiet. No dramas. there was unproven gossip round the campfires that a shadowy figure called the Beer Baron was the man to see about getting booze, and he was a Limey.

The Beer Baron:
On operations the US Military were always dry - no booze - unlike us Brits who were on a so called two-can rule. The two-can rule was loosely enforced at Camp Souter where A Company 1RGBWLI were based, and the blokes played the game. The RGBWLI team at the Afghan National Army Training Centre ANATC was another matter. They had their own in-house bar, and my old mates DM and Cyprus Eddy were based there, happy days.

Being a PSD, I had free range in Kabul and there just happened to be a Filipino supermarket at the Airport complex. With my future wife being Filipino, I was able to speak basic Filipino even though all the staff spoke English, so we used to do a bit of business. The Boss used to have back channels with various NGOs - Non-Government Organisations in the green zone and was always having to grease palms. All I'm saying is that the identity of the 'Beer Baron' was never uncovered.

MRE Madness:
Living on the Yank base was an adventure. The USMC lads that we were imbedded with were good people. Generous, friendly, and very professional. We as a team also got on very well with the American Military Police on camp as well. Most of the other Yanks treated the Yank Military Police like dirt, apart from us and the USMC team.

We Brits had our own TV Room and rest area which the RGBWLI team was responsible for. There were a few Brits on camp, mostly Senior Officers who left us alone or would scrounge lifts, but the Boss dealt with them and the

British RMP CP Team on camp did there thing. Tony, their boss, was a top bloke who knew the score so we would do him favours. A few select Yanks were made Canadian's and welcome in the new 'Commonwealth' TV Room, for the various sports matches due to our SKY TV dish.

There was only one drama in the TV Room, thanks to 'Jacko.' One of my lads had pulled two Yank female soldiers and bought them to the TV room to watch the rugby. They were a pain in the arse and kept asking stupid questions. At half time, the 'Boss' called me outside for a chat and told me Jacko and his latest girlfriends had to go, they were doing his head in! They weren't no fucking oil paintings either. Jacko sulked for days after getting kicked out, and he got blown out by the birds.

The Yanks would swap anything, especially our windproof smocks which were becoming extremely popular due to Big Country and The Von wearing them when we were out on Ops. Badges and bush hats were big business too. I was always getting phone orders from the lads spread over Afghanistan from the RGBWLI because I had unlimited access to the Yank PX on camp. Some of the lads from the Regiment were getting ripped off by a few jack cunts from HQ Company 1RGBWLI overcharging on PX items, which pissed me off.

'Kane' and 'Taff' were up in Mazar-i-sharif with A and B Companies 1RGBWLI, so after a phone call and a catch up, I was soon buying PSPs at PX prices for the lads up north from the Yank PX on Camp Eggers, then sending them up with the mail.

'Taff' was a proud Welshman, and one of the most un-flappable blokes I ever served with. The voice of calm and reason, and a Jedi style management system to always be able to calm things down. He could be dry and sarcastic without breaking into a sweat.

I had a phone call one day as I was getting ready to do my usual Friday admin run up to Camp Sutor. 'The duke' and 'Sledge' wanted a word when I was in Camp.

'The duke' was the QM and senior man in the Battalion. He was the voice of reason and experience, a quiet diligent bloke, and when he spoke you pinned your ears back and listened. You didn't want to be on his radar. He got his nickname from his days back in training in medieval times! The Duke of Edinburgh's Regiment, 1DERR was always under manned, the same as

1GLOSTERS, and The Duke was the only recruit for 1DERR in his training Platoon - hence the nickname The Duke.

Sledge was the RQMS, and I had known him since the amalgamation when he was a full screw. He was a big, black man with a booming laugh, and fancied himself as John Barnes due to his love of playing football. He was a bit of Jack the lad, but he always looked out for me. Sometimes I called him 'Dad'.

As we pulled our wagons into camp, and after unloading our weapons I sent the lads to do their bits and pieces. I went to the QM's trying to think what I had done wrong. Fucking wankers were winding me up, the QM needed a favour off the Yanks and Sledge was calling his 'son' to take care of business.

Due to resupply problems and most of the Operations A Company were conducting, rations out on the ground were becoming an issue due to the fact that giving the blokes a 24-hour ration pack for a 4–6-hour deployment was unviable, plus MREs were easier to carry and eat out on the move. I was asked if I could I see my Yank mates and get 200 MREs for the Company - two for each bloke for their crash out kit.

'Droz' in the clothing stores had already sorted me out a goody box of bits and pieces, including windproof smocks which were the big-ticket item. On arrival back at Camp Eggers I went for a coffee with my Yank mates. I was then taken to a little compound off the beaten track in Camp to RV with Tex who was the know proud owner of a pair of my spare LOWA boots. He then proceeded to open his magic shipping containers!

Christmas had come early for PSD Delta. The boxes of MREs came in 10's and because of the Yank Unit's turnaround Tex informed me he would give me 50 boxes - happy days! A quick phone call to Sledge and the Duke, and an hour later three snatch Land Rovers from 1RGBWLI arrived for tea and crumpets, followed by a swap meet in the British TV room. MRE madness was successfully completed. At the end of the tour, I drove out of Camp Eggers with just the clothes on my back!

CHAPTER 40

"Those Brits are a strange old race, they show affection by abusing each other, will think nothing of casually stopping in the middle of a fire fight for there

"brew up" and eat food that I wouldn't give to a dying dog! But fuck me, I would rather have one British squaddie on side than an entire Battalion of Spetznaz! Why? Because the British are the only people in the world who when the chips are down and there seems like no hope left, instead of getting sentimental or hysterical, will strap on their pack, charge their rifle, light up a smoke and calmly and wryly grin "well are we going then you wanker??"
Words of an American Soldier

'Jolly Boys' Outings' was the code name the Boss gave when we were out on the ground away from Kabul with the USMC DAIG team. It was usually a long drive to the massive Coalition Base at Bagram Airport, followed by being out on task with the North Alliance Fighters up in the Panjshir Valley. It was 14 hours a day of hard pounding. It was also a good laugh and loads of banter with the Yanks. The Boss, never one to miss a trick and play on American cultural sensibilities, nearly caused a few international incidents.
We had made good time to Bagram on this particular day, so off we all went for a coffee before heading up the Panjshir Valley. The Boss was talking shop to some Yank, full bird Colonel that had come out to play with us for the day, when the subject of the team manning and make up was being discussed. The Yank military are very rank conscious, and were amazed that I, as a mere Lance-Jack, was a PSD commander. In the US military the position was held by a Staff Sergeant, or a Warrant Officer. The Yanks were amazed at the responsibility the Brits gave to their JNCO's. The Boss just laughed and then dropped today's windup on the Yanks.

He proceeded to tell the Yanks a yarn about his family having land and titles back in the UK. He also told them that my family had always served and worked for his family since the days of British Empire in the West-Indies. I was then bought into the conversation, where I confirmed with my serious face on, that my father had served The Boss' father as his Batman, and now I was serving The Boss as his driver and radio operator because 'Batmen' were long lost like the Empire - it was how things worked.

The gullible Yank fell hook, line, and sinker for this little gem. He was getting a bit upset about what he perceived as *bloody British snobbery*. He nearly had a heart attack when I collected all the cups up, cleaned the tables, and paid the bill on behalf of The Boss. When all us Brits started laughing at this, it finally dawned on him that it was a windup. He was not a happy man. He just didn't get the British sense of humour. As per usual The Boss was at it.

Another time we were up in the Panjshir Valley, we had to RV with the Local Yank Liaison Team. As per-usual our joint UK/USMC Team were in a mix and match collection of Brit and US uniform, with warm kit worn over the top. Our beat-up Land-Cruisers and Ford Rangers blending in with the local vehicles. The next thing the local Yank Liaison Team rocked up in Humvees and were being a bit heavy handed with the locals there, taking it far too seriously, waving weapons about and making loads of unnecessary noise.

The Panjshir tribesmen were hard as nails, a proud and honourable people. We had a good rapport with them and were smack bang in the middle of their manor. One way in - one way out! If they wanted to kill us, they would kill us! They could do it anytime they wanted. It was their valley.

The Boss did his usual trick and fucked the Liaison Team off by leaving his rifle in the wagon and playing cricket with the kids and our USMC lads. Big Country and I had a cup of Chi with some of the tribesman who we had got to know on earlier outings. I had taught them a few Bristol phrases, the favourites being: 'Alright son?' 'Proper job', and 'Gert lush.' The look of utter disbelief on the Yank Liaison Teams faces when this craziness was happening, was a picture of disbelief.

'The Gimp' was the bane of my life in Kabul. He was a fat Civilian Government Civil Service adviser to the British General on Camp. On my handover with the Gurkhas, they had warned me off saying he was a dickhead. The first time I met the clown he said to me that he was the same 'rank' as a Brigadier! I told him that I was responsible for his safety and wellbeing whilst getting him from A to B, and he would put his seat belt on, sit in the back of the wagon, keep his mouth shut and follow instructions from myself or 'Rob' my Team's Second in Command. A great start - not!

The first drama I had with the clown was down to his laziness and arrogance. Camp Eggers was compact, and parking was a nightmare. Lucky being PSD-Delta, we had our own parking spaces out the back next to the American Vehicle Workshops. So, the drill was that if ever we had to taxi anybody around, the principle would meet me and the boys at the wagons - simple.

Not The Gimp - he wanted picking up outside HQ at the flag poles. So instead of coming to me with this issue, he when whinging to the UK Female RLC Adjutant who was feathering her own nest and was another REMF who didn't get the situation on the ground outside the wire. I was on the mat getting told off because The Gimp couldn't be bothered to walk 50 meters.

To make matters worse, the USMC lads got involved with taking the piss out of him in the cookhouse. They would walk past him and say, 'Where is the Gimp?' 'The Gimp's asleep', doing their Pulp Fiction voices. The Gimp knew it was my team that gave him the nickname but couldn't prove it - he was livid!

The second big drama was down to The Gimp fucking the lads about one cold winters night. I had the perfect storm of too many jobs on one day, and not enough manpower. Lucky for me, the Yanks provided me with two more crewed wagons so I could complete my tasks for that day.

I was on task with my wagon and Big Country with his USMC crewed truck. Rob with the other Brit wagon and Andy Curzon and his USMC crewed truck making up the numbers. That day we had an afternoon embassy run with The Gimp and another task.

I got back to Camp about 2200 hours and was surprised that the lads weren't back from the British Embassy. I got on the phone to see what the score was, and Rob briefed me up that The Gimp finished his meeting at 1600hrs and had decided to go on the piss in the Embassy Bar, leaving the lads sat in the car park missing scoff to hurry up and wait. Plus, it was fucking freezing.

That was it. I lost my temper! I apologized to the Yanks and said we had to do another job round to the British Embassy. Fair play, Big Country was trying to calm me down, but I was Mr Angry.

When I got into the Embassy, I left the lads with the wagons, told them to fire up all four wagons and prepare to fuck off back to Camp Eggers as soon as I dragged The Gimp out of the Bar. I didn't unload my weapons or de-kit my rig, I just walked straight into the Embassy Bar, tapped The Gimp on the shoulder and told him we were going now!

He started to babble some shit, and I was having none of it. 'Get your coat, we're done here.' Lucky some of the Hereford lads wandered over and gave him the look, because they thought he was a prick as well. As he was getting his coat and saying his goodbyes to his wanker civilian cronies, the Hereford lads told me he was pissing the Embassy staff off with his antics and gave him the international wanker sign. The silence in the wagon was deafening on the drive back to Camp Eggers.

We got into Camp Eggers, did our unload drills and post patrol checks after dropping The Gimp off at the Flag poles. I thanked the Yanks and apologized for the fuck about. It was bloody embarrassing. As I was walking back to the accommodation, The Gimp was waiting for me by the flag poles, he wanted a word. I told the lads to crack on - I would deal with the Gimp.

The Gimp was half cut and started gobbing off on how I had embarrassed him, and he was going to have me demoted. I just laughed in his face and told him he was drunk, and that thanks to his behaviour he had put lives at risk because moving around Kabul late at night was a coalition no-no, and he had also upset the Americans. He was like a schoolboy that had been caught stealing from the tuck shop, he stormed off in a huff. I just wanted to knock him out the prick!

I texted The Boss to let him know what had occurred, and fair play to The Boss, he stood us down the following day, and would come and find me at some stage for a brew and a de-brief. I don't know what got said, but The Boss squared it all away and there would be no more unassessed journeys for the rest of the week. The Gimp dealt with The Boss direct and would always meet us by the wagons from now on. All The Boss said to me was, to be polite and professional towards The Gimp - end of chat. Only pick the battles you know you can win.

I was chuffed to fuck when The Gimp finished his tour. We had our sweet revenge on the prick at the Airport through contacts in the RAF Police, they gave his kit a full search and there was a dirty rumour his bags got left behind or lost by accident on the tarmac - shocking news - I was gutted for him.

His replacement was another civilian, but the bloke was brilliant. He was from Ulster, really onside and the attitude was, 'I will work round you lads, just tell me when and where, and I will give lads plenty of notice on what I need'. Big respect. He was a breath of fresh air and a really nice bloke. He proved to me that not all the civil Service types were wankers.

ANNAT Christmas day:
The RGBWLI were always big on Christmas and being deployed wasn't going to spoil the fun. As a team, The Boss had called in some favours, and we were stood down Christmas and Boxing Day.

The Yanks did things a bit different from us, and as far as they were concerned, us Brits on camp were welcome to have an American Christmas Day or do our own thing. 'Mac,' 1RGBW Camp Sergeant Major of UK Camp Sutor, had already booked my team and attachments in for Christmas Dinner festivities. We were all looking forward to Christmas Day with A Company, 1RGBWLI, Camp Souter.

The Chef's did a fantastic Christmas dinner for everybody at Camp Sutor, the Yanks couldn't believe how good the scoff was and they enjoyed the 1RGBW Christmas experience. We then got on the trucks and drove over to the ANNAT for Christmas night fun and frivolity. Mac the Camp Sergeant Major was dressed as an Elf, with his pace stick covered in tinsel which was brilliant. It ended up as a full-on Christmas piss up in a supposedly dry Muslim country not! Fair play, the Brits, Yanks, and Kiwis had a great time. DM and Cyprus Ed were on form with the party games and generally fucking around.

Boxing Day morning, as we loaded up, we all looked like death warmed up. Making our way back to Camp Eggers was a rerun of the Wehrmacht Retreat from Moscow. The American Military Police stopped us at the front gate for a spot check due to reports of alcohol being smuggled out camp! Shock horror - who would cause such a scandal? After a quick search, we were on our way back to our accommodation to get our head down - beauty sleep time.

'The Sheriff' was our nickname for the Chief of the US Military Police on Camp Eggers. He looked like Stone-Cold Steve Austin the WWF Wrestler, but bigger. He was firm but fair and knew the score. He was a big fan of Mr Bean, so he got the British Banter and one-liners. He also had his suspicions of the identity of the Beer Baron. His party trick would be shouting 'Tea and crumpets chaps!', every-time we entered the cookhouse, or as the Yanks called it the Dining facility. We would then always chow down 'eat' together.

I was just about to crawl into my pit after saying Happy Christmas to some of our American cousins, when the Sheriff felt my collar. I was lifted up by the hand of God, and gently pulled into his office. 'Clarence my favourite Lammy, just an observation son, it's Christmas so let's not ruin the holidays by me doing a field sobriety test on PSD-Delta and your pet Devil Dogs shall we? So, I don't want to see any of your bozo's for at least 12 hours check!'. Good night and Happy Holidays chump. I had been given the gypsies warning loud and clear, Texas style. Op Low Profile, and a No Movement Order was then placed on DIAG and PSD Delta.

The Circus Comes to Town:

Being on tour is always a crazy place for bumping into random people. There were no secrets amongst the GLOSTERS/RGBW network, and rumour control HQ was always on the airways and cookhouse gossip was always jibber jabbering in the background. Word on the street was that I was on a good screw with the Yanks and was cutting my own detail.

One morning, the American Guard Force for the camp came and found me, due to an ongoing incident at the front gate involving UK Black Op's assets who had asked for me by name. My brain was working overtime trying to work out this information overload. The Boss delt with the Embassy and Hereford, as this was well above my pay grade.

As I walked down to the interior security gate with just my pistol for protection, there was a beat-up Toyota in the search bay and two blokes that looked like something out of the CIA Afghanistan Training Manual. Then as I got close, I was greeted by a shout of 'Get the brews on wanker!'

'Big Ed' and 'Ginge' were to former members of the Regiment that were doing Close Protection contracting in Afghanistan and had decided to pay me a visit. As I was trying to process all this, the Yanks were bemused, and they had difficulty in understanding West-Country language mixed with the usual squaddie banter and slang. When dealing with 'Big Ed' there was always the 'Ed factor' - what favour did he need this time?

After vouching for the two clowns and the Yanks doing their security checks, we all retired to the camp 'Green Bean' coffee shop. I sent 'H' to go and open the wagons and get my goodies box, because I knew I was going to get 'Ed factored'.

After a catch up and a coffee with them, I took them to the PX so they could go 'shopping'. Only after they had left camp, PX staff had discovered that a few items had disappeared from the shop. Some nefarious felons had robbed the place. I'm not pointing the finger of blame and suspicion in Big Ed's direction, but if I were a betting man, I would have put good money on his involvement. A leopard doesn't change in spots - if it weren't nailed down - Big Ed would have it away, the great big flaming galah!

Epilogue for an American Act of Kindness:

One afternoon I had a phone call from The Duke. I knew then it was bad news. 1RGBWLI had taken casualties, and details were still coming through. Op Minimize had been called.

That afternoon it was a quiet drive up to Camp Souter. Fair play, the Yanks had gathered that the coalition had taken casualties, and knew it was my unit, so they drove and gave us space till I got the full details.

On arrival at Camp Souter, I was taken to one side by Sledge and given the details. Back at Camp Eggers, I got my lads together in the accommodation and told them that 'Shirley' from Support Company had been killed in an ambush up in Mazar-i-Sharif, and 'Benny boy' had been severely injured.

The lads took it with stoicism and fortitude; and were a credit to themselves over the next couple of days. I was gutted. Thirsting for revenge due to the fact they were both good friends of mine. Benny Boy and I had done the same JNCO Cadre.

RIP 'Shirley'. A top bloke and good laugh, gone but not forgotten.

The Boss came across with the Yanks for a chat, and it was good to be amongst a good bunch of lads and tight team during this difficult time. I will always be grateful to the Americans that night. Word had quickly spread around camp about what had happened.

As a team we went for evening meal. The Sheriff was waiting for us and had cleared a space on a table away from it all for some peace and quiet. He had also arranged for the US Army Parade to come over and eat with us, and if we needed a chat, he was available. The Von, Big Country, and the rest of boys wanted to treat us for coffee later.

Enter our RLC female adjutant who marched up to the table all arrogant like, 'Corporal Heal, if there's anything I can do don't hesitate to ask', she says with insincerity. Fair play, The Sheriff told her to move on before I could speak!

The next day, it was back to work as normal life goes on. The Yanks were spot on. Top draw, I will always be grateful for their friendship and support that night.

Having done a double header, due to my previous Iraq Tour I was on one of the first flights home, The Duke said I had done enough and needed a break. Plus, I had paperwork to do back in Bristol due to the fact I was getting married. I was keen to get back to UK sort my kit out, and head to Southeast Asia to see the Mrs, and get married.

My happiness at being back in UK was destroyed two days later with the devastating news from Afghanistan that during one of the last 1RGBWLI patrols, 'Tin Head' had been killed. It was a sad and dark night sat in my room with 'Gary' digesting the awful news. RIP Tin Head my friend. It was a great honour and privilege to read your Eulogy at your funeral and speak to your family. RIP mate.

'The Brit' written by Corporal Jason Richbourg - USMC:
This has taken longer than necessary, but when asked to write about a friend, it seems harder than expected. I had been back in the Marine Corps for five months, had just gotten married, and had a daughter when I went to Afghanistan in November 2005. I was sent to fill the billet as the J3 (Operations) NCO, instead I ended up running security and convoys for the J2 (Intelligence). It is in this capacity that I would come into contact, with one of the most interesting, honourable men I would have the pleasure of calling friend and brother. However, niceties set aside, that is not what I thought when I first met 'Clarence'.

I was introduced to Lance Corporal Heal through our convoy/security team leader who simply called him "the brit". I keep this in lowercase to simply annoy him now as he reads this. LCpl Heal was not what I expected when though "British". I had a perceived notion, much like the perceived pronunciation of the English language, but I was wrong. Heal, much like his vernacular, was more "Cockney" and very much not what is "proper". We call this character in the States, or as we always called it "The Colonies". He was not 6 foot 2 inches, he was more like 5 foot 6 inches, and instead of pasty pail with blue eyes, he had dark skin and brown eyes. His candour was insulting, his vulgarity would make a sailor blush, and this all added to the idea that was LCpl Heal, "the brit".

When we met, he talked fast, used slang I was not used to, and I asked him to slow down and speak English. Our friendship began then. "I am speaking English you bloody colonial, what you got sand in your ear? You sound like your inbred." It was from here that he gave me the moniker "Big Country". And it stuck. Any time we met; he would always bust my balls: ask me how it was being married to my cousin? Do I call my father "Dad?" or "Uncle?" I would return the favour and ask if he was sure he was British and not from Pakistan. He looked like he was going to jump up and slap the freedom out of my head.

I was impressed at his professionalism. All the shit we would talk to each other, and crap we would say would make most people outside of our circle assume we hated each other, but nothing could be further from the truth. When it was time for a mission, all shenanigans would cease, and it was business time.

I was able to join him on a few convoys as a "blocker" vehicle. Basically, I drove like a mad man from the back of the convoy to the front, blocking traffic and making sure the convoy doesn't stop. I was honoured that he asked me to join. Afterwards I said, "thanks for adding me." He said, "Anytime, I would rather lose a treasonous colonial than a proper Brit". It took me a second to realize what he had said, and I stopped and stared at him. He winked at me, slapped me on the shoulder and said, "Let's get a cup of tea mate." I said, "I hope you get the shits!" By no means was it as smooth as his line, but I was still in shock. This was "the brit", witty, funny, and the king of tact - Not!

My wife sent me a picture of my daughter in a Christmas stocking as December rolled around. I put it up on the wall next to my desk. Heal had come into our office and saw the picture and commented on how cute and beautiful she was, and that she must take after her mom. I laughed it off, and then he said, "Well if she did not get her looks from the 'missus', must be from the postman". Again, I had to stop for a minute, "Bro, what the fuck!" "It's all good Big Country, don't get your panties in a wad, come on over to our camp." He made it up to me with a few beers that he and his team had. I had been away from the military for a few years, and nothing could get you back into the swing of things like a combat deployment and working with someone like LCpl Heal.

One day Heal busted into our office, "Hey you damn colonial! Let's go, Captain Von is coming also". We went down, "The twins are coming too" he shouted, then started loading the troops up. Other members of our team including 'The Brass' suddenly appeared.

We began driving out of the city and towards an area close to some mountains. What we would find out was a NATO shooting range for weapons. LCpl Heal had got us ammo and set up for us to shoot some. It was a great time, something different and relaxing, working the different drills, assaulting on the targets, talking shit to each other about poor grouping. It was a much-needed reprieve, and solidified LCpl Heal as the unofficial leader of a band of misfits from the colonies. As always it got competitive between us and the Brits. A few days later, Clarence confessed that he and 'Mad Max', the British Colonel in command of our team, had cheated to win the shooting competition!

Every night you could see LCpl Heal route marching with his full kit and gear throughout Camp Eggers. I asked him why he was doing this, "I'll be back on the lines in Battalion when I'm done here, I have to be ready, I won't have a big dumb colonial around to attract all the bullets." He got me again, I replied, "You know if you guys would have tried this hard a few hundred years ago, we may still be part of the Empire." He stopped a minute, "Fuck you, inbred colonial".

We met at the coffee house afterwards. Life was never dull or boring with our team of US/UK misfits. What always amazed me was the banter and mutual respect between us all, and the interaction and banter between Clarence and Colonel Mad Max was always amusing to us Yanks. The Colonel would always jump on the banter and give Clarence grief, but once out of the wire they were well oiled team. Even the Colonel addressed Clarence by his nickname!

CHAPTER 41

> *"Bah, It's humbug still! I won't believe it."*
> *Ebenezer Scrooge, 'A Christmas Carol'.*

Chester Cheshire UK – December 2006:
After getting married in the Philippines and Honeymooning in Singapore, it was back to normal jogging; like in UK Post Tour and preparing for the wife to arrive in UK.

Relocation of the Mortar Platoon HQ:
When I signed for and moved into my Army Quarter on the Pad's Estate in Chester, I was rapidly preparing for the arrival of the wife callsign. Sky TV gave

me a fantastic deal just in time for the World Cup. So, thanks to 'Norm' and 'Gonzo,' Mortar Platoon HQ was relocated to my Married Quarter, where I promptly lost control of the TV remote. Team Fiji got in on the act as well, reference: The Rugby.

The constant trickle of blokes, cars, motorbikes, and mountain bikes coming and going soon got the curtain twitchers gossiping, and my name firmly on the Family Officer's radar.

How to Upset the Commanding Officers Wife:
One random Sunday morning after a night on the piss, there were random blokes from the Platoon in my house, when there was a knock on the door, which a half-naked and hungover 'Gonzo' answered.

To my horror, it was the Commanding Officer's wife, with a pot plant and a welcome to the Regimental family greeting! However, she was greeted by mad, mental Mortars. She looked at the assembled parade of reprobates, grinned and commented, 'I take it your wife hasn't arrived in UK yet then Corporal Heal? Good morning gentleman'.

Monday morning, I was tabbing the mat getting told off for the various goings on at Harrington Road on the Pads Estate. I also got another mouthful off Brummy for being selfish and antisocial - how *dare* I turn off the SKY Sports Bar and Grill round my house and spend time with my new wife - I was bang out of order. Not a team player.

De-turfing Disaster:
My wife quickly settled into married life within the Regiment and was busy with work and adult college. Her pet project was her veggie patch in the garden. I came home from work one day, and the wife had turned our back garden into one large grow your own veggie patch. I had tried to explain that we have to hand the Army Quarter back when we got our own home bought, sorted, and moved out.

One year later, we bought our own home in Chester, so we were in the prosses of preparing the Army Quarter to be handed back. It had to be spotless. I didn't want to get a bill from the civilian Company that was now responsible for the Pad's Estate and Army housing. I had completely forgotten about the back garden, which now looked like a ploughed field. I had a bit of a flap on.

For once in his life Brummy came up with a cunning plan. On a cold dark night, myself and certain individuals went onto the Training Area and started a long process of de-turfing, transporting, and relaying them in my back garden, followed by laying grass seed. It was a long night, and my garden was finally ready for handover a few days later.

That morning, 'Sledge' popped in for a chat laughing his head off, saying that due to the houses getting mothballed ready for the Royal Welsh coming back from Cyprus, the gardens weren't a big deal. All I had to do was spread some grass seed around. I asked why he didn't tell me this earlier. He just laughed and said it was funny as fuck seeing me and the lads sweating and sneaking about, digging trenches and de-turfing the Training Area. Wanker!

Stag Night Storm:
Brummy was getting married, so a Stag weekend on the piss was organized for the Mad Mental Mortars in the fair city of Nottingham, with the fancy dress theme of Robin Hood and his merry men. Due to the fact that myself and Clarkey were both recently married, we were just going down to Nottingham for the Saturday night fun and frivolity. We had booked into the same hotel as the rest of the lads, and the RV was planned for 1200 hours Saturday.

On arrival at the hotel, I walked into the usual Mortar Platoon booze filled drama and scandal. The best man, Crowbee, had been sacked from his role. Nobody was really sure what was going on, and everybody was putting his 50 pence worth in the conversation, arguing and squabbling like children. Crowbee had been sacked by Brummy, because Crowbee dressed as Robin Hood, had stopped Brummy dressed as Maid Marion, from putting lipstick on and kissing random women in the various pubs and clubs. Typical - pissed up Brummy behaviour upsetting everyone within a three-mile radius! Hilarious!

The other drama was caused by Norm and Danny Dogshit who nearly got us all kicked out of the hotel. These clowns, in their drunken state, had convinced themselves they were rock stars - Rolling Stones style which resulted in their hotel room getting trashed. It was an awfully expensive weekend stay for those two clowns! I should have given them the bill for my role as the UN mediator.

It was a good weekend had by all and in hindsight, due to situations out of our control, was one of the last times we would all be together for a jolly boys outing. The actual wedding of Mr and Mrs Brummy was a fantastic day out, with little drama or scandal.

Christmas Chaos:
Christmas in the Regiment was always a great time in the RGBW, and because we were in Chester as a stand-alone Battalion it was a happy time. I was on duty over the Christmas period which made sense because I was married on the patch.

My wife decided that on Christmas Day we were going to have an open house. It was a great afternoon, with some of the Fijian families popping round, with my wife spoiling the kids and so on. Then the drinking and buffoonery started. Brummy had been on the piss all day before he decided to pay us a visit, and it all ended in disaster with tears before bedtime.

Santa Claus Chaos:
Brummy decided to play Santa Claus for the kids. Instead of coming down the chimney like a normal Santa, he decided to climb through my kitchen window due to the fact that my Army house didn't have a chimney and was not going to spoil the Christmas spirt.

He was well pissed up, dressed like Santa, and definitely *not* Spiderman as he came crashing through my kitchen window. On that cold Christmas evening, Brummy AKA Santa Claus, fell through my kitchen window like a bouncing bomb, breaking the window and managing to catch is bollocks on the latch, whilst losing his trousers in the process. All in attendance had a good laugh. It was also the wife's first experience of UK Christmas Army style. Brummy's wife nearly died of embarrassment.

CHAPTER 42

'Here's forty shillings on the drum for those who volunteer to come, to list and fight the foe today, over the hills and far away'.
John Tams

HQ Rifles Warminster/Winchester and Rifles Support Team Shrewsbury 2007-2009:
'The Social Hand Grenade' was my new boss and 'God' within the new Regiment. He was the King Maker. He was nicknamed The Social Hand

Grenade because for an officer and a gentleman, he was a blunt talking, bull in a China shop kind of bloke, and capable of upsetting everybody in a 50-mile radius. He was on a mission from God to form, create, and mould the Rifles into the best Infantry Regiment in the British Army. He was straight talking and didn't suffer fools gladly. Plus, he was up for the banter.

One day I had a row in camp with some REMF SNCO bloke, who was giving me grief for not parading for PT and Corporal's Mess functions. When I explained to him that I worked over in HQ Infantry for the Rifles Divisional Colonel and worked weird hours, he wouldn't see me at all because I was nocturnal. I also told him I did my fitness with the Rifles Recruiting Team over in Bulford with 4RIFLES, and he could always email the GYM for my MATT's. He went ballistic!

I just walked out his office as I couldn't be bothered with the aggravation. Talk about being a big fish in a small pond. Fair play to the Social Hand Grenade, he was in a chipper mood later that day when I bumped into him. He explained that this REMF SNCO had phoned him to have a whinge about me. The Boss had dealt with it in his own tactfully unique way.

That afternoon I was moved out of the accommodation and put into a new room out of the way in the old Officer's Mess at the back of camp. Result. My next-door neighbour was a Fijian Para Regiment lad who worked for the Para Divisional Colonel. He had also had a row with the same bloke, so we were outcasts together. We did our own PT, and there were no mess functions for these callsigns.

'The Mouth of South' was also on camp at Support Weapons Wing - Happy days! I had a good time at Warminster, where I met and worked some interesting characters within the new Regiment.

Taff, the head honcho of the London Recruiting Team, together with his partner in crime Del-boy were a double act of complete and utter carnage wherever they roamed. At work they would do there recruiting duties, but they always had something else on in the background, or Del-boy would be wheeling and dealing.

A prime example of this was the day Taff needed to use the staff car, which was the best and cleanest vehicle in the fleet. I lent it to him, saying that I needed it back Sunday night because I had to pick up the Divisional Colonel

Monday morning. Typical Taff, something went wrong and there was no staff car Sunday night!

There was no fucking way 'God' would want me driving him round in the Recruiting Team's black Toyota Land Cruiser in Rifles livery! The interior was a bio health hazard due to 'Lez Crowther' and 'Dutch Holland' smoking, living on a diet of fast food and energy drinks, with the wagon being their own private rubbish tip and mobile administration area.

The only thing I could do was throw myself on Captain Baz's mercy and go to confession round his house in Warminster. I was like a condemned man when I phoned Baz and told him I had fucked up big time with the vehicle allocation for the week, and there was no staff car available for the Colonel, Monday morning.

Baz being a LE Officer and Jedi Master, put two and two together and told me to get round his house like yesterday - bring fags and a gum shield. On arrival at his gaff, he threw me the keys to his Army Estate wagon, which was spotless, refuelled, and ready to go. 'Leave me the Toyota ant hill mob wagon coco the clown! And I don't care how you do it but get the bloody staff car back! The Divisional Colonel will fill you in if you rock up in the bloody Hilux! You bloody clown!' were his words on wisdom that night. Lesson learned - big time!

After Warminster I was posted to the Rifles Recruiting Team Shrewsbury, which was a good laugh. Closer to home, and full of interesting characters from around the newly formed Rifles Regiment.

'Tell Me a Story Rory' was a late entry officer who was also a Civilian Light Aircraft Pilot who always a had a yarn to spin, and a cup of tea welded to his hand. He was always in a good mood and laughing about something or other. His other claim to fame was that he was always in a bother for getting parking tickets, speeding fines, or other driving offenses.

'Punk Arse Ed' the team PTI was a bloody nightmare. Whatever task the team was on, we always had to consider in the Ed Factor due to his habit of dropping everybody in the shit within a 30-mile radius. The rest of the team were 'Jimbo' 'Adie Gold tooth' and 'Stevie' a good bunch of lads and unique in the recruiting group because of team had a member from all the former Regiments that made up the Rifles. Ed was a generous, fit as fuck joker from Nottingham, who provided good morale for the team. Here a few examples of the Ed Factor!

Ed and I were tasked by 'Adie Gold Tooth' the Team Commander, to go down to Hereford Rifles Reserves to conduct a PFT 'Personal Fitness Test,' so the TA lads could get the tick in the box required for their bounty. We arrived in Hereford by the early afternoon, and because we had to conduct the test in the evening, we had time to kill. Ed decided to have a few beers, I was dry because I was driving.

Ed took the test with a few beers on board. I ran it as the 'sweeper' in a time of 11:30, so the name of the game was for the TA lads to beat me in - this equals a pass. For once in his life Ed conducted the test by the book, with result being that half the lads failed! This didn't go down well with the TA Head Shed, and because Ed was full of Dutch courage, the last thing I needed was Ed kicking off with the TA Head Shed. The times were amended, and Ed got his head down in the passenger seat all the way home to Shrewsbury the wanker! Another fun filled day with Punk Arse Ed. To add insult to injury, I got a speeding ticket in the wagon on the way back.

The biggest Ed Factor drama was a high-profile job at the Police College in London, where we were running the assault course competition for the Police Cadets. We were on our best behaviour, and I was in the ultimate command appointment because Adie was away.

Ed ran a really professional walk and talk through on the Saturday for the Police Cadets, ready for the main event on the Sunday morning. We were invited into the Police Bar that evening for a few beers.

Ed did what he usually does and got into an argument with some copper because the copper was telling Ed how he should run the assault course competition in the morning. It then went nuclear when Ed told the copper to fuck off and wind his neck in! I was called over because I was in charge and the copper was threatening to arrest the whole team for being drunk and disorderly! Of all places to have a drama was a Police College full of the Five-0! You couldn't make it up!

So, I'm now having a row with some irate copper over a bloody assault course thanks to Ed, who had now disappeared down to the Union Jack on the piss, and to hang one on with his mate Ricky who was the manager there.

Luckily for all concerned, the copper kicking off was known for being a clown and was extracted from the bar by the Police College CSM. The rest of the team retired for the evening, and in the morning after a nice chat with the College CSM over a cup of tea and a kit swap, all sins were forgiven, and the cadets had a fantastic competition.

Ed was late and hung over for the rest of the day. He sulked all the way home when I made him sit in the back of the wagon and shut the fuck up for the trip home to Shrewsbury. Ed's final nail in his coffin happened after I had just left the team, due to getting promoted and posted back to Battalion.

On one Christmas evening, Ed had decided to gate crash the Officer's Mess Christmas function at Copthorne Barracks. Because Copthorne was a Brigade HQ, there were officers, civilians, and Reserves - every man and his dog.

Ed didn't give a shit, he just wanted to get a beer! It ended badly a few hours later when it transpired that Ed wasn't on the guest list! He was asked to leave by the Brigade Commander's Aide which ended up with Ed having a row and threatening to fill him in.

The story goes, that after a scuffle Ed retreated in good order and was back in 5RIFLES by the following lunchtime. Life was never due when Ed was on the 'Ed factor'.

CHAPTER 43

Swift and Bold!
'I hate those Grasshoppers! The name given to the Green-Jackets by the French as they would appear behind them, stab them, and disappear just as quickly.'
Napoleon.

1RIFLES Chepstow, Afghanistan 2008-2009:
On return to Battalion, I was straight back into the mix and found myself a few months later back in Afghanistan as a newly promoted full screw on a Land Rover WMICK with the 1RIFLES OMLET 'Operation Mentoring Teams'. Teams working out of FOB 'Forward Operating Base' Tombstone run by the USN/USMC. In a nutshell our job was to babysit the ANA and run supplies all over Helmand.

It's All Gone Davey Lane, 1RIFLES, Afghanistan 2008 – 2009:

'Rambo' was my new boss, a RIFLES LE Officer from the RGJ, who on my first impression was a grumpy, miserable old git! My first nickname for him was Mr Happy! I was proven very wrong on our first operation which went noisy and ended up in two weeks of medieval total war in Nadi-E-Ali. Rambo was given to him in respect to his Jedi Master skills in commanding troops in war and leading from the front.

'Fight Club', was a Royal Engineer Officer who was attached to us for the duration of the deployment. He was given his nickname due to his habit of getting into disagreements with the ANA. On one particular day, due to the Afghan macho male cultural trait, he was offered out for a fist fight by the skinniest human rodent Afghan solider on the patrol, much to our amusement. He was in his element blowing things up with Bar Mines.

'Jugsy,' another lad posted into the Unit from 264 Signals from Hereford. He had already been christened Jugsy due to his Mickey Mouse ears! A very professional solider and also our TACSAT Jedi. He was always up for the banter and willing to help out when we were maintaining the wagons and doing the dirty work. At the time of writing this book, Jugsy sadly passed away due to PTSD induced issues. RIP Jugsy, you are now in Valhalla drinking in the hall of heroes my friend.

REME Dave the Silver Fox is the best mechanic I have ever known, and I was always bumping into him throughout my Army career. He got his nickname through his silver-tongued success with the women. More kids than the Old Lady in the Shoe, and more fan mail than the average boy band. The Swansea, Welsh, Silver-tongued Cavalier!

'Ricky Spanners' was our other REME Recovery Mechanic who was given his nickname by The Boss due to his mythical skills in fixing things and dragging vehicles out the shit. He was also that laid back he was horizontal.

'Dockers' was a young rifleman, the baby of the team. He had more front than Blackpool! Always opening his mouth before engaging his brain. Due to his good nature and hard work, everything would turn into laugh with him. He was great for team morale and got his nickname due to his surname.

'Davy Lane' was a TA Signals SNCO bolted on to us as our Signal's guru. A big, good natured black lad from London who was one of the nicest people you could ever meet. Unfortunately, the team saying 'It's all gone Davey Lane' was thanks to him, because every-time he dropped a bollock, or was just plain unlucky, everyman and his dog knew about it! So, when anybody else fucked up or things went wrong, it was now known as 'It's all gone Davey Lane'.

I See Some Ships:
During one of our small arms contacts, I gave a Fire Control Order to get rounds down to supress the enemy. His rounds were going everywhere but on target! Tracers don't lie.

It happened a few hours later as well, so me and The Boss were thinking we were going to have to bore sight his rifle. Dockers then confessed that he had left his glasses back in camp! The Boss when fucking ballistic - I mean he fucking lost it - I thought Dockers was going to get a slap.

Jugsy and I went round the back of the wagon sniggering like naughty schoolboys while The Boss lost his temper and Dockers looked like a scolded puppy. Top tip: Always check your blokes have their glasses. I also wore a bollocking for not checking Docker's kit before Operations.

Smoke-tastic:
One night, somewhere north of Nawa, we were operating on NVGs when we encountered a possible IED and ambush. Some locals had been sighted looking rather suspicious by Andy up on top cover.

Rambo withdrew the wagons to a nice over watch and fire support position, and we were all stood to ready for a possible contact. Rambo then ordered me to put some white light up over the Wadi. We had just been issued with latest Para-Illumination Flares which were supposed to be the dogs-bollocks.

The one I fired soared into the desert sky with a small flash, then that was it - nothing much to see. I thought it must be a dud, so I fired another one. The same thing happened. So, I fired one more off, then started to rummage around in the wagon for more flares etc. Then I heard Fight Club shouting me to get up in position and observe my ARC's, calling me a mong in the process. Andy had lit the area up with a 40mm UGL Illumination Round, and to my horror the Wadi was covered in a dense smoke screen. I had fired Para-Smoke instead of Para-Illumination due to not checking the markings on the tubes in the darkness and being in a hurry. School boy error on my part, and a few hours piss taking off the lads. Top tip: Always check your kit in the darkness.

Ali Baba and a Pair of Lowa boots:
During the battle prep for the operation to push Terry Taliban out of Nadi-Ali, we were sleeping on, or by, our vehicles in a secure ANP camp. We were also co-located with the ANA in a confined space. Davy Lane, who was part of the Forward Medic set up was also with us. He was on the Pinzgauer Battlefield Armoured Ambulance with the Doctor. Due to the heat and the climate, Davy had decided to sleep on a stretcher next to the wagon on his gonk bang, with his boots off under the stars.

The next morning the peace and quiet was shattered by Davy Lane not being a very happy teddy bear! He was cutting around the area in his flip flops to the amusement of all present. Because at some stage during the night, somebody had stolen his boots.

After a bit of a CSI investigation TIME, Fight Club, and myself went to have a little chat with the ANA. Abdul the ANA CSM then decided to throw his toys out of his pram when it was suggested that one of the ANA soldiers might have come into possession of a pair of Lowa Boots. He took it as a personal insult that we were accusing the ANA of being 'Ali Baba' thieves in the night! At that exact moment, some random ANA solider bimbled by in Davy Lanes boots which looked like clown boots on this scrawny Afghan kid size feet! The ANA then calmed down and were keen to return the Lowa Boots due to a 'mix up' in the dark. From now on, it was keeping your kit away from the locals and don't trust any of them because they would rob you blind then lie to your face. The saying 'It's all gone Davy Lane' was born.

Afghanistan 2008/09 holds various memories for me. A three-way split between sadness - shame of the loss of friends and lives ruined because of that conflict; and pride and elation at being part of a Band of Brothers and being on a two-way range for real. Last of all being witness to some simple acts of kindness and friendships forged in fire! Here are a few examples of this:

Our Leon was part of a small team being flown into the Nawa District Centre, when the chopper he was on took incoming rounds. The aircraft didn't hang around after dumping the troops out. The end result being, Our Leon was minus his Bergen and ended up living out of his daysack for the foreseeable future.

As a concurrent activity, my call-sign was fighting its own little war punching into Nadi-Ali then on to Nawa DC. After a week of being in contact we were out of ammo and water, plus we had to tow Rambo's wagon into the DC for repair while we were resupplying.

As we pulled into the Nawa DC looking like extras from the retreat from Moscow, the first person I bumped into was REME Dave. He and his crew, including Ricky Spanners had come out to repair our broken-down wagon. Dave was in shock at the state of us and he said I had aged 10 years in a couple of weeks; looking like I had been on the Atkins Diet for the last year.

He then gave me an ice cold can of pop he had be saving. It was like the nectar of the gods as I passed it round for the boys to take a swig. This was typical of Dave thinking about other people. Dave told me later on that he had been cutting around the area in an unarmoured Bedford Recovery truck for a week, the bloody lunatic.

After the leaving the wagon, REME Dave and I went to go and find Our Leon. It was my time to be shocked when I caught up with him. He had grown a beard due to lack of water and had lost a lot of weight due to living on rations. He then started to give me grief for worrying him, because all he had heard from our call-sign was me sending contacts reports and the sounds of it all going off in the background. I then gave it back to him, saying what kind of complete bell-end gets himself shot down! The wanker. After that bit of brotherly love, we went over to my wagon and had a whip round of kit for him, including wash kit, because he had the clothes on his back. That was it.

The last act of kindness I witnessed was during some dark times for me personally. Danny Dogshit had been killed in action. It had happened whilst we were out on the ground operating in Support Company's TAOR. We had heard some of the radio chatter on the net.

As we entered the SP Company location there was none of the usual banter and ribbing. The OC and Sniper Dan were waiting in the vehicle for our wagons to rock up. Rambo and I were taken to one side and given the bad news. I was upset and angry but was told in no uncertain terms by Rambo to get my head in the game because we're had a patrol to complete, and I had responsibilities.

A few days later, we returned late at night to our base location at FOB Tombstone. I was not in a good place. As we were unloading the wagons and doing our Post Patrol Administration, the RSM appeared down the ISO containers looking for me. Fair play to REME Dave, he got wind of it and took over my wagon as the RSM called me over.

The RSM the took me over to the Yank side of camp out the way of prying eyes, gave me a hug, and said he had been waiting for me to come off the ground to check I was doing OK because he knew how close the old Mortar Platoon boys were from 1RGBW. He then sparked up a couple of cigars and we put the world to rights for a while.

That night in my gonk bag I thought fair play to the RSM, he has the whole Battalion to think about and he came and found me at my lowest ebb. That was leadership and looking after the boys in difficult times.

CHAPTER 44

> 'Those men in the green tunics …. Oh, what I could achieve with 10,000 of them.'
> Napoleon.

UK and return to Afghanistan 2009 – 2011:
Being back in UK was a bit of an anti-climax. It was back into the normal swing of things with Battalion exercises and courses. I was now the Battalion Driver Training NCO. I had a good team of lads, including Papa Bear, Chris, and Mac. Because we had super-fast civilian broadband down my driver training hanger, we were very popular for troops popping in the hanger for a brew. We were all busy running various driving courses and training for the lads.

Corporals Mess Capers:
I soon found myself in charge of running the Corporals Mess Bar, which proved to be a very cushy number, and opportunity for me and my hand-picked crew.

'Dan Mac' was the PMC of the Mess, and an old friend who had been posted into the RGBW Mortar Platoon straight from Depot when he was a 'CROW' to make our numbers up. He had fitted in well, had an excellent career to date, and was knocking on the door for promotion to Sargent. He was also a bit of a 'Lad' who was happy with the Mess Bar. As long as the beer was flowing and everybody was having a good time, he left me alone to do my thing. I also knew his father 'Jed Mac' who had served in the Glosters and was a famous artist back in Bristol, who also happened to be one of my adult instructors in Bristol Army Cadets.

'Saulo Roko' my partner in crime and 2IC of the Corporal's Mess Bar we had renamed as the 'Nuclear Sub'. Roko was the first Fijian recruit I had met back in the day and is still a good friend. Roko was a squat, powerful rugby player and former Fijian national sprinter. He was also a nightmare with booze and birds. The lunatic has more kids than the Old Lady in a Shoe!

Due to Dan Mac's wheeling and dealing, and massive support from 'Rob' the Battalion Domestic Pioneer, the Corporal's Mess was transformed into a great venue on camp, including a pool table and Sky TV. Over the years we hosted weddings, christenings, various functions, and of course Fiji Day celebrations.

The Regiment Accountant provided finance where I would sign out a sum of cash which I would pay back, plus 10% for the Regiment. Any profit would go back into the Mess for Sky TV or improvements. I had to provide receipts for everything and keep a Mess ledger, so it was all above board. I would round everything off to a pound or fifty pence. It was also cash bar which the lads were happy with. I had several wholesale cards and a contact at the local biscuit and crisp factory, so stock wasn't a problem.

What happens in the Mess, stays in the Mess!

One afternoon, Papa Bear asked for the Mess to be open for Fijian Church, and tea and coffee afterwards. Sure, no problem. I was busy working in the hanger that afternoon, so I left Saulo Roko with the keys to the kingdom.

As I walked over the Mess after my evening meal, I was surprised to see the lights still on and things happening. I had to laugh; rugby was on Sky - 'Church' was watching the rugby! The Mess was full of all the Fijian's and their families having a great time watching the match! 'Church' was now the code word for "Rugby match piss up'.

On another occasion, a few of the lads approached me to open up for a football match which quickly deteriorated into an unplanned monster piss up. Word quicky spread around the Battalion, so every man and his dog were in the Mess on the piss. We had to go to Tesco to restock. The only trouble being, the QM wasn't very happy due to the Battalion recycling bins being filled up with Mess rubbish, and he gave me fuck all for not informing him I was open for the big match! School boy error on my part.

The Last Hurrah Afghanistan 2011 Patrol Base 2 Helmand Province:
My final operational tour was as a member of the Commanding Officers TAC 'Taxi Service' Group. The brief I got from The Boss was whatever happens, the three 'Husky' TAC trucks had to operational and on the road at all times, because they were the only armoured vehicle asset in the Battalion TAOR.

The nearest gun trucks being the PMG 'Protected Mobility Group'. The PMG were 30 minutes away, based at FOB Price, plus they had to navigate the Abbasakk Wadi which was nick-named the Rose-Garden due to the amount of IEDs littering the place. So that was me for my last tour, guns, and trucks 'R' us.

Camel-Boy Jay was a strong, switched-on Rifleman who was one of the top cover gunners. He was a gym queen who was built like a tank and as strong as an ox. He got his nickname due to his facial resemblance to a camel.

His claim to fame being that he got drunk a week before deployment and took a Husky Armoured Fighting Vehicle around camp for a spin. The bloody lunatic! On return from the tour, he was given a rather large fine.

The Hobbit and Fiji Gus were the Laurel and Hardy of CO's TAC - a right pair of jokers. The Hobbit got his nickname due to his surname and body shape. He was a proper Hobbit from Devon. Fiji Gus was a gentle giant, a monster of a man, with a booming laugh and a Jedi Master in avoiding work. He was given his nickname due to his long and complicated Fijian surname. 'Gus' was easy for everybody.

The Yank Balloon Boys:
The Balloon Boys were the American Department of Defence Contractors who operated the surveillance balloon that covered the TAOR which was based in Patrol Base Two with us.

'Thin Crust' was a quietly spoken, rather large chap from Arizona who was known for his kindness. He was given his nickname for his size and love of pizza.

'Al Dez the Italian Stallion' was your typical Italian American, a Gandalf the Grey beard, dark Mediterranean looks, and loud outgoing personality. A former US Navy Combat Engineer, and ex US Forces Operator that knew the score. He was always smiling, and he got the British accents and squaddie banter.

'Wolverine' was a former US Marine gym queen and being a native of Alaska he had his admin and job proper squared away. He was also one of the most intelligent blokes I have ever meet. He got his nickname because with his sideburns, he was the spitting image of the Marvel Comics Superhero - Wolverine.

The biggest threat to the PGSS Balloon wasn't the Taliban, but the local kids! They would use the balloon for target practice with their slingshots, and bows and arrows, especially when the balloon would come down for maintenance.

Luckily, we had the man for the job in Anglo-Afghan relations in the form of Fiji-Gus. The ANA soldiers looked at Fiji-Gus as some sort of warrior king, plus he had picked up the lingo quite well, and was always doing deals with the ANA or going for Chi over the ANA side of camp. So, if the local kids would play up, he would go and get the ANA to jog the kids on.

He would get fresh live chickens via the ANA from the local Bazar for the Balloon boys to cook up. I would also lend AL the quad bike for doing his bits and pieces, so life was good for our Anglo-American relations! Plus, the Yanks had internet access and aircon which was a welcome relief for a 20-minute chill out away from the midday sun.

The Great CIMIC ISO Give Away:
Due to R and R, Operations, and various other issues I was CQMS for a few weeks. It was a welcome break but could be a nightmare when dealing with everyman and his dog from Battalion HQ.

Civil-Military Co-operation Teams (CIMIC) were part of the hearts and minds campaign in the TAOR. In reality, it was a complete waste of time because the locals/ANA and Taliban were all at it, and on the make trying to make a quick quid.

There were no hearts and minds in Helmand; everybody hated ISAF and just wanted to be left alone. The CIMIC Team at PB2 was run by some STAB Officer who was a throw-back from the bad old days of the Cold War, British Army. Officers were gentleman, and the other ranks were the scum of the earth. This clown had a bad rep amongst the lads because he was arrogant and a snob. He even complained about the food on the PB. I personally thought 'Butch, Turkish and Paddy' the chefs did a fantastic job of feeding the troops with rations, limited fresh food, Afghan climate, and in the middle of a two-way range.

Due to limited space and ISO container storage, word had come down from the QM that I had to make room in one of the ISOs for bottled water. The summer was in full swing, and water was becoming an issue, so we had to stockpile just in case.

CIMIC never left camp, so as far as I was concerned their ISOs were fair game for a clean-up. Old Major Problem was on R and R, so I had the keys to his kingdom. It was like Christmas when me and the boys had a rummage around with the CIMIC free shit to give away to the locals ISO! Even the CO ended up with some nice bottles of iced tea and Afghan blankets. The ISO was soon emptied and restocked with bottled water.

It was amazing at the end of the tour how many blokes had Afghan flags as souvenirs. Major Problem wasn't a happy teddy bear when he returned from R and R. 'Dry your eyes mate life is unfair!'

United Nations Intervention for the Balloon Boys:
About once a month, 'TAC' would drive up to Camp Bastion for various taskings and resupply. The CO hated going into REMF Central because there would always be drama and scandal.

It was always good to catch up with 'Banger' and the lads from the QMs Department. Banger would always be wheeling and dealing, getting treats and goodies for the lads on the PB line, including slabs of pop for the back of my wagons so when we used to roll up at various locations, we had a morale boost for the troops.

AL and the Balloon Boys had an issue with their rear link over the American side of Camp Bastion – Camp Leatherneck. They hadn't received mail or resupply for a few weeks, so their morale was lower the whale shit!

'Scott the Dickwad' was the PGGS rear link at Camp Leatherneck, so me and Fiji-Gus borrowed Bangers quad bike and went to go and have a chat with Scott and grab Al's mail.

When we arrived at the PGGS compound, it was like arriving on another planet. It was like the bloody Ritz Hotel, plunge pool, and ice machine included. Scott the Dickwad lived up to his reputation for being a typical petulant bureaucrat with a face and mannerisms that said please punch me in the face! I was trying to be all diplomatic and polite, but Fiji-Gus just dealt with the situation Fiji style, including a life lesson for Scott about the error of his ways. We soon left with the mail and resupply. Scott was rather quiet and subdued and had rather a red, sunburned looking face – with his face being that red, if I was a suspicious man, he looked like he had been bitch slapped...

'I'm a Firestarter' was the nickname given to the original PB2 TA CQMS. He had a rather bad day which ended with him up in flames. One of the jobs of the CQMS was to burn the rubbish from camp in a purpose-built burn pit, which was just out of camp, covered by the super-sanger.

Dennis Wanjiki was the CQMS's odd job man and general labour force. Dennis was a good-natured Kenyan Rifleman who was known for his friendliness and general pleasantness. The story goes one morning, that the CQMS decided to back the ATV all the way into the burn pit to unload the rubbish, Dennis was against the plan due to the pit still smoking from the day before. The rubbish was promptly dumped in the pit, when disaster struck - the ATV got stuck in the pit and the rubbish then decided to light up!

Dennis had to jump into the pit with some of the LECs to push the ATV out and rescue the CQMS who by now was smouldering and suffering from flash burns, hence the nickname I'm a Firestarter. The CQMS was medevacked to Camp Bastion for treatment and never seen again. Johnny Mouth of the South was inserted into the CQMS position at PB2.

Most evenings, I would wander down to the CQMS ISO and shoot the shit with Johnny. We would get the deck chairs out and have some banter. It was also good to take the piss out of people walking past, or myself getting ripped for my latest fuck up. Trouble is, Roko would join us. Then Mikey would rock up. Soon, it was the unofficial meeting place with even the RSM joining in. Ask anybody that served in PB2 with 1RIFLES about running the gauntlet outside Johnny's ISO.

This was my last hurrah and final Operational Tour. I had the pleasure of serving with some good lads and consider myself fortunate in walking away in good order. This chapter is dedicated in memory to 'Jugsy' and C/SJT Kev Fortuna who were killed in action during the tour. Also, this chapter is written in remembrance of the other casualties from the 1RIFLES Battlegroup including 'Maldoon and John Mac'. RIP Lads. Stand easy, you have done your duty.

CHAPTER 45

'Woman asked a Rifleman on Op Olympic if he was enjoying himself. 'No Madame, I would rather be on the holiday that I booked with my family'. She replied, 'Well at least you are not in Afghanistan'. 'No madame, I was there last summer and will be in Africa next year.'

Op Olympic 2012:

On return to the UK, it was back to normal Army life in Chepstow – full of hurry up and wait. I knew my time in the mob was coming to an end, and civilian street was on my radar, coming in thick and fast.

My whole focus now, was on sorting myself out, ready for punching out, and going back into the world. Before I could sort my life out, London 2012 was going to throw a big spanner in the works.

The first whisper that the Battalion was going to get dicked, was whilst watching the BBC News, known in the Battalion as 'The Baghdad Broadcasting Corporation' due to its anti-Army and left-wing bias. The security plan put in place by the Government and G4S, was despite the media spin that was going down faster than the Titanic and becoming a right cluster-fuck.

Watching the news with 'Papa-Bear' down the Hangers, we were having a laugh about the usual left-wing lovies whinging about The Royal Artillery setting up Rapier SAMs 'Surface to Air Missiles' up on some tower block, down the smoke London-town. Bloody clowns - don't they remember September the 11th?

A week later, I found myself attached to A Company staging down the O2, or as the knobs called it, The North London Olympic Arena. As per usual the Army got screwed by the politicians. We were sleeping on camp beds in some disused 1980's throw-back shopping centre Tobacco Warehouse down the East-End.

Coca-Cola Cowboy, Papa-Bear, and I, found that we were running the nightshift on the 02 Vehicle Check Point with some of the A Company lads, odds and sods including the Polecat.

After a few days of getting my head in the game, we had a good relationship with the old Bill and the Coca-Cola sponsors. One night I was having a chat and a brew with the Coke Logistics' Manager who was telling me his young lad was Army barmy, so we had a quick whip round to get the lad a beret and some 'Rifles' bits and bobs. The chap was made up, plus 'Nez' the A Company CQMS got some glow sticks and a Rifles water bottle for the lad.

The next night a Coca-Cola truck rocked up at the check point. 'How many drinks you need mate? It's all free,' the driver asked me. Not wanting to be greedy I said, 'I've got about 40 blokes so a couple of slabs of whatever you can spare would be much appreciated by the lads,' was my reply.

The Cockney laughed at me and said 'You're going need a bigger mini-bus son. As he wheeled out a tri-wall pallet of soft drinks. I had Papa-Bear doing a shuttle service in the mini-bus back to Nez in Tobacco Warehouse sharing the love! It was the start of a beautiful Rifles/Coco-Cola friendship. The QM's van from HQ Company back in Chepstow even turned up one night for a sugar fix.

Chicken nugget nosh up:
Because we had a mini-bus on site, Papa-Bear was always doing admin and scoff runs throughout the nights. We had Greater Manchester Police staging on with us one night. A great bunch of people who knew the score and were up for the banter and buffoonery.

We were doing a McDonalds run, which the Coppers were up for, and after the usual banter this bloody huge copper said he could do 40 chicken nuggets in a oner. So, I laid a bet on with him that one of my lads could do 60 with space left! This soon started a frenzy of betting and potential kit swaps all over the checkpoint. I then deployed my secret weapon - Papa-Bear.

The minibus was deployed to get 100+ chicken nuggets for the challenge. It was like some man vs food satellite TV show, when the two gladiators faced off in the tent that night. In the end, Papa-Bear won: 62-43 in the Great Nugget Eat Off. I still feel sick to this day when I see our smell chicken nuggets.

Chipmunk the Chump:

As per usual, there was drama and scandal one night. There was a concert at the 02 celebrating 'Jamaica's 50th' It was the anniversary of Jamaican Independence, so every man and his dog from the Jamaican community was on the piss at the O2. The people that came past were as good as gold and stopped for happy snaps and all sorts with the troops.

I was called down to the Checkpoint about 20:30 hours because there was a drama! As I walked down from the admin area, Papa-Bear joined me. There was this bloody great stretched limo parked in the search bay. The driver, some well-dressed, polite, black bloke was having a chat with the lads, and I took an instant liking to the lad.

As we got into a conversation, he was explaining that he needed access to the parking in the VIP area, because he had the headline act in the limo, but didn't have a pass. No worries. I would make a phone call speak to the police and try and sort it out. Then from the back of the wagon I heard some weasel voice gobbing off saying 'Don't you know who I am brov?' He was bumping his gums and demanding access there and then.

I was trying to diplomatic, but things quickly escalated when this fucking huge, gorilla of a bloke got out of the front of the wagon and just stood there looking me up and down. I thought, *here we go*, chuffed I've got Papa-Bear with me because this bloke is a monster.

From the back of the wagon, the weasel piped up again, 'Don't you know who I am I'm Chipmunk?' I replied, 'Never heard of you mate, aren't Chipmunks supposed to be fury animals?', which got a laugh from the lads. The limo driver was trying to keep a straight face.

Chipmunk then threw his toys out of the pram much to everybody's amusement, like some sort of petulant child. I couldn't leave it without having another dig, 'Aren't you supposed to be on some kids cartoon program with a bloke called Alvin?' Even the gorilla stated grinning at that one-liner. There was silence from the back of the wagon.

In the end it didn't take long to get the limo in and parked up. I thought fair play to the driver keeping cool and being a good bloke, Chipmunk must have been a right wanker to drive around.

Being tech savvy, some of the young Rifleman found out that the Chipmunk had been on his social media, whinging and whining about getting delayed by the Army. Fair play, I think the entire Regiment got on the web and took the piss out of Chipmunk, the chief chump!

Chapter 46

'The only man I envy is the man who has not yet been to Africa, for he has so much to look forward too.'
Richard Mullin

Kenya and Flood Relief Operations 2012-2014:

My last two years went quite quicky, including an exercise in Kenya which was a nice jolly to end on. I was acting MT Sarge, working for 'Boycee' the QM.

The highlights of the exercise being the QM, being a God like figure, sacking on the spot an incompetent officer, much to everybody's amusement! Also having Dennis Wanjiki as my interpreter was a God send, because the Kenyan's were worse that the Bosnian's for trying to rip us off and take the piss.

Dennis was a Kenyan Rifleman that was one of the hardest working, and friendliest lads you could ever meet. As a reward we were able to cut him away on R and R early, down to Nairobi to see his family. I had to laugh, we had a bone-idle Ugandan lad who had been a pain in the arse for the entire exercise always sloping off, ear stuck to his mobile phone, generally being a selfish prick. He was always pulling the race card, or a sick chit. I had great delight when he tried to get away early with Dennis, explaining in a nice, fluffy, PC way that Dennis had earnt his extra time off and was being rewarded by the QM direct. Chris and Carl two of the MT Lads that were fed up with his shit were snigging in the background. Top tip: in the 'Rifles' we are a relaxed multinational multi-ethnic outfit, we are all Riflemen! Don't be a Jack cunt.

There was severe flooding in the spring of 2014 all over the UK, Support Company, 1RIFLES were deployed to the town of Hereford to assist the Emergency Services. I deployed with my trucks and Support Company which was a good laugh, and this being the last thing I ever did in the Regiment. It was a good way to finish my time in green.

It was a bit of a nightmare drive, paralleling the River Wye up the Hereford from Chepstow, but our SV Man trucks were brand new and up for the job.

'Ginger Snap Daver' was a local Hereford lad, and a Support Company character due to his mythical ability to avoid work, chill out, and still come out the other end smelling of roses. Fair play, he played a blinder, and for once in his life worked his arse off and was invaluable with his local knowledge and contacts.

The people of Hereford were absolutely brilliant with their generosity and fortitude in dealing with the flooding. Unfortunately, it all went horribly wrong when our three-ship formation went out on task to the hamlet of Hampton Bishop.

Hampton Bollocks:
It had been a long, cold, day sand bagging and helping the locals when our ad-hoc formation was re-tasked to the hamlet of Hampton Bishop. The local copper who was attached to our call-sign told us off the record, 'Mind how you go in Hampton Bishop, because the locals there are two-bob snobs'.

It was dark and late when we rocked up at Hampton Bishop, the lads were chin-strapped, everything was soaked, and we were running out of sandbags.

As we started to unload and get to work, the local Parish Councillor, or self-appointed big wig rocked up and started gobbing off - Lady Bloody Muck. She was bumping her gums about *why we were late*, and *how come we only had a limited number of sandbags?* She was not happy and was going to complain. Fair play, 'Greg' an up-and-coming full screw, and all-round good bloke who was due for promotion, was trying to be all diplomatic with this clown and was starting to get pissed off. This bloody woman was having none of it. Even the copper was getting grief from this two-bob snob.

As Daver and I wandered down from the SVs to see what was happening, all I heard was this woman gobbing off saying, 'Don't you know who I am? I'm such and such. I will be complaining to the local MP and your Commanding Officer!' I thought, *you cheeky bloody cow.*

I didn't want any blow back on Greg, so I walked over to put my two pence worth into the escalating drama. 'All right my love how's it going sweetheart?', was my opening line! The look on her smug face was priceless. She started spluttering, how dare the peasants speak to their betters like that?!

I then told her my name was 'Clarence' from 1RIFLES, and she should be grateful that the lads were here doing Assistance to the Civil Power. Also, that the lads were tired and wet, and had been on the go for over 20 hours, so she and her ilk should show some bloody respect. Old Lady Muck then went up like a bloody rocket!

I then started taking the piss, asking her if she had been sacked from the 'Charm School?', which got a good laugh from everybody present, including the copper. Fair play, Greg ordered the troops to mount up. We were bugging out due to weather. The look on Lady Mucks face was bloody priceless.

To add insult to injury, 'Daver' jumped in his SV and reversed over her well-maintained lawn leaving a few ruts, and the Garden Gnome became a casualty of war.

Bollocks to Hampton Bishop! I never did find out if she complained or not the stupid cow, I was punching out. ENDEX.

ENDEX:
I drove out of the camp gates for the last time on 11th June 2014. The last day was a bit rushed. All I wanted to do was get trucking back up to Chester. The wife had stayed on in the Philippines doing the family visiting thing, because I was busy doing my resettlement and was keen to get a McJob sorted out. I was lucky, because a mate of mine, Dave Trev, was in the process of getting me an interview with Airbus Security.

My Last day in 1RIFLES consisted of a brew in Gonzo's office, breakfast round Mikey and Kat's with team Fiji, a final brew at NAAFI break with some of the lads, followed by a brew in 'Bones' office, who was now HQ CSM.
Then that was it. Endex. Throw my daysack and quilt in the back of my wagon, gain some height, turn to the right, turn the key, and drive on son.
The barrier went up, the young lad on the gate said, 'Take care Corporal Clarence,' and that was it. 24 years down for Queen and Country. No regrets.

Roll on my last pay day and check my pension on the 14th of September.

Fair play, the G3 clerk, 'Karl' did ring me on that date to make sure that it was all squared away. That was it, no regrets. I had taken the Queen's shilling and was now drawing my army pension. I was now a Veteran on Planet Civilian Street.

'Stumpy' was a Welsh Cavalry Veteran, who had lost his lower leg to an IED in Iraq, hence the nickname.

Stumpy and I had mutual friends because he went to school with my mate Baz's stepson. Stumpy had a nice little property empire going and always in the gym. He was a bloody nightmare on the piss, but 'Long John Silver' had nothing on Stumpy.

On Remembrance Sunday, we ended up on the piss all day. About 21:00hours I was well pissed. Fair play, Harry Crumb's wife was playing babysitter, picking us all up to get us all home safe. Not bloody Stumpy! He stayed out in town on the piss. About 01:00hours I was awakened from my drunken slumber by my mobile, bloody Stumpy! So, I turned my phone off and went back to sleep.

Monday lunchtime, I had a call asking if I had heard what had happened to Stumpy? It turned out Stumpy had fallen over pissed up and had broken his good leg! He was in the Countess of Chester Hospital getting treatment and he had tried to call me last night.

Stumpy still gives me grief to this day for abandoning him in his hour of need to this day - the wanker!

EPILOGUE:
Fast-forward to November 2016, Stumpy had called in a favour, so I was rattling a tin for the Royal British Legion Poppy Appeal in Waitrose, Chester. Stumpy was up to his usual trick of snaking some Danish bird while I was manning the booth on my own, bloody typical of him.

An older veteran had come over for a chat, he was out shopping with his son and had lost sight of him, so he came over for a chat. I got the brews on and had a really nice chat with the gentleman about his time in the mob while we kept a lookout for his lad. 10 minutes later, his lad turned up, so we started taking the piss out of the poor bloke for elder abuse and losing his father in the shop, which he took with good grace. We ended up having a brew.

Then these immortal words were spoken to me! 'Listen mate, my name is Major Mike Lee. I command the Kings School Chester Combined Cadet Force.

You're the sort of man I'm looking for. You fancy coming into school next week for a chat and a brew? You will meet Tony the SMI from the Welsh Guards; I think this could be good for all of us.'

Old Soldiers Never Die They Just Fade Away… Not This Bloody Call-Sign Son!
Lt Julian 'Clarence' Heal, RIFLES, Kings School Chester Combined Cadet Force Contingent, Chester, England.

Notable Mentions Not in the Book:

Bungalow – not very bright bloke – nothing upstairs just like a bungalow. This was a popular insult given to people doing stupid things within the Regiment.

Bino's – Lance-Jack from the DERR's - given his nickname before the amalgamation due to his huge National Health Issue eyeglasses. They were proper Joe 90 specs. They looked like Army issued Tank Commander Binoculars.

Caesar – The spitting image of Julius Caesar himself. The only thing missing was the laurel reef on his head, Roman style.

Harry Potter – One of the Mortar lads that got his nickname due to his Glasses, Harry Potter Style.

Dead-Head – A young lad always doing stupid things, nothing between his ears.

Dog Head – QM's bloke that had a head that looked like sheep dog. He had the face of a border collie; a stores Jedi that was known throughout the Battalion by his nickname. A very useful bloke to know and keep on side.

Eddie Mallet – One of the Battalion Intelligent cell NCO's that would later transfer to the 'Green Slime.' He was the Support Company boxing Jedi and all-round good bloke. He got his nickname his surname was modified to 'Mallet' due to the kids TV presenter, Timmy Mallet.

Fred West – One of the lads from the Rifle companies who got caught out in a honey trap, bagging an underage bird that told him she was nineteen whilst he was on a night out in Gloucester. It went all the way to court. Common sense prevailed, so he was found innocent, but he still got grief off the lads and given the serial killer nickname, Fred West.

FARSM (Fake Acting Regimental Sargent Major) - A complete winner of a bloke, with amazing people skills - not! Attached to the Regiment in Afghanistan, he thought he was the real RSM, even though he was only acting as the RSM of one of the teams, not the whole Regiment. Not a good role model or leader.

FONC (Friend of No Cunt) - one of the Officers. Had no friends and was very unpopular across the board in the Regiment.

Gunny Anning – The exact clone of the Clint Eastwood character, Gunny Highway from the movie Heartbreak Ridge. Old school solider from the Devon and Dorset, who was a human cyclone that looked after the lads but was hard core.

Straight Hair Curly teeth – RSM of the RGBW. A ginger bloke, top man. The original ginger ninja whose claim to fame was his Vauxhall Astra breaking down and blocking the M25.

Shit Life – Ricky a bloke that had been in care as a kid and had a shit life before the Army. Had a tough upbringing but found a home in the Regiment. Because he had been through the care system was known as Shit Life!

Too Tall – A seven-foot giant of a man from the Royal Welch Regiment. A gentle giant always up for a laugh and a beer.

Pumpkin Head – CSM with a head like a giant pumpkin. Nobody would call him that to his face.

Punchy – Was one of the most loyal and honest blokes you could have in your corner. Trouble is, he would never back down and had a volatile temper when push came to shove. Hence the nick-name Punchy. He was always getting into fights. He has mellowed out in his old age and is now a gentleman farmer and family man.

Poll Tax – A misunderstood SNCO that was about as popular as the 'Poll Tax'.

Kev the Orc – One of the Senior Lance-Jacks in the Regiment that looked like an Orc of Lord of the Rings - straight out of Mordor. With his Wiltshire accent he needed a translator to communicate. As one of the Royal Irish lads commented, 'Can you send a bloke over the block? We can't understand the Orc in the baseball cap!'

Womble – A random solider from another unit that spent his time working down the Saddle Club in Cyprus picking up rubbish and doing odd jobs. He was abandoned by his parent unit. He was left in Cyprus.

Abbreviations and Army Slang

ANA – Afghan national army
ANP – Afghan national police
ATGW – Anti tank guided weapon, Milan or Javelin
ANATT – Afghan army national training team

Basha – Shelter/Poncho/Ground sheet
Brew – Cup of Tea/Hot Drink
Benny – A resident of the Falklands Islands, taken from the old TV show Crossroads
Bollocks – Something that is complete rubbish
Bimble – To walk non tactical
Bug out – To leave/withdraw

Cpl/Full Screw – The rank of Corporal
Chin Strapped – Exhausted
Cook House – Eating area in camp or fixed location
Crow – Combat replacement of war, new member of the unit

DERR – Duke of Edinburgh's Royal Regiment
D&D – Devon & Dorsetshire Regiment
FFR – Land rover fitted for radio
Fold up – Cash in note form

Gonk Bag – Sleeping bag
GPMG – General purpose machine gun 7.62 mm
Gats – Guns
Glosters – Gloucestershire Regiment

IED – Improvised explosive device

Jack – A person that looks after themselves 'I'm alright jack'
Jack it in – To finish something

Lance jack - Lance Corporal

MID – Mention in despatches award
Mong – A stupid person or a clown
Monging – Being tired or not switched on

Nav-Ex - Navigational exercise/map reading

Re-sup – To resupply
REMF – Rear echelon mother fucker, not a front line solider
REME – Royal electrical and mechanical engineers
RLC – Royal logistics corps
RIFLES – The Rifles Infantry Regiment, an amalgamation of the Devon &
Dorset's, RGBW, Royal   Green Jacket & The light
Infantry battalions.
RGBW – Royal Gloucestershire and Berkshire regiment

Snaking – trying to pull a woman by slithering and sliding just like a snake.

Tac – Tactical operations centre

USMC – United states marine corps
USN - United states navy

Yanks The Americans

After-thoughts - Words of wisdom from Clarence Heal

Life is all about growing up my son, and life is tough for any kid!
Don't be a hero son, the graveyard is full of them.
Don't piss down my back and tell me its railing sonny.
Life is unfair son! how did you think my wife felt on our wedding day!
If you were any thicker you would set fool!
You are living proof that Dopy and Snow-White had sexual intercourse!
Life is unfair son, dry your eyes and wipe your nose and move on.
Don't be shy your mother certainly wasn't

If you enjoyed this book, found it useful or otherwise then I'd really appreciate it if you would post a short review on Amazon. I do read all the reviews personally so that I can continually write what people are wanting.

Thanks for your support!

Printed in Great Britain
by Amazon

12954531R00108